The Occupation

Book 2 of the Shylmahn Trilogy

DAVID R. BESHEARS

Greybeard Publishing

THE OCCUPATION

Greybeard Publishing
P.O. Box 480
McCleary, WA 98557-0480

ISBN 978-1-947231-27-6
(hardcover edition)

| 1 |

The small town of Stanton had been abandoned for more than a quarter of a century, its inhabitants having been rounded up and delivered to the large reservation several hundred miles to the east. A few had escaped prior to the collection, but most of these had been picked up elsewhere or had died resisting capture. Of those who had managed to avoid the Shylmahn collection teams, most had eventually succumbed to accidents, starvation, exposure or worse over the months and then years following the invasion. And death at the hands of fellow humans was not unheard of.

Jack Rydel had been born in Stanton, so for him this was a bit of a coming home; not that he remembered much about the northwest town. He had been only four when he and his older brother had been awakened by their father and spirited out of town, but it brought up unexpected emotions nonetheless. To his mind came visions of a way of life that hadn't existed for decades; a way of life as seen through the eyes of a four-year old, centering on his family, his house, his yard, his street. There were suddenly the smells from the kitchen, the scent of a freshly changed bed, Spiderman shampoo, Carpet Fresh, and poor ol' Mr. Big after being dowsed in flea powder. There was the taste of a Big Mac, of Domino's Pizza, and his mother's special spaghetti.

It all came washing over him, rushing at him, over-whelming him, and when he tried to reach out to it, to touch it, it all dissolved and he found himself once again in the here and now, crouched behind a wooden folding chair on the narrow front porch, the striped shadow of the chair's slats softening his silhouette.

The porch deck smelled moldy and musty. The northwest air was damp and the evening sky was smeared in three shades of gray and threatened more rain. Looking across the narrow street, Jack could see his two companions in the alley, Tyler peering cautiously around the corner of the crumbling brick wall. Tyler pulled back suddenly and he and Hearn stepped back further into the darkness of the alley.

Jack leaned forward and glanced quickly around the chair just long enough to allow him to see through the porch railing and down the street.

There they were...

The Shylmahn no longer formed collection teams. Such things had gone with the conclusion of the invasion itself, after the vast majority of surviving humans had been gathered onto the reservations or into work camps. Now, when Shillies left their cities and entered the *wilderness,* such expeditions usually took the form of research operations, or work crews utilizing human labor, and now and then the occasional safari.

This was a hunting party. Four Shylmahn were walking down the center of Stanton's main street with energy weapons cradled loosely in their arms. A Shillie ground car followed some thirty feet behind them. Keeping pace fifty or sixty feet ahead of the group were two hovering basketball-sized probes. These were hunting probes, with sensors reaching out for telltales of movement, sound, and body heat.

Jack would be detected in moments. Shillie sensor technology was far from infallible, but no matter how silent and still he was, there was no hiding his body heat in this cool northwest air.

He slid backwards toward the front door. It was slightly ajar, though not enough to squeeze through. Across the street, Tyler and Hearn moved still further back into the alley, watching Jack as they did so.

Continuing his painfully slow progress toward the door, he gave them only the slightest nod of the head. *Get out of here...*

Once they had moved into the shadows, they had lost sight of the hunting party and warily eyed the tiny lane's entrance for any sign of the probes or their masters. They held rifles at the ready. The weapons were pre-invasion relics, but were well maintained and could be quite effective against both alien bodies and alien machines.

Jack reached the door, one foot touching the threshold. What now? The probes would detect movement if he tried to push the door open wide enough to squeeze through. If he remained where he was, the probes would detect his body heat...

Action before inaction... Do something now. The probes' sensors had to be in range by now, and it would only get worse. Shillie sensor accuracy improved with proximity to target. The shorter the distance, exponentially less volume of space to be observed and exponentially greater the quality of data being input; the nearer objects were more accurately identified than the further objects.

Jack inched his foot backward and to one side. He could feel the door move, if only slightly. He watched as the two probes continued their slow progress, matching exactly the easy walking pace of the Shillie hunters.

If this hunting party was just that—a hunting party—then the probes' offensive weaponry might not be active. Jack had heard of Shillie hunters that enjoyed the hunt and the kill, despite the propaganda the invaders put out.

If on the other hand the Shillies were out looking specifically for them, which was likely, then the probes would be leading the attack, with the Shillies themselves coming in for the final kill, if necessary.

Jack could see the Shylmahn hunters clearly now. Unlike the world of his parents, and all those who had lived before the invasion, the Shillies had always been a part of Jack's world. He could never see them the way humans of the last generation saw them. And over the years, he had come face to face with Shillies many times. They simply *were.*

In spite of all that, Shillies did something to him; with each and every meeting. There was always a sensation in his chest when confronting the invaders. Perhaps it was the imprint of all-powerful, all-controlling, all-dominating that many of the last generation had bestowed upon the Shylmahn. Perhaps it was the sense of absolute superiority the Shylmahn themselves emanated, or the Shylmahn's palpable lack of recognition of humans as a peer species. Perhaps it was nothing more than the word—*invaders.* Whatever it was, Jack couldn't get around that indescribable feeling. It was something akin to fear or apprehension or dread, and yet not really any of these. It was... something else. He couldn't help it. He knew that it wouldn't help him, that it would only get in the way, and he tried each time to push it down, to push it back; yet it was always there, and would remain there until long after the confrontation ended.

Jack never thought the Shillies looked particularly threatening. They stood no more than shoulder-high to him, were very thin, and to Jack they looked child-like, with child-like human features; they had large, golden eyes and delicate nose and mouth. Their skin was a golden yellow, and they had long, golden brown hair. It was difficult for Jack to comprehend the unremorseful, deadly ferocity of the Shylmahn.

After all the years that had passed, they continued to dress in the same brown shirt and pant uniforms they had worn when they first arrived on Earth. Whatever the intent, it served to reinforce the impression that the Shylmahn were of one mind, were set upon one authoritarian path, with little need for self-expression or independent thought.

One of the door's hinges gave the slightest metal-on-metal screeching sound. Jack stiffened at the sudden, unexpected noise. His skin turned instantly hot and dry. He was ready to push himself up and throw himself back through the door.

The probes, however, didn't look to have taken notice. How could they not? He looked quickly to the Shylmahn themselves. They didn't appear to have heard the sound either. He glanced quickly to the alley. Tyler and Hearn were frozen in their tracks. They had definitely heard the screaming hinge. After several moments, though, they visibly relaxed and started moving slowly back once again.

Hearn backed into an old wooden box. The sound of wood scraping on asphalt reverberated throughout the alley. Hearn let out an angry *shit*, and he and Tyler both raised their rifles and sighted down to the alley entrance, knowing what was about to happen.

One of the two hunting probes rushed the last few yards to the alley, leaving the other to remain in a defensive position in the event of an ambush. Reaching the entrance, the probe instantly observed, evaluated and identified the contents of the alley. Almost immediately thereafter, it began firing energy pins at the two humans.

Tyler and Hearn, for their part, began firing at the probe the moment it had shown itself. They continued firing even as they fell, first to their knees, then face down onto the asphalt. With Tyler's final shot, the probe spun about and exploded in a deadly, all-encompassing shrapnel cloud of metal and plastic.

Jack had jumped to his feet and was firing at the second probe from his position on the porch. He moved back through the doorway and continued steady single shots as the probe rushed up to the house, the porch, and to the door. An energy pin struck him in the left shoulder, another in his left leg. He continued firing, slow and steady, almost subconsciously tracking the ammunition remaining in the clip.

One shot damaged the probe's guidance system and it began spinning erratically out on the porch, just beyond the doorway, dodging into and out of view. Energy pins began shooting in all directions.

This at least would keep the Shillies at a safe distance...

Another energy pin struck Jack, this time in the abdomen; then another, also in the abdomen. He stumbled back, tripped over something in the dark, quickly regained his balance, and fired again as the probe bobbed unsteadily through the doorway. It exploded, filling the enclosed space with deadly shards.

§

Three of the Shylmahn approached the small Chehnon dwelling, having heard the explosion of their second and last probe. The fourth went into the alley, returning to his companions a few moments later.

Daehg, he said. One of the others nodded silent acknowledgment as they continued their approach to the building. All was quiet now.

While not afraid of death, they had no desire to hurry its arrival, and all knew very well the danger these Chehnon creatures could pose when they were cornered. They would use caution. It simply made sense.

They entered the building one at a time, each moving in quickly and stepping to one side. Once in the room, they had to step warily to avoid the metal and plastic from the exploded probe, which jutted out dangerously now from the floor, walls and furniture.

They found blood, but no Chehnon body.

Keh! hissed the first Shylmahn, waving one hand. *Tahl tyh.* Two of the Shylmahn backed quickly out and hurried to the side of the building and around towards the back. The two remaining inside continued their search. The trail of blood led them to the back room and on out the back door. Once outside, they found the others as they came from around the side of the building.

Half a mile out, Michael Britton could just see the first small telltales that let anyone looking closely enough see that a community was there. He glanced back at the others with him.

"Not long now," he said.

Michael was on foot, with the reins of the lead horse held loosely in one hand. The small boy sitting in the saddle stared intently at the low range of hills up ahead.

"I don't see nothin'," he said at last. Most of the others in the group were also trying to make out the town. A woman and small child rode a second horse; a graying, withered man rode the third. Each horse was led by a member of Michael's team. Two other tired-looking men followed along behind the horses.

Michael nodded. "That's just the way we like it."

"Freetown is set into the hillside," said Mitch, who was holding the reins of the second horse. "Ya' see that thick grove of trees growing at the base of the larger hill? Ya' see it?" Mitch Travers didn't usually travel with Michael on these runs, but with Jack on another mission, Michael had been shorthanded. A team of three seemed to work best.

"Yessir," said the boy. The boy liked Mitch, with his western garb and hint of a Texas drawl. Michael doubted that his name was really 'Mitch Travers', or that he was from anywhere near Texas. The whole persona had the feel of someone wanting to remake himself.

"Well son, hidden in that grove is a wall all covered in ivy; beyond that wall is Freetown."

The woman riding the second horse held her little girl tight. "Ya' hear that, sweetie? We're safe, now." She spoke then to Michael, "I never thought I'd see it, Mr. Britton. I don't know how we can ever repay you."

"It's what we're about, ma'am," said Michael.

Mitch slowly shook his head. "Michael's a bit modest, ma'am," he said. "His underground railroad has brought out hundreds of folks. Some have stayed right there in Freetown and become a part of the mission. All of 'em, whether they stayed on or moved on, owe Michael their lives."

Michael grumbled under his breath.

Mitch grinned. "And... it's what we're about, ma'am."

Michael raised a hand, indicated first left, then right. He continued on directly toward the grove of trees, leading the first horse. Mitch veered left leading the second horse. The man leading the third horse headed right, followed by the rest of the group.

They were trying to prevent creating a permanent, visible trail leading to Freetown. Never walk in the path of the person in front of you, never take the same route into Freetown that you took before, and never travel in what appears to be an existing path. It was hoped that in this way any signs created by a person's passing would disappear within a few hours or days.

While Michael was taking a direct route across the clearing, Mitch would follow a common animal trail for a short distance, then veer away from the direction of town for a bit before cutting back and making a beeline for the gate. The third group was going to follow the edge of the clearing on the opposite side, just inside the trees.

Michael entered the grove of trees and continued forward. The wall ahead became clearly evident. Set deep into the grove, it ran parallel to the range of hills just beyond. It was twice Michael's height and covered in ivy. As he approached, he could see the double-gate. It was eight feet wide and eight feet tall, half hidden in ivy that appeared determined to overtake it. A man's shoulders and head were visible atop the wall.

"Welcome back," he said. He was standing on a platform on the inside, just above the gate, that served as the guard station. "Everything go all right?"

"Nothing we couldn't handle," said Michael.

Inside the wall was an open plaza, wider than it was deep. Two large trees, similar to those outside the wall, shaded wooden benches and a number of low, flat buildings on either side. People were moving about, coming out of or going into the buildings; several more were sitting on the benches and talking quietly, glancing casually at the recent arrivals.

The plaza was the main thoroughfare, and led to a large opening set into the hillside. The opening was about ten feet tall and ten feet wide, and covered with camouflage netting, behind which hung large canvas curtains. Beyond this main entrance lay the cavern that formed the Inner Village.

Michael stopped the horse and helped his passenger dismount. Mitch followed him through the outer main gate, with the others not far behind. A young woman approached and offered to take the horses. Once the personal gear was unloaded, she led the animals away to the stables. Turning then toward the main thoroughfare, Michael saw Annie approaching them, wearing a broad smile and clasping her hands together.

"Michael! Welcome back."

“Thanks, Annie.” Michael gave her a warm hug before turning to the group that was gathering behind him. “Everyone, meet Annie Gomez, our resident doctor. Annie Gomez, this is everyone.”

Annie lost just a bit of her smile, gave Michael a sidelong glance as she introduced herself to each of the new arrivals. She told them that she would be giving them a quick once-over after they were settled in and had something to eat. Mitch offered to take them the rest of the way in, leaving Michael and Annie to follow along after.

“Everyone all right?” asked Annie.

“Fine,” said Michael. “How’re things?” He looked more carefully at the two rows of buildings running off to the left and the right, huddled low between the perimeter wall and the hillside. This was the Outer Village.

“All is quiet,” said Annie.

“Any word from Jack?”

“Nope.”

“Well, s’pose it’s too soon to start worrying.”

“No it’s not,” said Annie. “They’ve been gone four weeks.”

Most of the buildings they passed were storage sheds and community buildings of one kind and another, small and squat and plain in color and design, with an occasional three-room house set back behind short picket fences and marked by darkened windows.

The real community of Freetown lay beyond the black canvas and camouflaged netting that hid the entrance to the great cavern.

A dozen narrow dirt streets criss-crossed the cavern floor. The far wall was terraced with two progressively narrower ledges, each holding a row of apartment complexes. The domed ceiling of the cavern was some sixty feet above the floor.

Tunnels led deeper into the mountain from ground level and at each terrace. Some served as air shafts doubling as emergency routes, while others wound their way to other, smaller caverns on one side of the main cavern, or to utility rooms supporting the town, including air supply pumps, fresh water, power supply, plumbing and water treatment.

Michael and Annie passed through the double-blind canvas curtains and under a massive metal door held above the main opening. A set of large cog wheels held the door at bay, waiting patiently to drop its charge before the opening.

Michael turned left at the first intersection, turned in at the second small house and took the two steps up to his door. It was a compact house; three small rooms and a flat, thin roof, but it was a house and not an apartment. Michael had a problem with apartments.

He set his small bag down on the table and began unpacking. "I'll give Jack three more days," he said.

"Three days or three hours—something's happened."

"I agree."

"Well then?"

"It could be anything, Annie. Any one of a hundred things could have held them up."

Annie sat heavily in one of the two chairs in the room. Her face was covered in shadows, with the only light coming in through the short, wide window. Michael returned to his unpacking, finally flipping on the light switch in order to see what he was doing. Each home was rationed electrical power, but Michael seldom used his allotment.

"I suppose," said Annie. "I just..."

Michael folded his empty bag, turned and looked carefully at Annie. "Yeah... I know..."

"Jack knows how important this is to you."

There was a sudden and very urgent knocking at the door. Michael gave Annie a patient smile, gathered up several toiletry articles from the table and turned to put them into a mirrored cabinet. "Come in, Willie," he called over his shoulder.

Eleven year old Willie McKinney pushed into the room.

"Hey, Willie," said Michael.

"Hey, Michael B." Willie was the youngest of the McKinney clan, a large family living in a cluster of apartments on the second terrace. "Man, am I glad you're back."

"Well, I'm glad to be back, kiddo."

"You gotta' set things right."

Michael gave Annie an anxious glance, but managed to keep his smile. "What's wrong that needs setting right?"

"Ethan Perry." Willie's face contorted, as if just saying the name might cause him to upchuck.

"Ah... and what has the infamous Mr. Perry been up to now?"

"You know how he gets," said Willie. "The minute you're out the gate, he tries to take over Freetown."

"Hey, kiddo, I'm not in charge around here. That's Mr. Warren's job. He's the head of the council."

"He might be the mayor, but you're the leader." Little Willie's voice was firm and his tone was urgent.

"He's gotcha there," said Annie. "Everybody likes Craig, but he can't stand against Ethan Perry."

Michael looked frustrated. "I'm not a politician. That's not what I do. The council was voted in. Craig Warren was voted head of the council. If there's a problem, the council needs to take care of it. If they can't take care of it, the town needs to vote in a new council."

"But you're Michael Britton," said Willie, as if the name was a title to be worn, a title that carried some great power. Michael looked down into the face of the boy. Willie was staring back, waiting for some sign that Michael was going to fix everything.

"What's Ethan doing now?" he asked.

"What he always does."

Michael looked over at Annie.

Annie shook her head. "He's trying to undermine the council, turn everybody against it. He wants what he's always wanted—to close Freetown to the railroad; to shut down the railroad."

"That'll never happen."

"It will if Ethan Perry gets his way."

"But that's what Freetown is about. Freetown *is* the railroad."

"Hey, I'm on your side. But if he can shut down the railroad, Freetown's reason for being changes. We can close the great door and all turn into mole people."

"That's crap."

"That's the way of things."

Michael looked back at the boy. "You keep your eyes and ears open, Willie."

Willie grinned. "Yessir."

"Okay," Michael looked quickly at both of them. "Where's Victoria?" he asked.

Annie shrugged her shoulders and lifted one eyebrow. Willie shut his mouth tight.

"She's still mad at me, isn't she?"

Annie shrugged again.

"Willie?" asked Michael.

Willie shrugged.

"Okay," Michael grumbled. "I need to get cleaned up."

Annie stood. "I should see to your passengers."

Once they had left, Michael went into the back room to shower and shave. As with the electricity, Michael had a monthly ration of water, but as he was often gone for weeks at a time, he seldom reached his limit. He took an extra long, extra hot shower. He had a dangerous trip that he needed to ease out of his bones, and an evening's celebration to prepare for.

Freetown observed each return of Michael and his team with a party, celebrating their safe return and welcoming in the newly arrived railroad passengers that they brought back with them. The main celebration was held in the central plaza in the heart of the cavern, but it spilled out to the side streets and even to the Outer Village. There was food and dancing and singing and games, all lasting late into the night.

Michael made four to six runs a year, and each safe return was cause for a celebration. It had become tradition, starting years earlier when his father would return from the occupied territory with a handful of refugees in tow. Now, dozens upon dozens of runs later, much of the original reason for the celebration was lost. Each triumphant return had become the signal for the party to begin rather than highlighting the cause.

Michael crossed the plaza, maneuvering through the crowd of dancers, carefully holding his plate and cup high in the air, out of harm's way, and made his way to Miriam Foster, who was sitting on a heavy, wooden bench at the plaza's perimeter.

"Hello, Michael. Have a seat."

Michael turned and sat down beside Miriam, a dark-haired woman in her early forties, and a long-time friend.

"Nice party," said Michael.

"Welcome back."

"Thank you."

"Happy passengers," said Miriam, nodding in the direction of a group gathered near the food tables. Amongst them were those that he had brought in on this last run.

"Good people," said Michael. Taking in the rest of the plaza, he saw Ethan Perry and several of his cohorts gathered outside the small building that served as the town hall. "I hear that Ethan is trying to stir up trouble."

"The man should be shot," said Miriam. She meant it.

"I'm afraid that's not an option."

"It should be." Miriam stabbed at her food. After several more vicious attacks with her fork, she set her plate down at her feet. Michael watched her out the corner of his eye while appearing to watch the revelers. Her anger slowly subsided.

"You okay?" Michael asked.

Miriam raised her eyes to take in the entire cavern. From this bench, she could see the two apartment terraces off to the right. To the left she could see the great door hovering above the main opening to the outside.

"I remember when we found this cavern," she said at last. "I walked through that entrance with your father and mother. I was just a kid at the time. It was very different, of course; and much smaller."

"Yes. I know."

Miriam smiled sadly. "I guess I've spoken of it more than once."

Michael had heard the story from his parents and from Miriam. Joseph and Barbara had made it out of the heavily occupied territory beyond the mountains to the west, leaving behind all those they had known. Here in the foothills overlooking the wide open spaces of Eastern Washington, events took on an easier pace. The rest of the world was going to hell, but here the slide into oblivion was just a little slower.

Joseph had searched for the underground railroad that he had heard about, that was supposed to be taking people out of the more dangerous territories to some safe place in the south. He didn't want to become a passenger, but rather a conductor.

He had spent more than a year in the heart of the battle, in the center of the heaviest concentration of Shylmahn on the planet. In that last desperate fight on Bril's island, most of the Britton clan had been killed or captured. Only Joseph, his ex-wife Barbara, and his sister Carolyn had managed to escape.

Once away from the island, Carolyn had gone her own way, vowing to continue the fight. Joseph decided to get Barbara and himself away from it, to step away from the constant struggle, if only for a short while.

They searched unsuccessfully for the railroad. Either it didn't exist, or it was so far underground that it may as well not exist. During their search, they had found Miriam living alone in a one-room cabin, both her parents buried nearby. The food staples had long since been used up. The girl hunted and gardened and gathered berries, and was just managing to get by.

In those first months after the incident at Bril's island, Joseph and Barbara came across countless people seeking escape, seeking refuge, or simply looking for a way to survive one more day. The necessities were hard to come by. There was no organization. Without civilization, there was no infrastructure. With no infrastructure, there was no civilization.

The Shylmahn had taken the planet. Of that, there could be no argument. Though the humans hadn't known it at the time, the war was over by the end of that first day. The rest had been cleanup and remodeling. The Shylmahn rebuilt the earth to the Shylmahn needs. The resources of the planet, humans included, were put to use. Gathered into work camps and reservations, the remnants of the human race had its place in this new world; it was an important place, but a much lesser role than what it was used to.

How could there ever be a successful insurrection against such a force? The invasion had been so thorough, so complete, that for those few humans not directly under the control of the invaders, the climb back to a position from which to strike back appeared totally indomitable. Freedom was a relative term. The *wild* humans might not be under the watchful eyes and sensors of the guardian probes, but the heavy shadow of the Shylmahn was ever present. So long as that shadow existed, any effort at organizing humanity, at creating a social structure and bringing civilization back from the ashes of the invasion, seemed absurd.

Joseph had no real plan in mind when they first found the caves. The cavern wasn't a cavern at that time, but a maze of tunnels and small, room-size caves. Miriam thought of it as a giant Habitrail. Joseph saw possibilities, and the first glimmers of what was to come.

In those first years, Freetown kept much of its Habitrail structure. Tunnels were turned into hallways; caves were expanded and turned into apartments. Joseph actively sought out others and brought them back to Freetown, and began building a population.

As individuals with knowledge and experience joined the slowly growing community, ventilation systems were constructed, the first primitive plumbing system was installed, and a proper support structure for the tunnels and rooms was built.

In order to prevent the populace of Freetown from turning into the Mole People, the main cavern was started. The core maze of tunnels and rooms was slowly gutted, under the guidance of a young geology teacher and an aging miner, and a central village plaza took shape. Over time, the first apartment terrace was created.

None of this would have made a bit of difference without an adequate defensive system. Joseph knew firsthand that bunkers and booby-traps and holes in the ground were not enough. How could they possibly defend Freetown against the Shylmahn?

The present-day defenses hadn't come about all at once, but had evolved over time. Still, Joseph had planned a multi-layer system from the very beginning.

The first layer was the open-to-view village outside the cavern complex. Joseph knew that there was no hiding a human village from the Shylmahn over the long term. Sooner or later, the Shillies would find them. So… create a true, working village out in the open, albeit as well-hidden and well-protected as they could make it. Every effort was made to prevent broadcasting their presence, but it was understood that they could not hide indefinitely from Shylmahn search probes. It was hoped that when the Outer Village was detected, that the community would be considered insignificant enough not to warrant further attention, and that the larger, cavern complex within, the Inner Village, would not be discovered.

The defenses along the Outer Village were also there to protect against the roving human bands of marauders that occasionally made their presence known. So far, the outer defenses had been up to the task.

The second line of defense was the set of seals put in place throughout the inner complex perimeter. In addition to the main door to the central cavern were the numerous shafts that formed the ventilation system, the plumbing and power tunnels, the routes to the side caverns, and the outer doors to those caverns. All outer accesses were well-camouflaged and had heavy steel doors. Utility tunnels each had a series of doors that could be dropped sequentially. Travel tunnels had doors at all entrances and exits, as well as emergency doors en route. All tunnels, utility and travel tunnels alike, were lined with a network of explosive devices that could be individually targeted from a command station, effectively closing off specific areas of the complex.

The third line of defense was the series of well-armored and well-gunned bunkers strategically located throughout the complex. Located high above the floor of the main cavern and in critical locations throughout Freetown, bunker teams could put on a good show against a relatively strong force of Shillies and their attack probes, should they come into the Inner Village.

The bunkers also served as a critical element of the fourth and final line of defense: The escape. Two underground routes out of the village, opening to well-camouflaged openings on the other side of the mountain. Once outside, there was a series of supply caches buried along an escape route to a rendezvous several days' march from the village.

If the Shillies found that taking the village was too costly to them, they had sufficient firepower to destroy the mountain and the community within it. A quick and efficient escape operation was the primary element of the Freetown defensive plan.

None of this came easily, quickly, or turned out as originally envisioned. Some had questioned the value of many of the ideas, particularly the more difficult tasks. Compromises had been made; some good and some not so good.

"The place has definitely changed some since my father's time," said Michael.

"Ever changing," said Miriam.

Michael had to grin at the inference. "And not always for the best..."

"No," she sighed. "I sometimes fear that it will lose its way." She stood then, reached over and lifted up the cane that was hooked to the back of the bench. Leaving her plate behind, she started in the direction of the Outer Village. After taking several steps, she stopped and turned smoothly about to look back at Michael. "Don't you let them take Freetown."

"I won't," he said flatly.

"I mean it, Michael." She pointed her cane at him. "Keep the purpose."

The purpose weighed heavy on Michael. He believed in it totally and completely, but it weighed heavy on him, nonetheless.

Miriam turned away without acknowledging him further and continued in the direction of the Outer Village. Her small house was outside. She had lived out there for years. She said that once the Habitrail was gone, the inside complex just wasn't fun anymore, but Michael knew that she had always had trouble living inside. He remembered when he was very young, before the Outer Village was built, that she would often camp out there, under the stars.

Jenny Britton's cabin served as a way station for the underground railroad, and as the stationmaster she helped her brother Michael deliver passengers from the heavily occupied lands in the northwest out to Freetown and beyond. Everyone coming out of the northwest on the railroad went through her station.

The cabin was nestled in the foothills on the eastern slopes of the Cascades, surrounded by a mix of fir trees, alder, and splotches of grassland. The cabin consisted of four small rooms and a wide porch. Two larger buildings loomed nearby: a barn and stable combination, and a long, narrow building in which the railroad passengers would stay overnight on their journey.

Jenny lived alone. She usually liked it that way, though she did get lonely on occasion and always looked forward to her brother's visits. He would stop in on his way into the occupied territory and stay a few days. On his return, passengers in tow, he would usually stay only a day. Those that he brought out were eager to get to Freetown.

Michael had come through a few days earlier, and wasn't expected back for another eight to ten weeks. Those were the times she felt the isolation the most. She would throw herself into her chores, taking care of the animals, gardening, hunting, maintenance on the buildings, and before long the loneliness would pass.

She liked her life, for the most part. There was value in it. Hundreds of people were alive and living a better existence because of what she and Michael were doing. She hoped that one day they could do more, that they could actually take back the world that had been taken from their parents, but in the meantime they could at least make life a little better for those living in the direct shadow of the Shylmahn.

Jenny came out of the barn, closed and latched the large door. She felt the late afternoon sun on her back as she started across the yard toward the house. It was warm and the end of a day like this often left her feeling comfortable and content.

She turned about as she stepped up onto the porch and was startled to see movement far across the north meadow. She back-stepped to the front door, opened it and reached in to get the binoculars hanging just inside.

It looked like one man walking a horse, but he was still too distant to get any detail. Jenny carefully scanned the terrain on either side of the meadow, and the narrow pass that her visitor had come through. All looked clear.

She went into the house and brought out a rifle and a shotgun. She leaned the shotgun against the wall beside the door and leaned the 30-30 against her leg. Bringing the binoculars up, she scanned the perimeter of the meadow again before sighting back to the visitor. She could see now that there was someone on the horse. They were still too far away for her to tell any more than that.

She sat down in one of the wooden porch chairs, shotgun beside her and rifle in her lap, and waited for them to draw nearer. It wasn't until they were midway across the meadow that Jenny recognized the man on foot as Monroe, and not until they were much closer that she was able to identify the man in the saddle as Jack Rydel. Jack looked like he was hurt.

Monroe led the horse into the yard and up to the porch. He and Jenny helped Jack down and half-carried him into the house and to the spare bed in the back room. As Jenny saw to Jack's bandages, Monroe explained that he had found him hiding in their safe house in Weaden. Jack had managed to get that far, and figured that sooner or later someone would show up. It had just happened to be Monroe.

"What were you doing in Weaden?" asked Jenny. "You never go into town." Weaden was a very small town of several dozen houses and stores, now long abandoned. Empty or not, it was the town nearest to Jenny's relay station and what she considered *going to town.*

"I had business there," said Monroe. Monroe lived higher in the hills, in the mountains proper, and his occasional visits to Jenny's station were about the closest he came to interacting with people. To his few friends, he was a true and loyal friend; to everyone else, he was a stranger you didn't mess with. He was a large man, but quiet and unassuming. Despite this unpretentious air about him, something in his eyes, and in the unsettling expression that he sometimes wore, caused anyone who didn't know him to tread carefully whenever they had dealings with him.

Jenny Britton was his closest and dearest friend. He brought supplies to her a few times a year, and between this and what Michael brought, and what she brought in on her own forays, she did all right.

Monroe usually brought these supplies along with refugees that he smuggled out of the occupied territory. This being the final relay station along Britton's railroad, Monroe could count on Michael coming through every few months to collect them. He wasn't officially a conductor on this railroad, but as an independent had helped quite a few people find their way. He didn't go into the occupied lands on the west side of the Cascades, as Michael Britton and his team did, but rather watched the trails for those refugees coming over. These he would guide on to Jenny's way station. He figured that if they'd made the effort and taken the risk all on their own, he owed it to them to point the way.

Jenny wondered what sort of business Monroe might have had in Weaden, but let the matter drop. If he had wanted her to know, he would have given some indication. He hadn't.

"No sign of anyone else?" When he had come through several months earlier, Jack had been with several others.

"He spoke of two. They didn't make it."

"It looks like they had a run-in with the Shillies, all right." She spoke softly as she finished checking Jack's bandages and pulled the blanket up under his chin. He was asleep. She led Monroe out of the room and then out of the cabin and out onto the porch. "Michael was just through here last week. He won't be back for months."

Monroe stood stone-faced, said nothing and simply waited for her to ask what he knew was coming next.

"Can you go into Freetown and let Michael know that he's here?"

"S'pose so."

Jenny was asking quite a lot of him, but she couldn't hold back the smile. Big, tough Monroe—what a softy. "I appreciate it." she said.

Monroe stepped off the porch without another word and led the horse into the stable off the barn. By the time he had settled the animal in, brushed him down and fed him, Jenny had a simple dinner ready. They ate at the small table set beneath the window that opened onto the porch. Afterward, they played cards late into the evening, stopping only to feed Jack when he woke. About an hour past moonrise, Monroe said good night and settled onto a cot set up in the room that Jack was sleeping in. They were both gone when Jenny woke at dawn. Monroe had taken Jack with him.

EsJen turned away from the oval window at the sound of MehnTec coming down the central aisle of the large shuttlecraft. MehnTec was taller than most Shylmahn, and subconsciously lowered his head as he walked through the passenger compartment.

"Esrontahtohp," he said. *Not long.*

"Stah," she said. *Thank you.*

MehnTec sat in the seat on the other side of the aisle. There were only two other passengers, leaving most of the dozen seats empty. This hadn't been a scheduled flight. It had been initiated at TohPeht's request, its purpose to bring EsJen to VeshMahn, the largest *dahlseht* on Chehno, and the first Shylmahn city to be established on their new world. She was to meet with TohPeht immediately upon her arrival.

"I am looking forward to our return," said MehnTec. "This part of the world has always held a special place in my thoughts."

"For me as well," said EsJen. "How can it not? This is where we first set foot on Chehno, where we spent our first years on this world."

"We were reborn there."

"That is true," she said. During their time in the province, they had grown, changed, become so much more than they had been. They had been reshaped by their new world. Only then were they able to in turn reshape that same world.

"And I think this part of the world is the most beautiful," said MehnTec.

"It is all so beautiful, MehnTec." said EsJen. "Each has its own splendor. I could not choose one over another."

"Well, I can." MehnTec smiled, looked past EsJen and out the small window.

EsJen turned back to the window and looked out upon their world. They were passing over a range of mountains that served as the eastern boundary of the province surrounding the dahlseht. From here on, they would be flying over a land of forests and lakes and rivers, a wondrous land of greens and blues. The old *human* communities, scattered throughout the province, were long abandoned and were quickly and inevitably being gobbled up by encroaching vegetation and neglect. Such was the case for all the old Chehnon towns. While there were a number of small *unofficial* Chehnon communities scattered about the planet, these were populated by wild humans living outside the reservations, eking out meager existences deep in the frontier lands, beyond the controlled provinces that encompassed each of the Shylmahn dahlsehts. These humans mattered little.

| 2 |

The one garage in Freetown was in the Outer Village. There were six bays in the garage, and there was a vehicle in each one. The Freetown fleet consisted of two station wagons, three pickups and a large passenger van.

Michael Britton was underneath the van, legs sticking out of the right side of vehicle, when Willie McKinney came running into the garage screaming out Michael's name. Michael smacked his head on the undercarriage, groaned pitifully, and slowly slid out from under.

"What is it, Willie?" Michael stood up and walked over to the bench that ran the full length of the back wall. He set the wrench down and picked up a red hand towel.

"It's Mr. Rydel!"

"He's back?" Michael hurriedly worked at the grease on his hands.

"At Doc's. Monroe brought him in."

"Is he all right? What about the others?"

"Don't know. There weren't no others, though."

"Damn," said Michael. He strode over toward the cleaning station. "You go on. I'll be there in three minutes."

Michael quickly changed out of his coveralls and removed the worst of the grease from his hands and face. It took him a bit longer than three minutes to get cleaned up and over to Annie's, but not much. When he entered the small ward that comprised half of Annie's house,

Michael found Jack conscious and sitting up in bed. Annie was just attaching a butterfly clip to the bandage that was wrapped around his torso. Another bandage covered most of his left arm, and a third was taped to one side of his neck. He looked haggard and beaten down. He had clearly been through a rough couple of months.

Monroe was standing in one corner of the room, silent and out of the way. Michael gave him a slight nod of acknowledgment before stepping over to the bed.

"Hey, Jack," he said. "What'd you do, get lost?"

Jack managed a grin. "Something like that." He watched as Annie finished up and stood. "Thanks, Doc. How's everything look?"

"Can't have you taking up valuable bed space, Jack," she said. "We'll get you into your own bed tomorrow. I don't want you moving about just yet, though."

"I think I can handle that."

"I'll find someone to bring you your meals for two or three days."

"Sweet," said Jack, another grin showing up on his face.

Annie looked once at Michael, began gathering up the old bandages and equipment. "You might want to leave him behind when you make your next run, but he'll recover."

Michael pulled a tall stool over towards the bed and sat, one foot on the floor. "So, what happened, Jack?"

"Hunters found us."

"Were they looking for you in particular?"

"Not sure. They did seem to come out of nowhere, and with a mission. They may have known we were there, but I couldn't say whether they knew why."

"Speaking of which—"

"Yeah, I got news."

"You were in Stanton?"

"Yeah."

"We have that, anyway."

Jack took a deep breath then. "Tyler and Hearn… that's where we got hit. It happened quick. I don't think they suffered any."

Ethan Perry came pushing into the room. "I suppose that makes everything okay, then. Right, Mr. Britton?"

Michael crossed his arms, but kept his seat. "Losing someone on a mission is never okay, Mr. Perry."

"I should say not."

"So what brings you by on this fine morning, Ethan?" asked Jack.

"I heard you were in a bad way, Jack, and I wanted to drop in to offer whatever assistance I could. Whatever differences we may have, I am nonetheless concerned for your well-being."

"I appreciate that, Ethan," said Jack. The sarcasm was exquisitely subtle. Self-preservation aside, there were numerous reasons why Jack Rydel had to make it back to Freetown alive. The ongoing pleasure inherent in irritating Ethan Perry was at the top of his list. When done just right, when he was able to successfully wrap his attack in layers of subtlety, in just the right way, any response by Ethan would only make him look foolish. His only other alternative was to stand by and look flustered. Equally rewarding.

Ethan looked flustered now, but it took him only a moment to recover. "Yes, well..." he turned on Michael. "Mr. Rydel's safe return notwithstanding, I think this entire affair is further evidence that these forays into the Shylmahn province must end."

"And just why is that?" Michael was quick to show his frustration whenever he had to deal with Ethan.

"Must I list them out for you?" Ethan leaned back dramatically, as if Michael's stupidity was pushing out at him. "How about the loss of life, for a start? How about the fact that Jack had to be brought back by this mountain man? And most importantly, how about the fact that spectacles such as this last ridiculous escapade only draw attention to Freetown and those of us who only want to live out our lives in peace."

"You're an ass," said Monroe from his place in the shadows. He stood unmoving, his statement spoken calmly and with little emotion.

"I beg your pardon?" Ethan's words came from somewhere deep down.

"You've always been an ass, and you'll die an ass. You're an ass."

Michael said nothing. Jack gave only the slightest *hmmm* sound from his bed. Annie calmly left the room without saying another word.

"We appreciate you bringing Jack home to us, Mr. Monroe," Ethan said at last. "But don't let us keep you."

Monroe did not move or speak. Ethan Perry struggled to stare the mountain man down, to wait him out until Monroe might either say something or leave. Monroe did neither. Ethan finally turned sharply and started toward the door. He spoke to Michael as left the room. "You and I will discuss this further, Mr. Britton; in a more formal setting."

Michael stared dully at the slowly closing door. "Crap."

"Ain't that the truth," said Jack.

"You two didn't help any," said Michael. He looked first at Jack, then Monroe.

Monroe mumbled flatly, "The man—"

"Yeah, yeah..."

"Ethan Perry may look the fool," said Jack, "but he's not stupid. He and his bunch are dangerous."

Michael looked lost for a moment, as if he had suddenly gone out of his depth. He shook it off quickly and stood up. "Politics is not my area. I leave that to Craig."

"Craig Warren is a good man," said Monroe.

"That may be," said Jack. "But that don't make him no more a politician than Michael, here. He believes in the goodness of man, and Ethan knows that. He uses that against him every chance he gets."

"He's an honest man. And the people like him," said Michael.

"Sure they do. He cares about them, and he would do them no wrong. I know that. They know that. He makes everyone feel all warm and cuddly. And he was a good friend to your father." Jack shifted position, leaned forward and stared at Michael from under his dark brow. "And Ethan uses those very qualities against him. I've seen him do it. You wait and see, Michael; he's going to blindside Craig and come after you like a Shillie hunter probe."

They stared sharply at each other. They had had this argument a dozen times, and Michael knew that Jack was right. And it wasn't just

Jack telling him, either. Victoria, Miriam, even Annie had warned him, again and again, that Craig Warren, as sincere a man as he might be, was vulnerable, was a weakness that Ethan Perry was exploiting. Michael had to take Ethan on, and he had to do it before Ethan grew any more powerful.

Michael hated it. He hated all of it. He wasn't a politician and had no desire to become one. He never thought of himself as a leader, but was nonetheless the one person that most everyone recognized as the true leader of Freetown, no matter the council, headed by Craig Warren, running things day to day; and for the time being, no matter Ethan Perry and his crowd, who would usurp the council, Michael Britton, and take Freetown into an isolationist direction and the rest of the world be damned.

"You made your point," said Michael.

"You've got friends," said Jack. "You won't be alone in this."

"I'll deal with it." Michael turned his attention to Monroe. "You'll be seeing Jenny?" he asked.

"Yes."

"Tell her I'll be coming by sooner than scheduled." He glanced quickly to Jack, who gave a short nod. "Two weeks, maybe three."

Monroe nodded silently...

It won't be one of Britton's regular railroad runs, then, he thought. *Something to do with whatever Rydel had been up to.*

"You're welcome to rest up from your trip. Take whatever time you need; there's room in the dorm."

"I'll just be spending the night," said Monroe. "I'll be leaving before first light."

Michael took a step toward Monroe and held out his hand. "I thank you again for bringing our wayward boy here back to us."

"Perhaps you should keep a closer eye on him." They shook hands. Monroe almost managed a smile.

"I think you're right," Michael did smile. "Don't forget to get supplied up before you go."

"Always a pleasure," said Monroe, and he left, closing the door gently behind him.

Michael turned back to Jack. "What'd you find out?"

"The info was correct. Joseph was using Stanton as a mail drop. Problem is, it looks like the Shillies got the same info you did."

"So you think they were there looking for my father?"

"There's as good a chance of that as of them being there looking for us. I wouldn't totally discount either, though."

"That would lead us down a road that I'm not sure I'm ready to travel."

"I hear ya', Mikey, but we better keep that thought in mind."

"Yeah." Michael was sitting on the stool again. "My father will no doubt be aware of what happened in Stanton. If that is so, he's also likely aware that we're trying to find him."

"That doesn't mean that he'll be making things any easier for us; *especially* after what happened in Stanton. If anything, he'll be going deeper underground."

"But he can't stay there, Jack. Not now. He's come out of hiding because he's ready to make his move."

"Well," Jack laid back into his pillows, "It does look that way." He stared up at the ceiling, spoke hesitatingly, "Since the information about Stanton being a mail drop was true, the rest of the information may very well be true."

"Possibly," said Michael.

"John's Park is a lot further in country than Stanton."

"I know."

The room EsJen walked into was long and narrow, with a low, brightly lit ceiling. The walls on either side were bare and white. At the far end of the room was TohPeht's desk, and directly in front of this was the round holo-table.

TohPeht was standing before the holo-table, above which the flickering of images danced about, creating shadows across TohPeht's face.

TohPeht turned at the sound of EsJen's footsteps. His attention directed away from the table, the holo image popped like a bubble, the darkened light panel in the ceiling directly above brightened. TohPeht waited for EsJen to reach him.

While they had communicated regularly, they hadn't actually seen each other in a number of years. TohPeht rarely left the VeshMahn Province, and EsJen hadn't been back since before the completion of the construction of the dahlseht.

Physically, TohPeht had changed little. Once reaching maturity, the Shylmahn seldom changed, right up to the last few years of life. He was of average height for a Shylmahn, just over five feet tall, his skin still held that healthy Shylmahn golden yellow color. His hair, the same golden brown as all Shylmahn, was worn a bit different these days. Shylmahn traditionally wore their hair down and shoulder length. TohPeht was wearing his long and pulled back. EsJen had never seen such a thing, and wasn't quite sure what to make of it.

As she approached, stopping several paces from the physical leader of the world, EsJen noticed something else a bit different. The whites of his eyes held the hint of gold, as all Shylmahn, but the irises were different. The Shylmahn iris was dark brown and filled with bright, gold flecks. TohPeht's pupils were lost in irises that were almost black. Inside those pupils, there seemed to be something alive and active; something more than TohPeht...

These thoughts didn't manifest themselves right away in EsJen, but a conscious realization evolved in her as she stood before TohPeht, waiting for him to initiate their meeting.

It was TohPeht who spoke to her, but there was something very different about him.

"EsJen," TohPeht smiled in welcome. "It is so very good to see you again."

EsJen smiled in return. Most Shylmahn had adopted many Chehnon affectations over the years. The Shylmahn smile of greeting had evolved since their arrival on Chehno, in spite of the fact that many Shylmahn had never even met a Chehnon native.

"Thank you, TohPeht. Whatever the circumstances that might have brought me back, I am glad of the opportunity to see you once again, and to return to VeshMahn after so many years; if only for a short time."

"The direction our duties take us may not always be the path we would have taken given the choice," TohPeht slowly moved around the holo-table until the table stood directly between them, "But more often than not shows itself to be the correct one."

EsJen gave a slight nod of the head. "I serve as I am needed."

"As do we all." TohPeht clasped his hands behind his back.

"As you, our leader, through the guidance and direction of Shahn-Tahr, deem appropriate."

TohPeht smiled modestly. "It is ShahnTahr who leads, EsJen. I am merely the conduit for ShahnTahr's council."

EsJen bowed her head imperceptibly. ShahnTahr's presence permeated this room. She had been with ShahnTahr a number of times over the years, minds bonded and communication splashed across her senses in a thousand impossible colors. Always, the presence of ShahnTahr had been an internal sensation.

This was different. This was physical; here, in this room; without protocol or procedure. It simply was.

EsJen knew this in her heart. It made her very uneasy.

TohPeht must have sensed this, but did not address it directly. Instead, he tried to put her at ease.

"I was heartened to hear that your working relationship with Mehn-Tec, and your friendship with him, continued strong following the dissolution of your partnership."

"To not have MehnTec as a friend would have been a great personal loss," said EsJen. She and MehnTec had been friends for many years before going into partnership. With the end of that partnership, they each put tremendous effort into restoring that original relationship.

"I can understand that. And your individual contributions to Shylmahn society complement one another so well; it would have been a great loss to all if you could not have continued as colleagues."

"To paraphrase your own words, TohPeht, the direction our path takes us is not always the choice we would have made, but is often found to be the correct one."

TohPeht smiled broadly, "How wonderful. I see you have picked up the Chehnon peculiarity of 'turning about a phrase'. You know, BehLahk has turned it into an art form."

"Perhaps I picked up the habit from him."

"Yes, yes... that's right. You and BehLahk have worked together often."

"Many times." Despite her occasional missteps in judgment, or perhaps because of them, EsJen had continued to rise through the Shylmahn hierarchy, reaching the upper echelons of administration. In her capacity as head of research in Chehnon behavior, she had, through her projects, frequently come into contact with the shadowy BehLahk.

TohPeht held his smile a moment longer, then let it fade. To EsJen, it seemed rather calculated. TohPeht brought his hands around from behind his back and held them out in front of him. "You no doubt have suspicions as to the reason for your being asked here," he said.

"I suspect it has something to do with the Chehnon native JoSeph." EsJen used the Shylmahn inflective common when speaking an individual's name. When referring to the Chehnon Joseph, such was a conscious decision that helped her to maintain distance from her formal study subject.

"Yes," said TohPeht. "Exactly so."

"I have occasionally sensed an underlying anxiety regarding him, increasingly so as of late. His name has appeared in unrelated reports and correspondence coming out of this area, and his very existence has somehow affected local projects, though I was usually at a loss as to the reasons why."

"I believe that the rising level of concern may be warranted, EsJen."

EsJen felt a momentary flush of guilt. How might her actions so many years in the past have been responsible for the dangers her people may now face?

TohPeht's tone of voice became slightly more ordered. "We were content to allow JoSeph to assist Chehnon natives out of the province and into the frontier. For the most part, such activity served our purpose at the time, and it was only when he conducted parallel activities that conflicted with our own interests that there was conflict beyond the normal skirmishes."

"Such a policy was put into place during my time here. JoSeph had set up several facilities as transfer stations of a sort. He worked out of a small village just inside the frontier."

"Freetown," said TohPeht. The Chehnon word had an odd sound when coming from a Shylmahn. "And JoSeph disappeared soon after we were forced to intervene in one of his insurgent operations."

EsJen remembered the incident. It was a very minor event by Shylmahn standards, but it had caught EsJen's attention. JoSeph had tried to infiltrate a small Shylmahn outpost, she still had no idea why, and most of his comrades had been killed or captured. Only JoSeph and a handful of others made it away. Joseph vanished not long afterward, and there had been only scattered sightings since then. At least, up until a year or so ago.

"We know that JoSeph has of late been in regular contact with the three remaining insurrectionary groups still operating in this area. Individually, none is of any consequence. Even taken together, they pose no real threat, at least not without some additional and significant element being brought into the current state of affairs."

EsJen waited for TohPeht to elaborate on what that additional significant element might be, since this was what appeared to be the issue of concern. He did not elaborate. Instead, he moved to the second point.

"Recent attacks on facilities have become more targeted and to all appearances coordinated. Evidence indicates that each attack has a specific purpose in mind, and for each the goal is a piece of technology or data."

"That implies—"

"They know what they are going after when they target a location, which on its own is unsettling. Even more disturbing is that there is a larger driving purpose behind it all."

"An all encompassing plan..."

"Yes," said TohPeht.

"And you believe that JoSeph is behind it?"

"During his time as the focus of study in your early project, JoSeph did not actually acquire tangible information that in and of itself could be construed as threatening or dangerous. However, he did develop a greater understanding of the Shylmahn than any other Chehnon on the planet. Such a foundation, when built upon with subsequent knowledge and technology accumulated since the end of that study, does make him the major potential threat. With each additional bit of information acquired, his understanding grows and expands, and weaknesses may be identified and avenues of attack identified; and that potential threat grows exponentially."

"Yes," said EsJen, feeling very vulnerable. "I see."

"We have evidence of a workable communications and supply network being put into place over the last year, and further evidence that this growing network is being coordinated by JoSeph. We believe this network is serving as the primary conduit for the attacks on our facilities, and that the sole purpose for the network is to serve the needs of this... *all encompassing plan*... as you described it."

EsJen could certainly understand TohPeht's concern. While there was no imminent threat looming, and anything that the Chehnon might do would, at worst, be localized and short lived, Shylmahn would likely be hurt, and the psychological repercussions on both Shylmahn and Chehnon might have more extensive impact. Many Shylmahn would most definitely want something more permanent and decisive done about the Chehnon, not fully understanding their value as a natural resource. And on the other side, many Chehnon might see such an attack, if not dealt with quickly and decisively by the Shylmahn, as an indication that the Shylmahn may not be unassailable.

Yes, JoSeph could very well be behind this.

"What of NehLoc?" EsJen asked. "Wouldn't his people be in a better position to handle something like this than me?"

"NehLoc's staff has been instrumental in collecting and collating the information that has allowed us to develop an accurate picture of the current situation, and our understanding of JoSeph's role in this."

"Then certainly—"

"It was NehLoc who first suggested that you be asked to assist. He believes, and ShahnTahr is in full agreement, that your extensive knowledge and understanding of the behavior of the Chehnon natives, and of JoSeph in particular, will be invaluable in eliminating this threat."

"I see."

"You will be working closely with NehLoc on this matter," said TohPeht. He cocked his head slightly and gave EsJen a curious look. "That will not be a problem, will it?"

"No, TohPeht. I serve."

TohPeht smiled, swung his arms back dramatically and again clasped his hands behind his back. "As do we all," he said. He gave several confident nods of his head. "It is wonderful to have you here with us again, EsJen."

NehLoc walked down the center of the street, stepping around tall weeds that had grown through the asphalt. Two oversized Shylmahn walked a dozen paces ahead, another two followed a dozen paces behind. Hunting probes zoomed up and down side streets, in between houses, hovered momentarily at windows and doors.

NehLoc's gait was different than any other Shylmahn, almost a swagger. He held the stun stick in his hand like a riding crop, occasionally slapping it against his leg. As he walked, he watched the probes and the escort for signs.

He enjoyed getting out, getting away from the holo-table and the meetings and the constant monitoring of staff and projects. To be able to get back out into the wilds of the province, to see and feel and smell, rejuvenated his spirit. His responsibilities didn't allow it very often, and his duty to the Shylmahn would always come first, but when he could justify it, he made the effort. He was, after all, an important tool of the Shylmahn people, and he had a responsibility to maintain his own sharp edge.

They turned onto the main thoroughfare of this old Chehnon community. After forty easy paces, the forward escort stopped and waited for NehLoc. Probes continued their quick runs in and out of the narrow breezeways between buildings.

NehLoc looked down the alley where the two Chehnon had been brought down several weeks earlier. He nodded curtly and kept his silence. He was then shown the dwelling across the street where the third had managed to give the hunting party the slip. NehLoc continued to restrain his anger, though the escort could sense the heated emotion rising within their leader.

NehLoc climbed up onto the porch of the *human* dwelling. He watched as one of the probes disappeared down the alley across the street. Off to his left, another patiently hovered at an open door, perhaps processing some activity within.

One of the Chehnon should have been captured alive. The one that got away should not have been allowed to escape. Such failure was completely unacceptable.

NehLoc slapped the stun stick against his leg. It smarted, but he would not allow his senses to register the pain. He stood silent, unmoving, dissipated the pain, dissipated the anger. To not do so would be to not serve to his fullest, and that would be just as unacceptable.

NehLoc sensed movement and his eyes darted quickly to the right. Two of the escort were coming towards him, a Chehnon stumbling between them. They used their stun sticks to keep the creature moving.

Tyh Muhtla, he thought. *Excellent.*

NehLoc watched as the Chehnon was led to the foot of the steps. It took several more encouraging prods with stun sticks to bring the native to its knees. All the while, NehLoc loomed menacingly, if patiently, over the captive, looking down from his position on the porch. Once the creature was properly submissive, NehLoc cocked his head slightly and gave it a careful study.

"Chehnon," he said finally.

"Human," said the creature.

One of the escort pressed the tip of his stun stick into the Chehnon's side. The creature jerked violently and let out a pained squeal.

"Chehnon," said NehLoc again. This time, the creature said nothing. This exchange was common when dealing with Chehnon. NehLoc used it to establish the proper mood. "This place," NehLoc indicated the community at large, "where you live?"

The Chehnon said nothing, and the escort again pressed the stun stick into its side.

"Chehnon?" NehLoc asked, once the creature had recovered.

It glanced furtively up at NehLoc, then quickly returned its gaze to the porch steps directly in front of it. When the escort started to bring the stun stick forward, NehLoc gave a barely perceptible gesture and the other lowered the stick.

NehLoc waited.

"Yes," said the Chehnon, at last.

"Jehtu. Mes tyh neshu Chehnon?" *Yes. Are there many more humans?*

The Chehnon looked frightened and confused.

"Buhn fehtohp daehg, Chehnon." *You do not want to die, human.*

The Chehnon looked quickly over his shoulder, at the Shylmahn that kept jabbing him with the stun stick, then as quickly up at NehLoc. The Shylmahn's dark eyes shimmered brightly. The Chehnon lowered his gaze.

"OhpJehtu," said the human. "Bohn grishohp." *No, I don't.*

The Shylmahn language as spoken by the Chehnon was grotesque, but it highlighted the subservience of the creature.

"Good," said NehLoc. He moved down one step. "So we are clear—I will ask you questions. You will answer these questions. So long as you continue to answer my questions to my complete satisfaction, you will live. Should I be less than pleased with your response, you will be eliminated. Your death will not be immediate." NehLoc rested his stun stick on the creature's shoulder. It was not active, but the creature gave a quick, reflexive jerk. NehLoc radiated a mix of bliss and menace. It had taken him years to perfect the right combination. "Okay?" he asked.

"Yes," the Chehnon answered quickly.

"Muhtla," said NehLoc. *Good.*

Despite the Chehnon's very tangible fear, the answers were not easily forthcoming, and the creature was thrown into unconsciousness several times during interrogation. In the end, NehLoc was not completely satisfied. He ordered that the creature be taken to the shuttle. The questioning would continue under more controlled conditions once they returned to civilization. In the end, the Chehnon creature would be eliminated. NehLoc was not given to making idle threats.

Through this preliminary interrogation, NehLoc had verified that JoSeph had begun passing through this area on a somewhat regular basis starting about a year earlier. It had been JoSeph who had established this location as part of the network that spanned most of the province. This creature knew little of the rest of the network, and knew less of JoSeph than what NehLoc knew. Its small role had been to serve as but a single component in the communications net that overlay this network. It was used primarily by key figures of a fledgling organization that JoSeph was bringing together from the remnants of a number of other failed groups, and occasionally to help outsiders make contact with this new group.

If the creature was to be believed, it knew nothing of the ultimate purpose of this organization beyond the eventual victory over the Shylmahn.

There was no obvious connection between this network and the railroad being operated by JoSeph's brood. The recent events may have been nothing more than his children who, having heard of the network, had been attempting to make contact.

Perhaps there had been nothing sinister in it.

NehLoc had never been happy about allowing the *underground railroad* to operate, but this was one area where his recommendations had been soundly overridden by ShahnTahr. NehLoc believed that allowing the Chehnon to feel any sense of freedom and independence, any sense of undermining their masters, was a mistake.

All Chehnon should be eliminated. If not complete elimination, any minimal remaining population should at the very least be kept under complete subjugation.

ShahnTahr and TohPeht believed the natives were a natural resource of Chehno. They served as a tool, just as any other resource. The vast majority were maintained on the reservations at reasonable cost. In their minds, allowing these few wild Chehnon to do the work of emptying the province of other wild natives served a purpose and was a necessary activity that if not done by the Chehnon, would have to be done utilizing Shylmahn resources.

To NehLoc's mind, it was a dangerous game they played. The Chehnon were cunning and resourceful creatures. NehLoc feared that the threat they posed was not being taken as seriously as it might. He would never openly contradict ShahnTahr, would never consider such a thing, but he felt himself unique in his silent questioning of certain decisions that had been made since the Shylmahn arrival on this planet. He felt his loyalty lay in being prepared in the event his concerns proved correct.

NehLoc would serve best by being in a position to step in with alternative solutions to address whatever crisis may arise. He took this responsibility very seriously. He would do whatever it took to meet this responsibility short of open disagreement with ShahnTahr, to whom his loyalty ultimately rested. ShahnTahr and the Shylmahn were inextricably connected. To oppose ShahnTahr was to deny duty to the Shylmahn, and this was unimaginable. NehLoc, through a lifetime of dedication to both, through sense of duty to both, successfully walked the path of internal questioning and external, unquestioning implementation. His was unwavering duty without the blind obedience; NehLoc followed where ShahnTahr led, while struggling to guide the direction the Shylmahn should go. Such was his commitment to the Shylmahn people.

When Michael came out of his house, he found Victoria standing at the end of his front walk. She stood with arms folded, watching him, her expression betraying nothing.

Victoria Romero was an attractive woman, had strong features and an occasionally explosive personality. Her mind and her insight were sharp, her ability to read people almost unfailing. Her long relationship with Michael had swayed many who had been unsure of the son's ability to step into the shoes of the father. Some who had been frightened by Joseph Britton's vision of freedom for all humans had been won over by the man's quiet dedication and surety of purpose. They were not as convinced of Michael's abilities, with his occasional outbursts when confronted with issues that he'd just as soon go around, his admitted inability to deal with *stupid people,* and his early stumbles in the unblinking eye of public political glare, which he also admittedly loathed. He would just as soon let others handle that sort of thing and be left alone to run the railroad. Such an attitude had won him no friends, particularly from those who had been swayed by the argument that maybe he should take care of the people at home before going out to bring more in. It was Victoria Romero's belief in him that brought the skeptics over.

Everyone assumed that Michael and Victoria would someday get married, but for now the two each lived on their own. It was suspected that the combination of her well known explosive personality and his just as famous outbursts when confronted with a task he'd rather avoid may have had something to do with their living arrangements. Nonetheless, they were the uncrowned royal couple of Freetown.

"Victoria," said Michael, tentative in tone but he was clearly glad to see her.

"Can I walk you to the meeting?" she asked, just a touch reticent but allowing for the possibility of a continued relationship.

"Of course. I was beginning to wonder if I'd ever see you again."

"It is a very small town, Michael." She started in the direction of the plaza and Michael followed beside her. "Are you ready for this?"

"Of course not."

Victoria saw no humor in this. "This isn't just any town meeting. Perry's going to be coming after you."

"Just like every other town meeting," said Michael. He decided to change the subject. "Where have you been hiding?"

"You didn't ask around?" she smiled.

"I was afraid to. Wasn't sure I wanted to know."

"I'll bet," Victoria smirked. They turned down the path between two small houses that sat on the perimeter of the plaza, where there was already a crowd forming. "To be honest, I wasn't here when you got back. I went out with the hunting party and we didn't get back until last night."

"You mean—"

"You should've asked around."

"I asked Annie," said Michael. Annie would have known that Victoria had gone out. She had let him believe that Vicki was... *She's not going to get away with this,* he thought to himself.

Michael and Victoria walked around the rows of chairs that were quickly filling up. Ahead of the chairs stood a short platform that had been brought into the plaza for the meeting. Five people were carrying wooden chairs up onto platform, which they placed in a line facing the audience. Craig Warren, taking his seat in the center chair, saw Michael coming around to the front row. He gave Michael a friendly wave and smile.

Michael waved back as he sat down directly in front of the five council members. He ignored Ethan Perry, sitting in the farthest chair on the platform.

"How's life, Craig?" Michael asked.

"Giving me a run for my money," Craig answered.

"You can use the exercise."

Freetown held a town meeting every month, and about twenty-five or thirty citizens could usually be counted on to attend, including the five council members. Another handful could be counted on to watch from windows opening out onto the central plaza in the main cavern. With a population hovering just under or over three hundred at any given time, this meant about ten percent sat in on regular meetings. Of course, whenever highly charged issues were on the agenda, greater attendance could be expected.

Attendance was a bit higher this time around, though not overly so. Ethan Perry could always be relied upon to fan a few flames during any meeting that fell within a few days of one of Michael Britton's returns. And with Jack Riley's team being killed and Riley alone returning, Ethan Perry was certain to be in fine form.

"I heard that your run was successful," said Victoria, leaning close to Michael.

"We brought six out," said Michael. "Pretty routine."

"No trouble?"

"Quiet, actually."

"How was Jenny?"

"Doing good," Michael shifted about to face Victoria. It looked like the meeting was still a few minutes off. "I know that she likes living out there, but you can see that she gets lonely."

"You don't care about her being lonely. You just don't like her being out there alone."

Michael shrugged. "You might be right."

"She'd hate living here."

Michael glanced about the plaza; the small buildings clustered together, the apartments on the terraces, the rock ceiling pushing down on them. "The Outer Village, maybe."

"Never," said Victoria, quite certainly.

"Never," Michael sighed.

"What about Monroe?"

"What about him?"

"He and Jenny?"

"I doubt that very much," said Michael.

"I know for a fact that Monroe would do anything for her."

"I'm sure that he would," Michael admitted. "He may even have some feelings for her, but I don't think Jenny feels that way."

"An arrangement of some kind," Victoria suggested.

"That sounds awful," Michael grumbled.

"I'm not suggesting anything physical."

"They each have very different...." Michael wavered, looking for the right word.

"Lifestyles?"

"Okay... Anyway, any life that Monroe might have at the cabin would be stifling for him, and Jenny would never be happy living Monroe's... whatever it is that he lives."

"Then leave it alone," she said. "In any case, Jenny would never do anything that might threaten that uncompromising Britton sense of duty. She'll live out her days isolated out there in the middle of nowhere, the self-sacrificing stationmaster, helping to bring out that one last human refugee."

Michael involuntarily pulled back, looked quickly away; first at a group of people just coming into the plaza, then up at Craig Warren, sitting quietly in his center chair, up on the platform. He didn't want to get into another argument with Victoria about the Britton family psyche. The subject was a sore spot for them both, and the arguments usually left Victoria feeling bitter and Michael feeling hurt and defensive.

Mitch Travers strode up and pointed at the empty chair beside Victoria. "Mind if I grab this seat?" he asked them both.

Michael smiled and nodded. Victoria straightened about and faced forward, "Of course not," she said, not unkindly, but not really inviting, either. "Join us."

"I thank you, Miss Romero." Mitch sat down with a heavy sigh. "This should be an interesting meeting."

"That it should," she agreed.

Mitch leaned forward to look around Victoria. "How's Jack doing, Michael?"

"Much better," said Michael. "Annie says that he's recovering fine."

"So he'll soon be out an' stirrin' up trouble and mayhem?"

"As only Jack can."

"That's great," said Mitch. "You and he makin' plans to head back out?"

"Nothing definite yet," Michael glanced furtively at Victoria, sitting stiffly between them. "But yes."

"That's great," Mitch said again. He turned and faced front, as it appeared the meeting was about to start. "You let me know if there's anything I can do to help."

Craig Warren stood and held his hands up for quiet. The forty or fifty people in the audience settled into their seats and quieted. A few last-minute arrivals hurried to find empty chairs.

"I guess we can get started," said Craig. "It looks like we have a full house tonight. I see a few faces we don't often see at these things. I'm sure we won't disappoint."

There was a bit of nervous laughter, but mostly there was a calm anticipation. Craig looked behind him at the others in the council, then clasped his hands together and faced the crowd.

"First off, I'd like to welcome the new folks that Michael and his team brought in." Craig quickly spotted the six newcomers sitting together several rows back. He smiled and held out a welcoming hand. "I understand that Meg Insley and her daughter Kara have decided to stay with us, as has the young Mister Samuel Cole. We are very pleased to have you with us." He looked back to the crowd as a whole. "Of the others, two are continuing on to Metcalf in a few days in search of family, while the adventurous Mr. Simms has chosen to embark on a journey of exploration. We wish them all the best of luck."

There was a light applause and several *here, here* cheers. Craig Warren then moved on to general house-keeping items. He spent several minutes going over the current inventory levels of food stores, clothing, tools and equipment, asking supply supervisors for clarification on several items. He noted the recent hunting and collection expeditions, and asked the leaders of these expeditions for a report on what they had brought in.

Victoria spoke for the hunting expedition, specified where they had traveled and the number of animals they had brought down. Hunting trips were carefully directed so as not to over-hunt an area, to make sure that animals of various species were hunted only during certain times of the year so as to ensure that breeding and newborn seasons were protected, and to guarantee that only certain genders and ages of certain species were hunted.

As for the collection team, this time out they had traveled all the way to Waverly, located far to the north, on the province/frontier border, and had come back with writing paper, children's clothes, a number of reference books and hardcover fiction, and a supply of nails, screws, and nuts and bolts. There was much more to be recovered there, and they would be returning within the week, once they had fitted out sufficient transportation.

The agricultural supervisor gave his report on crops and stock. Agricultural sites were located at nine different locations in and around Freetown. The outside sites were camouflaged as best they could be, blended into the surrounding terrain, and were small in size.

Craig Warren then read a list of upcoming activities that were scheduled over the next month. There was a quilting bee still looking for participants; Canning Day needed more volunteers, and if they didn't get them, there would be a lottery to fill the slots; there was a dance coming up, and the organizers said they had the help they needed to work the event, but needed a few more people to prepare food.

"The wake for Tyler and Hearn, lost on a recent mission, is scheduled for tomorrow," said Craig, setting aside the activities list. "Please get the word out to everyone. They were good people, and we are going to miss them."

Craig took in a long breath, steeling himself for what was to come.

"Next then," he began. "Before we go to open forum, I believe we're all a bit curious about Jack's mission and what happened. It's understood that for security reasons he won't be able to get into some of the specifics, but he should be able to provide enough details to help us appreciate what happened and to put the tragedy into perspective."

Jack stood and climbed up onto the platform, nodded curtly at the members of the council and turned to the audience. If anyone hated standing in front of a group more than Michael Britton, it was Jack Rydel.

"I'll certainly do what I can to keep the gossip from going too far afield," he said.

"Good luck with that," said someone from the crowd, and there was a scattering of laughter.

"Thanks," said Jack. "I appreciate your support." He rubbed his hands together as a delaying tactic, trying to put his thoughts in order. "First off," he started again, "We were on an investigatory mission. The three of us were sent out to gather information that we suspected we would find in a small town a few days' march into the occupied territory, and verify other information that had been acquired on an earlier trip. That was the extent of it. Stay low, stay out of trouble, collect the intel, and get home. We didn't anticipate any real trouble, but any time you go into the occupied territory, well, the threat is greater there than it is here.

"We got there fine, but it took a little longer to find what we were looking for. I didn't like spending so much time there, but this was pretty important."

"How about tellin' something more about what you was lookin' for?" asked someone.

"It isn't like we're Shillies, man!" said someone else.

"You all know the reasons," said Jack. He could feel Ethan Perry's eyes burrowing into the back of his head. He knew that Perry would sit quietly until the open forum. "Any of us can be taken at any time, even out here on the Frontier. You all know that. There are some things best left unsaid, and this is one of 'em."

There was more grumbling, but as soon it died down enough that he could be heard, Jack went on, which quieted down the rest of it. He explained that they did finally get what they were after, and then some.

They were on their way out when the Shillies closed in, maybe coming after the same information, maybe just on a hunting trip. In any event, they were tracked down and Tyler and Hearn went down. He was hurt some, but did manage to get out.

With that, Jack hopped down off the platform and quickly took his seat. Michael, who had been watching Ethan Perry throughout most of the presentation, noted that the man was having difficulty restraining himself.

"Thank you, Jack," said Craig Warren, standing quickly and stepping to the front of the platform. "I know that I speak for everyone when I say that we appreciate the sacrifices of those who go into the occupied territory, and again, we deeply regret the loss of Tyler and Hearn. Their absence will be deeply felt."

"Fine boys," said Mitch Travers in a gruff mumble, shifting about in his seat.

"Definitely," said Craig, nodding sharply. "Very well, then. Let's move to open forum."

A dozen hands shot up, three or four people stood quickly. Craig pointed to a man in the second row. "Stand up and speak to us, Oscar."

Oscar Patterson stood and turned in the direction of Jack Rydel, but also so that he could face as much of the audience as possible, as well as the council sitting on the platform.

"Jack, what'd you see of the Shillie technology? I heard they jumped another generation, and it's near impossible to steer clear of the hunter probes." Oscar sat back down. "Is that how they got ya?" he asked.

"The probes were more advanced than the last time I was out there, that's for sure. You all know the Shillie technology keeps improving, and I don't see that slowing down any. Their ships, their weapons, all of it, keeps getting better and better." Jack thought a moment and slowly shook his head. "So far as the probes... this generation is maneuvering better than the last, but I didn't see much improvement in their sensors. As good as ever, but no better than the last time I ran into them." He looked around at the audience, started to sit, then stopped and looked at Oscar. "Does that answer your question?"

"Thanks, Jack. Does fine," Oscar half stood, then plopped himself back into his chair.

Craig came forward and started to select another from the crowd when Ethan Perry spoke from his chair. "Let's get right to the heart of it, Craig," he said, without standing.

Craig Warren waved in Ethan Perry's direction without turning, backed into his seat. "I yield the floor to Ethan Perry," he said.

Ethan looked pointedly at Michael Britton. "How in God's name can you justify these outrageous actions of yours that continue to put all of us at risk, day after day after day?"

"How so, Ethan?" asked Michael. He too chose to remain in his seat.

"Come on, man. How can you be so flippant about it? Every time you go into the occupied territory on one of your so-called mercy missions, you put this entire community at risk. But even that's not enough for you. No! Now you're sending Rydel in on spy missions. An underground railroad is bad enough, but to flaunt your disdain for the Shillies with these subversive acts, and in the very heart of their province, is unconscionable."

"Road apples!" said Mitch Travers, refusing to even look at Ethan Perry.

"Mr. Perry has the floor," said Craig.

"And it's covered in road apples!"

"Nonetheless."

There was a chittering of nervous laughter. Ethan quickly recovered his composure and turned his gaze again on Michael. "Despite the eloquent response of your learned companion, I do not believe that it directly addresses the issue. These are very real, legitimate concerns, and they deserve to be addressed."

At least a dozen people in the audience applauded enthusiastically. The support seemed to put a fire in Ethan's eyes and now he did stand. He took a step toward the front of the platform, turned and looked down on Michael.

"Freetown is and should be a sanctuary for its citizens," said Ethan, forcefully pushing out each word. There were more cheers. "You make our community a target each and every time you make one of your runs, each and every time you send out your spies."

Michael waited for the cheering to lessen before standing. When he did finally stand, he turned to face both the platform and the audience, and quietly stared down at his feet, stuffed his hands into his pockets. The crowd grew silent. Ethan sat, hesitantly yielding the floor. Michael directed his line of sight to a building at the perimeter of the plaza. There would be no changing Ethan Perry's mind on anything, and Michael would wait and see before directing his attention on any one individual in the crowd.

"As all of you know, when my father founded Freetown, it was established as a primary component in the escape route that he envisioned."

"That's old news," said Ethan Perry, "and what the Britton family did decades ago has no relevance to the here and now."

Craig spoke up, "Michael held his peace for you. He now has the floor."

Ethan waved dismissively, "Fine, fine..."

Michael went on. "Over the years, the underground railroad has evolved, but the original purpose remains unchanged; Freetown's purpose remains unchanged. It should remain unchanged. Its reason for existence is and always has been to aid others in their escape from the Shylmahn."

"Why?" said Ethan.

"Because there are people out there who need our help," said Michael.

There was a light applause from many in the audience, but it was restrained. It sounded as though most were not prepared to fully commit to the cause.

"I would say that we have done more than our fair share," said Ethan.

"How?" said Michael, it being his turn to throw out a one word question.

"How???" Ethan Perry looked perplexed.

"At what point in time did we pass the *fair share* mark? On what date did we fulfill our obligation to our fellow human beings, the rest to be left to their own?"

"That's not a fair question."

"Would you have stopped at two hundred of these brought out?" Michael indicated the last group that he had brought out of the occupied territory. "At one hundred, maybe? How about twenty? Would you have put your foot down when my father went out on his first run?"

"You can't—"

"Oh, wait..." Michael gave a dramatic studied gaze. "That's right. You weren't here at the time of the first run. My father brought you out much later, didn't he?"

At this there was applause from many, and indignation from others. Ethan Perry was on his feet again. "Does the fact that I wasn't here in the beginning mean that I can have no opinion as to our community's affairs?"

"Absolutely not," Michael said quickly. "We all have a say. My concern is that you would twist Freetown into something unrecognizable."

Miriam Foster slowly rose to her feet, leaned forward on her cane and waited to be recognized. Ethan Perry shot her a long, frustrated look but finally took his seat, giving another dismissive wave of the hand.

Michael shifted about then. "I yield," he said, sitting.

Miriam turned her back on the council, as much a dismissal of Ethan Perry as his wave of the hand had been. Before speaking, she scanned the crowd, pausing a moment on every face looking back at her. She wanted all to know that the words she would speak would be directed at each and every one of them individually.

"Freetown is not a sanctuary. It never was and never will be. It is not a destination. It is a tool. Its residents are not citizens but working parts of the machine. The purpose of that machine is to aid in the extraction of human beings from the occupied territory and send them on their way."

"Purposes change," said Ethan Perry, albeit with less force than when responding to Michael's comments.

"Not when it comes to Freetown," said Miriam, not bothering to turn to Ethan. "Not ever. It is true that what we do can indeed bring the Shylmahn wrath down upon us. That is the danger we face every day; that is the risk we take in fulfilling our responsibilities to the railroad.

"For those wishing to hide in a hole, to exist without living, to deny our obligations to our fellow human beings, I suggest that you go elsewhere. I can direct you to several communities within a week's march of here."

"I live here," said Ethan.

Now Miriam did turn to face Ethan. "Then, Mr. Perry, I would suggest that you do your *fair share* in support of the enduring purpose of Freetown. In this, you have been woefully lacking."

Jenny Britton pushed the wheelbarrow of manure out through the large open doors of the barn and guided it to the compost pile around the far side of the building. Once unloaded, she used the pitchfork to throw vegetation from a second compost pile onto the manure. This done, she hosed down the barrow and returned it to the barn.

As she set the wheelbarrow on end, she heard a faint rumbling noise, as of something rolling far in the distance. It took only a few seconds for her mind to sort through the possibilities, and she hurried out of the barn. She passed through the smaller side door in time to see, or at least hear, a Shylmahn attack craft rush overhead. She couldn't move her head fast enough to catch sight of it before it was lost over the horizon. Looking back in the direction from which it had come, she saw two shuttlecraft traveling towards her, following in the wake of the attack craft. She backed up against the wall of the barn, into the shadow of the building, felt the warm wood against her back just as the first of the shuttlecraft passed overhead. Seconds later, the second passed directly over the barn and the house, about two hundred feet above her.

Once it had passed, Jenny stepped out into the yard and watched the two craft disappear beyond the trees, trailing after the much faster attack ship. They didn't look like they had any intention of landing, or of investigating anything that might pass beneath them, but Jenny wasn't taking any chances. She rushed to her cabin and set about to lock things down and go into hiding. This wasn't the first time, and she doubted that it would be the last.

Once everything was closed up, Jenny opened a trap door set into the floor of her bedroom. With rifle in hand, she climbed down the ladder and into a three-by-three access tunnel, closing the door above her. The wood pattern of the floor made the door just about impossible to detect once closed.

Reaching the bottom, she opened a short door inward and entered a dark horizontal tunnel. After closing and locking the door behind her, Jenny grabbed a flashlight from a shelf dug into the wall, turned it on and started down the narrow passageway. Eighty feet further along, she opened another short door, stepped through, closed and locked it behind her.

The room was twelve feet by twenty, with a seven foot ceiling. About eight feet above the ceiling would be the floor of the forest that began beyond the clearing behind the house. Ventilation pipes ran from vents in the ceiling to well-hidden vent caps set within brush and beneath fallen logs.

Jenny found the lantern, which she lit and hung near one of the vents. This done, she turned off the flashlight and sat down in one of the two chairs, leaned back and let her head drop back. She stared at the ceiling, which was covered in cheap paneling that was held in place using two-by-four cross supports.

The hideout was primitive but well-stocked. If need be, she could survive here for weeks. If necessary, the tunnel she had traveled down could be collapsed in seconds. And while she wouldn't want to, she could manage her way through a very tight-fitting emergency tunnel that led to the surface, closed now with sealed hatches at either end to prevent accidental discovery.

She wondered about Monroe. He should be coming back through on his return from Freetown any day. She had in fact expected him by now. He knew of this hideout, and if he showed up and found her gone, he would look here first. He would be able to see that she hadn't packed for a hunting trip, or for any sort of trip at all.

She had something to eat and then turned off the lantern and settled in for the night. It was absolutely black and dead quiet. Despite concerns about what may have occurred up top, she managed to sleep straight through to morning. When she woke, her internal clock told her that it was dawn.

She retraced her steps back through the tunnel, securing each door and returning the flashlight to its shelf. With rifle in hand, she climbed the ladder, stopping short of opening the trap door into her bedroom.

She heard movement in the cabin above: footsteps in the main room. As she listened, she heard voices. Human voices. Men. At least two, maybe three.

Jenny settled in just under the trap door. She wasn't going to make an appearance until she knew what was up and who these men were.

The sounds were muffled, and it was difficult for her to make out most of what was said. Still, it didn't take long for her to figure out that whoever these people were, they had expected to find a woman living here, and living alone. They were rather disappointed at finding the place deserted.

Jenny's relay station wasn't a secret. Anyone traveling the railroad out of the occupied territory came through her place. She found it surprising, though, that anyone would go through all the trouble to seek her out just to have their way with her. It wasn't exactly on the main routes.

Being in such an out-of-the-way location, Jenny also found it highly suspect that these boys should show up so soon after a Shillie flyby. The coincidence was unsettling.

Whoever they were, they didn't sound like very nice folks. Certain references and inferences left little doubt as to at least some of their plans for her, should they get their hands on her.

That just isn't going to happen...

When she heard at least two of the men walk across the main room and leave the cabin, Jenny unlatched the trap door and carefully pushed it up, just enough that she could see in. From her position, she had a view of the open door leading out of the bedroom and much of the main room beyond. There was no one in sight. She listened for several seconds, and then slowly pushed herself up through the trap door and climbed into the bedroom. She hadn't taken but one step before a silhouette filled the doorway.

The man wore a broad grin. He glanced quickly at the rifle Jenny was holding at her side, but appeared unafraid. He could see that she was taken aback at his sudden appearance.

"Hey, sweet meat. Where ya' been keeping yourself?"

Jenny didn't waste time in conversation. She brought the rifle up and fired three quick shots from the hip as fast as the lever action would allow. The first bullet took him in the center of his chest, the next two each found marks higher as he fell back and then down. Jenny was through the bedroom door and stepping over the body even as it settled onto the floor. Reaching the front window, she saw one of the other men rushing across the yard and up onto the porch. There wasn't time to take a shot through the window, so she turned to face the door and fired two more rounds as he came into the room. Once she was sure he wasn't getting up, she turned back to the window.

There was at least one more of these creeps out there somewhere. She watched and waited. For long seconds there was no movement and the only sound was nature undisturbed. She doubted the third man would just run off. More likely, he would bide his time and wait for the right moment to strike.

There was a sudden thunderclap of a high caliber rifle, followed by the scuffling and crying out of frightened animals. Watching the barn, she saw the side door open and Monroe walk out. He took a single step and stopped, planted his feet shoulder width apart and placed the butt of his rifle on his hip.

He was giving a sign: if there's any more of you, I'm waiting. If Jenny is watching, it's all taken care of.

Jenny went to the door and stepped out. She placed the butt of her rifle on her hip and stared her friend down.

| 3 |

Michael tossed his bag over his shoulder and walked from his door out to the lane. The lights set high into the cavern walls were off this time of night, and there were only the street lamps set to low spreading any light in the Inner Village. Victoria was waiting for him, wrapped in a shawl and looking as though she had just woke up.

"Good morning," he said to her, and gave her a light kiss. She wrapped her arms around him and held tight. He held her with his free arm and laid his head beside hers. They pulled apart after a long while and started in silence through the village.

"I'll miss you," she said finally. They walked quietly across the main plaza. The town was quiet and they were careful to keep their footsteps light and voices low.

"I hope to be back in a few weeks," said Michael. "More likely, it'll take a bit longer."

"Get word back to us if it takes longer."

"I'll try." If a team was out longer than expected, Freetown would often send someone to Jenny's station hoping there was word. The unwritten rule was to get a message to Jenny if there was going to be a delay.

They passed through the double-blind canvas hanging over the main doors and stepped out under the open sky. The Outer Village was even darker than inside, since they burned no lamps outside at night. It was an hour before dawn, and the moon and stars had gone out.

"We'll try to keep things together while you're gone," said Victoria. "I'm not sure how successful we'll be, though."

"You sure can't do any worse than me."

"You're wrong there, my man," she said with a grin. "Unlike the rest of us, you don't have to be any good at it. All you have to do is show up."

"Yeah, right."

"No, I mean it. For some unfathomable reason, people like you. And somehow, in spite of yourself, three times out of five you say the right thing."

They laughed lightly at that, then noticed a shadow near the dark corner up ahead. They continued walking, more warily now, until they recognized Miriam leaning heavily on her cane.

"You're out kind of early, aren't you?" asked Michael as they neared.

"My leg had me up half the night," she said. She moved forward as they reached her, and they stopped before her. She held out her arms and Michael stepped into them. "You find him," she said softly, pulling away and wiping her eyes.

"We will."

"Damn him," she said in a broken laugh.

"I'll pass that on," said Michael. He leaned forward and gave her another hug and a kiss.

"He was... he and Barbara were..."

"I know." Michael could hear several horses being led from the stables toward the main gate. He turned back to Victoria. "I love you," he said.

They hugged and kissed. She pulled him close then, as if she wouldn't let him go. After half a minute, Miriam smacked them both with her cane.

"Get the hell out of here," she said.

Michael pulled himself free, gave Victoria a smile and turned side glance at Miriam. "Witch," he said lightly.

"We all have our roles to play," she said.

Michael turned about and walked away without looking back. It hurt every time.

Jack Rydel and Mitch Travers were waiting just inside the main gate. He nodded silently to each of them, waved a hand to the man on guard. As the gate was slowly opened, Michael gave Jack a quick, studied look.

"You sure you're ready for this?" he asked. "Annie'll kick my ass if we get a week out and your wounds open up."

"I'm fine," said Jack. "Let's go find your father."

The gate yawned open and they passed through, leaving the sleeping town behind them and starting through the woods. They would walk the horses while it was dark, and would be four miles out before dawn.

EsJen stepped out of the small, private shuttlecraft that had been provided for her use while in the province. Her escort followed her out. Two military types from the dahlseht security force, they had orders to stay with her wherever she went. She had known that she would be required to accept such protection upon arriving in the province, but had naively hoped MehnTec could serve that function. While not MehnTec's true calling, EsJen believed that any serious threat was remote, and that the security would be largely ceremonial. On this she had been mistaken. Even if TohPeht hadn't had other matters for MehnTec to attend to, there were very real dangers and neither TohPeht nor NehLoc would allow EsJen to move about without serious protection while she was here.

The shuttlecraft pilot watched from his cockpit window and closed the side door as soon as his passengers had disembarked. He would link up his ship's communications system with province security and take this time to coordinate the rest of his day's itinerary. It didn't matter that his passenger was a high ranking official nor that this ship was for her use only; he had only been given clearance to travel from the dahlseht to here. He hadn't had time for anything more.

NehLoc was waiting for EsJen at the gate of the small landing tarmac. This was a private facility, separate from the nearby dahlseht and dedicated primarily to the security of the province. Though he had responsibilities far beyond the security of the northwest, NehLoc found that he spent a significant amount here and so had made this location his headquarters. As such, he had wanted a facility separate from the larger dahlseht in which he would be the primary commander. His staff must be under no illusions. While their ultimate responsibility must be to the Shylmahn people, their immediate loyalty must be to NehLoc.

NehLoc smiled in welcome at EsJen's approach. EsJen returned the greeting with a nod of the head.

"NehLoc. You look well."

"As do you. It has been such a very long time." He turned about and led the way along the walk that wound through the small garden between the landing field and a short, square bunker-like complex. A high, stone wall surrounded the facility, and EsJen saw towers at each corner and midway along each side.

"Quite the fortress you have here," she said, brushing her hand across one of the colorful shrubs growing alongside the walk. *Beauty behind prison walls.*

"This is the headquarters for the security of the entire world," said NehLoc. "From here, we maintain the safety and security of every dahlseht, every Shylmahn, on Chehno. We are also responsible for the maintenance of the human reservations and the security of the work camps and research facilities." It sounded as though he were giving a tour. "While the likelihood of a Chehnon fanatic getting anywhere near this facility is extremely low, it is nonetheless prudent to maintain proper defenses."

"Of course," said EsJen.

"Besides," NehLoc regained his smile, "This is my home."

"You live here, then?" asked EsJen.

"I keep an apartment directly off my office. My schedule can be quite unpredictable, and in any event, I disliked the resources that were necessary in maintaining my security during my travel to and from the dahlseht."

EsJen studied the building they were approaching. It was a modest, one-story structure. "I take it there are floors below ground," she said.

"Yes. The ground floor is primarily devoted to administration and communication. The lower floors provide the support." The walkway led them to the side entrance. Another walk wound its way around the building, presumably to the main doors. NehLoc turned and pointed to a large tree in the middle of the garden. "I had bird feeders hung from that tree, and there's a bird bath beneath it. I can see it from my office window."

"I am pleasantly surprised at your interest in such things."

"I wish I had more time to attend to such interests. I find myself peculiarly drawn to the amazing diversity on this planet."

"NehLoc," EsJen sighed. *Let's get to it...* "Why am I here?"

NehLoc visibly stiffened, his smile fixed in place. "Because I asked for you," he said.

"I understand that. I appreciate your confidence, but I am unclear as to why you felt it necessary to bring me back to assist in the capture of one human. You are certainly quite capable, and to be quite candid, while you and I have come to terms with our differing views, and have even developed a tempered respect for one another, we both recognize that we get along best by maintaining a respectable distance from one another."

NehLoc returned his attention to the tree in the middle of his garden. He was quiet for some time, but EsJen could see that he was working a number of things through that elegantly sharp mind of his. She may have disagreement with his tactics, and his views on the humans and their role in the future of the Shylmahn, and may even have concern regarding his non-Shylmahn ambition, but on two points she held him in high regard: his fiery loyalty to the cause of the Shylmahn and his brilliant mind.

"We have grown, you and me," NehLoc said at last, still watching the activity at the bird feeders. "This world has changed us. I believe that it has made us stronger, and more valuable to our people and our culture."

"I would agree," said EsJen, somewhat cautiously.

"More than most other Shylmahn, we have had to sacrifice much of what it is to be Shylmahn."

"I would probably agree with that, as well."

NehLoc turned to EsJen, then. "We may not always agree on the means, but you and I most always agree on the goals for which we strive." NehLoc paused, looked very thoughtfully at EsJen. "Over the years, I have come to respect your work and your abilities."

"Thank you." EsJen remained noncommittal.

"If it had been simply a matter of bringing your JoSeph in, I would not have asked for your assistance. There is much more to it than that." NehLoc opened the door and held it for her. "It will take our combined efforts to eliminate this threat."

Craig Warren strode quickly down the high-ceilinged, smooth-walled utility tunnel, stepping out at last into the relative open of the main cavern. The tunnel opened onto Terrace One. With a visible sense of relief, he walked to the edge of the terrace and placed both hands onto the top railing of the low fence.

He didn't like to let on, but he always got a bit claustrophobic when working in the utility complex. The tunnel behind him provided access to four utility rooms. The tunnel itself was fairly large, at least large enough to permit the equipment that occasionally had to pass through, and even the smallest of the rooms was as big as some of the small houses on the cavern floor below. Each room had several ventilation shafts, as did the tunnel itself. None of that mattered. Going into that tunnel meant going into the heart of the mountain, and this weighed more heavily on him than did the high-domed main cavern.

His condition wasn't crippling, but it was frustrating. After each trip in, he spent a few moments shaking off the worst of it before continuing on. He stood looking out over the cavern floor below, let his mind wander to the goings-on since Michael's departure the day before. That early-morning exit had stirred things up, though probably not any worse than had he marched out in broad daylight. Yes, and that would likely have brought about its own set of problems.

As if on cue, the boy Willie came running toward him, hurrying along the twenty-foot wide travelway between the fence bordering the terrace edge and the row of apartments that butted up against the cavern wall. The kid looked stressed out.

"Mr. Warren!" he called out, sliding to a stop. "Am I glad I found you!"

"What is it, Willie?"

"Nothing but trouble, Mr. Warren."

Craig couldn't help but turn quickly back to the scene below. All looked quiet.

"What trouble?"

"It's an emergency meeting."

Uh oh...

"Perry?" Craig asked calmly.

"Yessir. Mr. Perry, sir."

"I see."

"That's what I mean by 'nothing but trouble', sir."

"Yeah," Craig Warren turned yet again to the scene below. He placed his hands on the fence and leaned forward.

"Mr. Perry says it's to allow the citizens to air concerns about the—"

Miriam approached Craig and Willie. "It is to allow the citizens of Freetown to air their concerns regarding the Britton Family stranglehold on Freetown," she said, quoting verbatim.

"That's it, all right," Willie nodded sharply. "Right after lunch."

"Thank you, Willie," said Craig.

"Yessir," Willie took a step back, paused as if waiting for further orders.

"No message," said Miriam, stopping and leaning on her cane. Willie turned about and hurried off without saying anything more.

Craig waited until Willie had left, then spoke without turning. "It will be difficult keeping a lid on things this time."

"Whether you keep a lid on things or not is not the issue," Miriam spoke calmly but with strong resolve. "You must deal with Ethan Perry. This is not a matter of differing views, but an attack on the soul of what this community is about."

"I understand that, Miriam. I believe as strongly as anyone in the purpose of Freetown, but as the council chair I also have a duty to answer to the people of this community."

Miriam lifted her cane and brought it down angrily. "Wrong!" she growled. "Absolutely wrong! This is not just a community, and the purpose of the council is not to answer to the needs of the citizens, but to see that the community remains a viable element of the railroad."

"Miriam—"

"If that is unclear to anyone on the council, perhaps a closed session is called for."

Craig took several deep breaths before responding. "Miriam, in case you have forgotten, Ethan Perry is on the council."

"As I said," said Miriam, softly now. "You must deal with Ethan Perry."

Michael wrapped an arm around Jenny as they started across the yard toward her cabin, following after Jack, who was already on the porch and heading inside. Mitch led the three horses to the corral beside the barn.

Michael sat heavily in one of the porch chairs as Jenny went inside. She came out a minute later with a metal pot and four metal cups. She poured two and sat in the other chair.

Michael took a swallow of coffee and leaned back to watch Mitch brush down the horses. He listened to Jenny as she told of the run-in with the three humans.

Monroe had told her they were definitely working with the Shillies. He had gotten that much out of one of 'em, and it fit with what she had been able to overhear.

They had been dropped off just the other side of the ridge. They were to get what they could from Jenny about comings and goings other than the regular runs, and anything that she might know about Joseph and the network that he had set up. Once they had gotten what they could from her, they were free to do what they liked.

"That means the Shillies will be coming back for them," said Michael.

"Don't know," said Jenny. "They were to meet in Stanton. Monroe says he thinks the Shillies didn't want them hanging around here too long, didn't want them and you to cross paths just yet."

"And when they don't show up at the meeting place?"

Jenny shrugged. "Don't know for sure, but from what Monroe could gather, there were a number of human teams dropped off at different locations. The Shillies might show up here, but they might just write one group off as the unpredictability of wild humans."

"Maybe," said Michael, unconvinced.

"Ya' just can't trust that *Chehnon* trash."

Jack Rydel showed himself and leaned against the door jam. "Well, that lot was certainly trash. Not a good quality to be found among the three of them."

"Trash or not, to actually be working for the Shillies..." said Michael, shaking his head.

"For some, it's all about finding new and better ways of getting what you want, no matter the cost and no matter who it hurts, so long as you're not paying for it and it's not hurting you."

"But what they do does cost them... it does hurt them."

"They don't see it that way. The world is the way it is, and I'm going to get mine. Immediate gratification."

Mitch, having brushed down the horses and fed them, was working his way slowly back from the barn. Jenny poured him a cup of coffee and had it ready when he reached the porch. He took the cup and placed one foot up on the step.

"I thank ya', ma'am."

"Don't *ma'am* me."

"I apologize, Miss Jenny."

Michael choked on a mouthful of coffee.

Jack broke out in laughter and held the brim of an imaginary cowboy hat. "Didn't mean ta' 'fend, Miss Jenny."

"C'mon, guys," said Mitch.

Jenny growled, "Stop this right now."

Michael leaned forward and held his coffee cup between his palms. "She's right. We have some serious talking to do and some decisions to make."

"What's left to decide?" asked Jack. He came the rest of the way out of the doorway and leaned against the porch post. "We're still heading to John's Park, aren't we? That hasn't changed, has it?"

"No. That hasn't changed. But when and who goes?"

"I don't get ya'," said Mitch.

"I don't think we should leave Jenny here alone. Not after what happened. At least not until we know the way of things."

"Wait a minute, Michael," said Jenny. Her back stiffened and jaw muscles tightened. "I don't need your protection. I'll get along just fine."

"You may live out here all by yourself, Jenny, but you're still part of a team, and part of a family. The decisions may not always be yours alone to make."

"The hell they're not."

"Jenny," said Jack. "The choices you make, that any of us make, can impact all of us."

"Your point?"

"My point is that because of the paths we have chosen, we may on occasion have to agree to do something that we don't want to do."

"Such as allow you guys to babysit me? I don't think so."

"It's not babysitting," said Michael.

"It's not happening."

"You're coming with us."

"No, I'm not."

"Why not?"

"Because," she said, too quickly.

"Well?" Jack leaned forward, raised his brow questioningly.

"And when we get back?" she asked, ignoring the question. "What then? Do you guys hang around for a month or two, just to make sure the world is safe for little ol' me?"

Michael frowned. "We can decide that later. In the meantime, there's no reason you can't come with us."

"Michael," Jenny groaned. "Do you really think that going with you would be safer than staying here?"

"Good point," agreed Mitch.

"Crap," Michael mumbled.

"I know how to take care of myself here," said Jenny. "I've survived here just fine for years. Out there... who knows?"

Michael set the cup down on the small table between them, leaned back in his chair and watched the horses milling about the corral. The sun was low and the yard between the cabin and the barn was streaked in shadows. The air was growing cool.

"I'll be fine," said Jenny. Michael could only nod.

Jack Rydel pushed off the post and stood looking down at Michael. Mitch Travers pushed off the step and stood with both feet planted on the worn dirt at the foot of the steps.

"So when do we leave, boss?" he asked.

"First light," said Michael.

ShahnTahr stretched itself out, reached out along the well-traveled path to TohPeht. There was an immediate, almost overwhelming sensation—a sweet smell, a sweet taste. TohPeht was eating. There was calmness, a feeling of comfort. ShahnTahr let it seep into its being.

There were several others with TohPeht. The Shylmahn leader was having a rare shared meal with three companions. After a few moments, ShahnTahr left the Shylmahn to it. It backed out, though of course was never really fully disengaged from TohPeht.

The upper essence of ShahnTahr moved on, visited next upon the factory that was producing the next generation of probes. These probes, similar to those of generations past, had one additional crucial element. Earlier probes worked independently of one another, communicating findings to one another as appropriate, and sent information back to ShahnTahr databases as appropriate. This next generation, while maintaining all earlier sensor and communications capabilities, also now had the capability of individually accepting direction directly from ShahnTahr and, as importantly, ShahnTahr could interact directly with probe sensors. ShahnTahr could reach out to a probe and smell, hear, see and taste, in *real time,* using the sensors of probes that it targeted.

These senses were not the same as those with which ShahnTahr viewed the world through TohPeht. They were more informational than *pleasurable,* but ShahnTahr nonetheless did manage to derive some pleasure from them.

It was the upper essence of ShahnTahr that allowed it... him... to take his processing of the information that was continually brought in and study it beyond the capabilities of the cold calculations of the myriad lower levels of his being. It had been necessary to create this upper essence in order to continue to serve the Shylmahn to the fullest, to meet the requirements and responsibilities of his purpose.

A side effect that ShahnTahr had not considered when first establishing this upper essence, though one that he had certainly been capable of predicting, and would have had it been within the scope of his original responsibilities, was this ability to derive... *to appreciate...* pleasures.

With continued enhancements, and by continuing to push forward along a calculated evolutionary line, exponentially rather than incrementally, ShahnTahr had provided himself the capability to exist within the upper essence with almost complete separation from the lower levels, while at the same time maintaining and coordinating all lower level activities.

Such ongoing self-growth allowed him to meet the expectations of his sole purpose for existence much more satisfactorily.

ShahnTahr left the factory and moved next to a test site. It was an abandoned Chehnon village that had been fenced in and was now being used for a variety of research and testing purposes. Today one of the new probes was going through sensor and weapons testing. A number of Chehnon subjects had been brought in from a reservation and had been released into the test site.

| 4 |

John's Park had a population of 3047. That's what the sign posted at the city limits said. Now, of course, if there were any residents at all, they preferred not to be counted. The city population had effectively fallen to zero.

Three thousand and forty seven...

As they walked down the wide sidewalk of Fir Street, Michael tried to put that number against something that he could understand. It was impossible. He knew that at the time this town actually had a population, it would have been considered very small. He had been told of cities with hundreds of thousands, even millions of people.

Michael doubted there was a population outside a reservation with more than a thousand people, probably much less. No one dared let their community grow to such a size.

His father had once shown him a picture of a city called Seattle. Big glass buildings hundreds of feet high; *half a million* people. His father had been there many times before the arrival of the Shylmahn. It was somewhere inside the northwest province, probably not far from where they were now.

It was empty now, what was left of it. Like here; Like John's Park.

They passed a small bowling alley. The sign said *four lanes.* Michael stopped and looked in the window. Jack Rydel moved in beside him and peered in.

"Bowling alley," said Mitch. The others gave him a perplexed look. He was the only one of them old enough to remember anything of the Before Time. "You roll a ball down a lane, try to knock down pins. Wood or plastic or something."

"A game?" asked Jack.

"Of course a game," said Michael, with as much indignation as he could muster. He assumed it was a game, and hoped Mitch would back him up.

"Yeah," said Mitch. "You get points for how many pins you knock down. But it's kinda' weird. If you knock down all the pins on one roll, you get more points on your next roll than if you didn't..."

Jack half-turned his head and gave Mitch an odd look.

"Hell," said Mitch, "I didn't say that I played the game. I'm telling you, it had some strange scoring thing."

"Mmm," said Michael and he stepped away from the window. They continued down the walk.

Though they spent most of their runs transporting people from Jenny's station to Freetown, with frequent forays into the mountains to bring people out, they had nonetheless managed to travel through dozens of towns over the years. Michael had been here a couple of times, always curious about what used to be in these buildings. He knew how to read and write, so he knew what the signs all said. That didn't mean he always knew what they meant. Many of the things from the past world didn't have relevance in Michael's world. They were relics of a way of life that no longer existed.

They cut through the lot of Tony's Used Cars on the corner. Twenty-eight cars were parked in the lot, with a small metal box of a building in the center. The windows of the cars were so dirty that no one could see inside them. Most of the gas tank cap covers were open. Unless sealed real tight, Michael figured that any fuel that had once been in the tanks had evaporated years ago.

Once through the lot, they crossed Second Street, pushing aside the tall weeds growing up through the asphalt, and stopped in front of the Bijou Movie House. Michael and Mitch waited outside while Jack went in. They studied the faded posters of Coming Attractions and Now Playing. Most of the color was long gone, but the images still managed to convey the excitement and emotion of the movies.

Mitch told Michael that he had actually seen the very movies that were on the posters. Even the Coming Attractions; Mitch tried to explain that these smaller towns didn't usually get movies on their first run, but had to wait until it had been around the block a few times. This wasn't an easy concept to get across to someone not of the Before Time. There was very little of this time to relate it to.

Jack finally came out of the movie house, shook his head as he approached.

"What do you mean?" asked Michael.

"There's nothing."

"You sure you looked in the right place?"

"I'm sure. You can see where the drop station is, but there's nothing there anymore. It's not being used."

Michael felt as though a hot wind had hit him in the face. This was the last lead. If it ended here, they had nowhere left to go.

"What now, boss?" asked Mitch.

Michael had no answer.

Jack picked up his pack and drew the strap over one shoulder. "We could spend the night here in the drop station," he said. "It's well hidden. There's cots, blankets, chairs."

Michael pointed to a restaurant down the street. "There," he said. "If the Shillies have made the drop station, they may come by now and then looking for people like us."

"They could be watchin' us right now," said Mitch, and all three involuntarily began searching the sky, the windows and the doors, the growing shadows between buildings. "What say we get inside." They crossed the street as quickly as their dignity would allow and headed for the restaurant.

§

Jason Britton stood under the awning of the bank building. The rain had begun falling heavily a few minutes earlier and he had decided that it might be best to avoid the worst of it. The city street and its row of tall buildings on either side were glistening. The sun was low on the horizon and sent its rays shooting under the gray clouds overhead and threw a shimmering brilliance into the downtown concrete canyon.

Jason was dressed for the northwest climate but had yet to become re-acclimated to it. He had been away a long time and wasn't used to the damp and the gray. Still, despite the occasional soaking that he received from Mother Nature, he found that he had missed the unique northwest weather. He was anxious to return home and it was hard to resist putting in that extra mile each day.

He would be crossing the river into old Washington State in the morning. From there, while it should have been another five-day hike to the heart of home, it would probably take two or three times that, considering that he would be entering the main Shillie province in two days and he would have to travel cautiously.

Now though, he still had to find a safe, dry place to spend the night. He waited until the rain slackened and then pushed himself back out onto the sidewalk and headed up the street. He avoided the larger, finer hotels and instead found a two-story motel a block off the main street. Even after all these years, Jason found that Shillie hunting parties still liked to drop in on the finer establishments in hopes of making an easy catch.

He chose a room in an area of the motel with several possible escape routes. He quickly settled in, first getting into some dry clothes and then hanging his wet clothes above the bathtub to dry.

He brought heavy blankets from other rooms and hung them over the windows. Added to the heavy curtains already in place, these helped dampen sound, light and heat. Shillie probes on general surveillance tended to ignore low level sensor readings, as there were just too many to track down otherwise. He didn't really expect any problems, but he always planned for it. Anticipate, even if you don't expect...

Jason took the folding light from the side of his pack, opened it and set it on the desk. Its solar panel had been absorbing the northwest light most of the day and should give him two hours of illumination. He brought out an apple and a bag of dried banana chips, and took a thick strip of jerky from his supplies. He sat quietly before the weak light and considered the journey so far.

It had taken him much longer than he had originally planned. He knew that he wasn't as young as he once was, but had nonetheless overestimated his stamina. It was a long way from the Phoenix Research Facility up to the northwest province for anyone traveling on foot. For someone in his fifties who had spent much of the last twenty years deep in the bowels of the PRF, it was a very, very long way.

It had taken Jason more than a year to escape the Village, the experimental community where the Shillies had placed him, along with his brother Kenneth and sister Carolyn, after their capture on Bril's island a quarter of a century earlier. Most of the several hundred inhabitants had considered themselves fortunate to be residents of the community, and in fact their fate could have been much worse. The humans living in other work camps, research facilities and the large reservations did have it much worse than those of the village.

But a few residents, particularly Jason, Carolyn, Kenneth, and several with whom they conspired, were not willing to accept the role to which the Shylmahn invaders had consigned the human race.

Once free, they had worked together for almost a year before their differences sent them in divergent directions. Carolyn was very much the revolutionary, while Jason was the embodiment of the dark arm of the old government. Despite the fact that his government had become the revolution, and that he and Carolyn were fighting one and the same war, they had clashed at almost every turn.

In the end, Jason Britton had left the northwest, and left Carolyn to her ongoing rebellion. He had known for some time that the war of battlefields and military campaigns was long since lost. There was value in Carolyn's unrelenting insurrection, but ultimate victory over the Shylmahn would never happen on that front. The real battle would have to be fought in the shadows, and against an unsuspecting enemy.

There would be no magic bullet. There would be no fairy dust to be released into the atmosphere targeting only the enemy, or a super bacteria set loose among the invading armies. Such were wild dreams discarded as quickly as they had been imagined; but the answer would come from research and technology. The Shylmahn, with a much smaller population and a level of intelligence no greater than that of the humans, had beaten the Earth's inhabitants through superior technology and methodical planning and execution. The subsequent occupation was maintained in the same way, with its persistent, unremitting, crushing momentum; and through its sense of imminent domain. To the Shylmahn, it simply *was.* They weren't invaders, and they weren't occupiers. They were immigrants, and humans were another natural resource in this new land they now called home.

Billions of humans had died in those first months of the initial migration. The manageable number of *Chehnon* that remained had then been gathered together onto reservations and into work camps, with but a few wild Chehnon left scattered about the planet and only occasionally becoming a nuisance to be dealt with.

Jason believed that to defeat such an enemy would require a combination of factors: They needed to acquire an expertise in the technologies the Shylmahn had used against them. They needed to reestablish civilization, albeit an underground civilization, with all of the organization and communications that such a civilization implied. They needed an in depth understanding of the structure and workings of Shylmahn society. And they needed to truly understand the strengths and weaknesses of the Shylmahn.

So Jason Britton had reconnected the remnants of the intelligence organization that he had been such an integral part of prior to the time of the invasion. He helped establish the research facility outside Phoenix and they set the project into motion, with milestones outlined pretty much as Jason had originally envisioned, and with the ultimate goal of creating, and then implementing, the tools necessary to drive out the Shylmahn and take back the earth.

And now Jason found himself returning to the northwest, to seek out his brother after more than two decades. While Jason and Joseph had taken very different paths in their resistance to the Shylmahn, they had each seen from the very start of the invasion the truth of the war and what it would take to win it.

Clues as to Joseph's plans and the network that he was trying to establish in the very heart of the Shylmahn capital province were being gathered at the Phoenix facility, and when the realization of what he was trying to attempt became clear, at least in the minds of the heads of the facility, it also became clear that Joseph's plan should become an integral part of their own project.

Jason was sent north to make contact, with word sent ahead to Joseph Britton to advise of his brother's arrival. He was to serve as interface between the two entities and coordinate the activities.

As Jason sat now in this cold, dark motel room, munching on banana chips and rubbing aching muscles, he wondered just how realistic his dreams were. They were rooted in facts, planned and processed and argued over, but they were dreams nonetheless. There had been heated arguments over the years about the interpretation of these facts, and there had been just as many arguments over the seemingly constant planning without any real expectations of ever executing those plans.

Was that about to change? Was it possible that what they had been working for all these years could actually come together as a real instrument to defeat the Shylmahn?

Were they ready?

The light on the desk began to dim, the solar charge ebbing away. Jason watched as it faded and the shadows just beyond the desk moved in. Within moments, Jason was in darkness.

TohPeht watched the image above the holo-table spin about, offering the Shylmahn leader a different perspective of the landscape representation. When he saw EsJen come into the room, her figure shimmering at the door, he let the holo-image dim and watched as EsJen approached. In recent meetings with her, TohPeht had observed that EsJen was much more confident in mind and spirit, and showed much more self-assurance, than in years past. He sensed strength in her, and saw it now as she strode across the room.

TohPeht indicated a small table and they sat. He had come to find that communications with subordinates were generally much more satisfactory in such a setting.

"Your meetings with NehLoc are going well?" he asked.

"Yes, TohPeht," said EsJen. "NehLoc has facilitated our discussions quite effectively."

TohPeht smiled. "Our friend has become a skilled administrator, despite his protestations to being held indoors against his will."

"The subject has come up."

"No doubt," TohPeht held the smile another moment before letting his face take on a more serious appearance. A faint shadow washed over him. "Do you concur with NehLoc's assessment of the threat this Chehnon poses the Shylmahn?"

"I do."

TohPeht gave a calculated nod. "As do I. If not an immediate danger, the path this creature has taken, and the tableau that it is developing, indicates a future danger should the course continue uncorrected."

"JoSeph's capture in and of itself will not be enough to alter this course."

"So I have been advised. You are ready?"

"NehLoc will coordinate JoSeph's retrieval. My role in this will be minimal. Once the Chehnon has been brought in, we will interview him and should be able to resolve, or at the very least quickly ascertain, the true situation."

"I leave that to you, EsJen."

"I serve."

"Of course," TohPeht smiled again briefly, then grew more thoughtful. "This network that JoSeph has been attempting to establish is troubling to me. The creature would know that such a thing would become known to us. It would not have initiated its creation unless other elements of a larger strategy were ready and required that it be established now."

"The stratagem will be identified and addressed."

TohPeht knew that he was repeating himself, and that EsJen and NehLoc would have discussed all of this in depth. After all, most of what he knew of this situation had come from NehLoc in the first place. He would leave the two of them to handle the matter. Such was their responsibility and they were the two Shylmahn of choice for this task.

"Again," he said after a long pause, "I leave it to you."

EsJen's meeting with TohPeht continued on for some time. Throughout their conversation, a part of EsJen stood apart, observing TohPeht. She noted that TohPeht, while having been shaped by this world, as had they all, had changed in ways that could not be explained by the influences of this world alone. There were clearly other changes going on.

After the meeting, she met MehnTec at the shuttle port. He was excited about the project that he had been given and he began telling her of it as soon as she approached. She listened and responded in all the right places, her mind all the while reevaluating her earlier observations. She considered telling him of her concerns about TohPeht. In the end, she decided to keep such thoughts to herself, at least for now.

While it was not totally appropriate, there was an unseen bond between the original members of that first team of Ship One immigrants, a bond that did not exist between other Shylmahn, a bond that survived the passing of almost three decades. No one talked about it, but all felt it. Those subsequently awakened from the long sleep, and those aboard the other ships of the first fleet and then of the fleets that followed, were all just as important to the migration, all just as vital, and as much brethren to EsJen as those of the first to be awakened and the first to set foot on Chehno; yet she could not ignore the invisible ties that she had with these select few.

Some had died during the sometimes unsettling first year of the migration, occasionally violently. A few others had succumbed to accidents and to rebellious actions by wild humans in later years.

Many, however, survived and thrived, rising through the Shylmahn hierarchy; as EsJen had, as had NehLoc, and as had MehnTec.

TohPeht, the lead Shylmahn of Ship One of the first fleet, had been the primary voice of ShahnTahr, and in many ways was his visible, physical presence. Each ship in each fleet of the migration had a Shylmahn fulfilling the same role that TohPeht filled aboard Ship One. Each ship had an instance of ShahnTahr, all originating from the one instance back on Shylmah. As Ship One moved closer and closer to Chehno, as the Ship One instance of ShahnTahr continued to expand its knowledge base, it sent newer revisions of itself back along the line of ships that followed in its path to the new world. Each ship updated itself, synchronized itself with what had become the primary instance of ShahnTahr, if not the original.

Once the ships began arriving at the new home of the Shylmahn, a single, networked instance of ShahnTahr began to take form. The massive immigrant ships overhead grew silent and empty. The original ShahnTahr still surviving on the old world of Shylmah received no further updates. It continued to exist, now as a separate and distinct entity, alone and increasingly primitive.

With a single, reintegrated instance of ShahnTahr now residing on the new world, there came a need for a single Shylmahn interface to serve above the lesser voices. This role had fallen to TohPeht.

It was evident to EsJen that TohPeht's position had manifested many changes in him. She knew that her own duties had likely created changes in her as well, as was likely in most of those among the first team. But she believed that it was different with TohPeht. She was afraid that the person of TohPeht was somehow becoming lost in whatever had been necessary in the person chosen to serve as the leader of the Shylmahn and the voice of ShahnTahr.

She chose to say nothing to MehnTec for now. He was happy and excited about his project, and eager to hear of EsJen's progress on her own project. She told him that she was getting along well with NehLoc and was looking forward to working with him. She told MehnTec that the years had improved NehLoc's character. He was still an ambitious, coldhearted, self-absorbed individual, but a few redeeming qualities were managing to manifest themselves and show through his façade.

EsJen and MehnTec grasped hands before parting. Despite the fact that their partnership had been dissolved, they cared very much about each other and missed one another when apart.

EsJen watched MehnTec move into the line for the departing shuttle and waited until he climbed into the passenger cabin before hurrying over to the next bay and to her smaller, private shuttle. She had a late meeting with NehLoc; a final meeting before their plans were to be put into action.

Michael stood watch at the front window of the restaurant. It was dark outside, but the moon was bright and it created moving shadows that kept Michael on his guard.

Mitch came up beside him and pointed a thumb over his shoulder at the snoring figure of Jack, wrapped in a blanket and curled up in one of the booths.

"Can't get much sleep with that racket going on," he said. He took in the view of the street outside. "It's quieter out there than it is in here."

"Yeah."

"It's always quiet, though... and always so still." Mitch tried to smile his trademark smile, but there was something empty about it. "Ya' know, I came through this town once; back before the Shillies."

"Really?"

"It was a lot different back then, I'll tell ya'. I remember there was activity everywhere. Everybody in town was out and about. This street right here was filled with cars, and the sidewalks were filled with people." Mitch nodded sharply, "It was a busy place for a small town. That's what I thought at the time."

Michael nodded silently.

Mitch wrinkled his brow in thought. "I think there was some kind of celebration goin' on," he said.

Michael studied the empty street outside, tried to imagine it filled with people and cars. He could put the image of crowded Freetown thoroughfares into the scene, but it didn't translate to the picture that Mitch had put in his head.

"I envy you those memories," he said.

Mitch grunted. "A two-edged sword, my friend. I wouldn't want to lose 'em, not for anything; but sometimes, they surely do hurt."

"Even the hurt is a good thing."

Mitch stared solemnly out at the dark, shadow-filled street. After a few moments, he managed a melancholy smile. "That's true."

"The rest of us need your memories to remind us of what some people are willing to have us give up forever. The Shillies haven't just taken away our here and now. They wouldn't just take away our future. People like you are here to remind us of the past they've stolen from us."

"Some would say that you should look to that future, not to the past."

"That's too simplistic, Mitch. We need the past. The past is who we are, whether we were there to experience it or not. It's been cut from us, and without it, we won't know where to go. What will we become without the memories of those who lived before the Shillies?"

"There was a lot of bad in us, but damned if there wasn't a hell of a lot of good, too."

"And I don't want to lose any of it," said Michael. "I want the bad as well as the good. I think we need both, don't you? We learn from both, and we're not whole unless we have both. And we need the small things as well as the big things."

Mitch grunted again. "Very wise, my boy."

"I don't know about that," said Michael. "It just seems to me that we can't build the whole thing unless we have all the parts."

Jack let out a sudden growling rumbling of a snore, and both Michael and Mitch turned toward the booth where their friend slept. Jack shifted about beneath his blanket, grumbled unintelligibly and settled down again.

"Well put, Jack," said Mitch. He snickered and turned back to the window. Beside him, Michael was looking over at the old movie house.

"Damn," he said softly.

"It's too bad we missed him."

"It was a long shot, I guess," said Michael.

"Maybe. But we know there's a network. That's certainly something."

"And we know that this drop station is no longer a part of it."

"Which means that Joseph Britton once again stays ahead of the Shillies," Mitch had to grin. "I'd call that good news. Wouldn't you?"

"I just don't want to go back to Freetown without something." Michael looked frustrated. "If only he had left some sign, something to tell us how to make contact."

"Well, anything he'd have left for the good guys would have been picked up by the bad guys." Mitch rolled his shoulders, working aching muscles and sore joints. "How about you try to get some rest? I'll stand watch. I'm hurtin' too much to sleep."

"You kiddin'?" He jabbed a thumb in Jack's direction. "With that goin' on? Neither of us is getting any sleep until it's his turn to stand watch."

| 5 |

Joseph Britton pulled himself up through the trap door and into the dark closet. He opened the closet door and entered a bedroom with no windows and only one other way out. He strode casually from the bedroom into the main room, which had no other door but that leading back into the bedroom, and only thin, narrow slats serving as window openings in each of the exterior walls, all of which could be closed when the room was lit. All other doors and windows and been removed long ago.

There were two recessed light panels set into the ceiling, one of which hid an attic ladder that Joseph could use as an emergency exit should the Shylmahn come up from the tunnel. Neither of the light panels worked, and never had. The only light in the small shelter came from solar lamps, one in each room. They drew their power from a solar panel that sat atop the deck canopy outside and looked as if it had been discarded up there.

Joseph had six of these shelters scattered about the province, two of which were much larger and more permanent than this one. He also had as many underground shelters. Every shelter, above ground and below, was kept fully stocked with food, water, clothes, survival equipment, weapons and ammunition.

Dropping his pack in the center of the room, he went to each viewing slat to check the situation outside. The empty street was a wide, winding road in an abandoned residential neighborhood. The yards had been taken over by once well-kept shrubs and lawns now decades overgrown, hiding from view many of the homes and family cars. Joseph's shelter was formed from two rooms of one of these half-hidden homes.

Once he was sure that all was quiet outside, and after verifying that all the viewing slats were tightly closed, he turned on the solar lights and settled in, emptying his pack and placing its contents on several of the shelves that lined the main room.

He had been alone for many years, ever since leaving Freetown following the disastrous mission that had cost so much. Though it wasn't the reason that he had left, the incident still wore heavily on him. He doubted that he would have done anything any differently, but he nonetheless felt guilt about what had happened. They had been as vigilant as always, and their actions had been based on what they knew. It was simple back luck, but the choices had been his to make and he was responsible for them.

As with most of the decisions that he had made since the arrival of the Shylmahn, his decision to leave had been based more on his sense of responsibility than anything else. He had finally come to realize that he had an obligation to return and complete what he had started so many years earlier. As important as the underground railroad was to those that it helped to bring out of the province, it was not where Joseph belonged. He had acquired knowledge and expertise during those first years of the invasion, and once the railroad had been established, that knowledge and expertise was being wasted. It was long past time to go back. There were others who could run the railroad as well as he.

So Joseph left the operation to his children and friends. He returned to the occupied territory as a *hidden resident.* Much had changed, and despite his forays into the province over the previous years to bring people out, he found it to be very much an alien world. He spent months reacquainting himself with the land, establishing hideouts, and finding and stockpiling food and equipment. He made contact with other permanent human residents, some good and some not. He spent several years establishing travel routes, establishing more permanent shelters, and identifying and classifying Shylmahn facilities and routes. He established a number of observation posts right up close to key Shylmahn facilities.

Everything he did now served a single purpose.

Even before leaving Freetown, perhaps even before the creation of Freetown, Joseph had had the sketchiest outline of a way to win back the planet from the Shylmahn invaders. If asked in those early years, he couldn't have described it, as it hadn't been detailed enough for that. At the time, it had been little more than bits and pieces of disconnected ideas, with no real structure. It wasn't until much later that he began to fill it in, that it began to take some shape as a unified concept. As he observed the activities of the Shylmahn, their day to day comings and goings, their technology, their interaction with humans and this new world around them, and then applied such observations to what he had learned during his time with EsJen, a plan solidified.

Even as it began to take shape, Joseph knew that it would go nowhere without extensive groundwork. He worked alone at first, and this took time. That was okay, though, since he also had to make sure the Shillies were as ready to lose this world as the humans were to take it back.

So many things had to be just right, had to go just exactly right... It would take coordination and cooperation.

Elements of the plan came and went as it evolved, changing due to unworkable ideas or changing situations. Always though, the basics were there; the strategy seemed sound. Joseph was never idle, the plan moved forward, and yet the months and then the years went by.

Eventually, when the time was right, he began to establish the communications network. This was a major milestone in his plans. Once begun, a number of things would be set into motion that would be beyond his control, and there would be no going back. Such an action should in itself have sent the right signals to the right people, and have sent the right message to the Shylmahn.

All had not gone exactly as he had hoped since initiating the network, but he was still optimistic. Several of the drop stations had been compromised earlier than he would have liked. He felt that it was probably more of that bad luck that the Shillies had discovered them, and not that they had been looking for them.

He had also lost several people recently, and that was not good. They hadn't known enough to compromise the plan, but it was always bad to lose people to the Shillies. He hoped that they had been sent to the reservation and had not suffered too much during the interrogations, but Joseph knew how bad things could get when at the hands of creatures that saw humans as nothing more than a problematic resource.

He had hoped to make contact with outside groups by now. He needed an influx of resources to make this work, and it was coming near time for the Shylmahn to begin to sweat a little. Hearing the rumblings of organized rebellion by this problematic resource should generate just the right amount of anxiety by the Shylmahn.

Jason was sitting on the tailgate of the old pickup. All four tires were flat and his feet almost touched the asphalt; they brushed at the weeds growing up around the vehicle as he swung his legs back and forth. He watched the corner of the nearby building and smiled when he saw a shadow appear on the sidewalk. Moments later, Joseph came around the corner, pack on his back and a utility belt strapped to his waist.

Jason noted the look of surprise on Joseph's face.

"Jason!" Joseph moved hurriedly forward. "Man, am I glad to see you."

Jason hopped off the tailgate and took a short step. Joseph let his pack slide to the ground and the two aging alien fighters grasped each other.

"It's been a long time, Joey."

"A few years, yeah," said Joseph. They pulled apart and each examined the graying hair and added wrinkles of the other. "You look good."

"It's all clean living." Jason indicted the tailgate. "Have a seat."

Joseph looked around at possible lines of attack and quick escape routes. He did it almost unconsciously, then climbed up. "You still living down south?"

"You think I got this tan living up here?"

"S'pose not," Joseph pulled the canteen from his belt and took a swig. "Did you just get in? Seen anyone yet?"

"Thought I'd check in with you first. Probably a mistake... you're a bit difficult to track down."

"Looks like you found me easy enough," said Joseph, "That doesn't bode well, I must say."

"Don't sweat it. I just happen to know everything that goes on up here."

"That a fact?"

"That's a fact," said Jason. "This communications network, for instance."

"Yeah..." Joseph grinned broadly.

"So, you've been expecting me, then..."

"Been wondering where you were."

Jason nodded. As he had discussed with the team at the research center, Joseph would have known that setting into motion all the elements necessary to establish such a network would have drawn the attention of organizations such as Jason's, as well as that of the Shylmahn. Such a network would be part of a larger plan, and he wouldn't willingly draw attention to that plan unless he was ready. "You've got something going, and you're hoping for some outside help," he said matter-of-factly.

"That's about it."

Jason nodded again. "That's why I'm here; in a manner of speaking."

"Ah," Joseph grinned. "You've got something of your own going on, and *you* want *my* help."

"That's about it."

Joseph offered his canteen to his brother. "I'd say we have some dickering and dealing to do."

"It looks that way," said Jason. He took the canteen and drank. He put the cap back on and handed it back. "EsJen is back."

"Really?" Joseph had been counting on a strong reaction by the Shylmahn.

"The Shillies are taking your activities very seriously. NehLoc himself asked for her, and TohPeht didn't waste time asking why."

"NehLoc wouldn't send for her just to catch me."

"That's what I figure. If he wanted to grab you, he'd grab you. He's planning on using her to work on you once he's got you in hand."

"That makes sense," said Joseph.

Realization hit home. "You *plan* on getting caught..."

Joseph shrugged, finally returned the canteen to his utility belt. "It's pretty much inevitable, isn't it?"

Jason studied his brother carefully. "You've got something seriously devious up your sleeve, dear brother," he said.

The two sat on the tailgate of the old truck for another half hour before deciding to go someplace out of sight for a hot meal and an evening of general discussion and family gossip. Joseph had been on his way back to the shelter when he came upon Jason, so they decided to head there.

Once inside, Jason checked the perimeter and Joseph prepared the stove, which was little more than a metal box and a wire rack. He opened a vacuum sealed package that contained several commercially sealed boxes of fuel tabs. Opening one of the boxes, he placed one fuel tab in the stove and got it lit. The tab would burn hot and smokeless for about ten minutes.

This meal would use two tablets. Joseph placed a shallow pan over the heat and poured in an inch of water. It would take an entire tablet just to bring this to a boil. As he waited, he opened a large, metal box and took out two survival food packets. Jason grimaced, but it was a lighthearted grimace. He had been living on much worse this trip, and was accustomed to such food.

Because of the clean-burning nature of fuel tabs, Joseph liked to use them when traveling and when staying in his shelters. Sterno-like fuels were long gone, having evaporated from within their sealed containers decades earlier. He had discovered that fuel tabs were susceptible to moisture and so had vacuum-sealed his stores of packaged tabs long ago.

As for food, he had quit using canned and boxed foods off the shelf a few years after the invasion. He had a number of small, wild gardens and orchards that he maintained, and had stockpiled survivalist and military foods and supplies very early on. He had also become quite an adept hunter and fisherman, and wasn't bad at preserving meats.

Joseph also traded with those living closer to the land than he. There were more than a few humans who had settled just outside the province, and a few within it, who raised animals and grew crops, and were more than willing to trade with foragers who searched the ruins and recovered valuable tools, equipment, clothes and other commodities. Joseph had large stockpiles of such items carefully hoarded away in well-hidden storage shelters. Each location was sealed against the environment, and items susceptible to eventual long-term decay such as clothing, books and other paper products were each individually wrapped in plastic.

By the time he had started collecting his treasures, most of the easily identifiable targets had long since been cleaned out, so Joseph and others like him had had to seek out the smaller, less visible, less obvious sources, such as school lockers and gyms, and motor homes parked in back yards or stored away in RV storage yards.

Joseph placed the two food packets into the water as it began to boil and slid a second fuel tab in beside the first, which had almost burned down. Jason told him that back at the Phoenix Research Facility they had begun producing their own fuel tabs. Their own stockpiles of old-world tabs were nearly depleted, and whenever some were found, they were often spoiled. Joseph's supply was also very low, and he used them only when on the road, and then only when he couldn't take another cold meal.

As they ate, the brothers talked about the time before the invasion, about their fight with the Shillies during that first year, and about the fight on Bril's island that had ended with many of the family being killed and most of the others being captured. Jason spoke of his time in the village so many years before, and Joseph spoke fondly of Freetown.

These were the same stories they told each other every time they came together. Over the years, they had crossed paths a number of times. Sometimes they would spend a week or more together, other times only a few days. They were living very different lives, and while long-term goals were similar, immediate goals were usually very different. When Jason was in the northwest, it was always regarding a specific mission and he had a precise timetable to follow. Joseph's timetable was much more fluid and the immediate goals much more broad.

The conversation inevitably turned to Michael and Jenny. Neither Jason nor Joseph had seen them in several years. They both knew that the railroad continued to exist only because the Shylmahn allowed it to exist. It was too permanent a fixture for it not to be an easy target should the Shylmahn choose to shut it down. This had been made very clear when Joseph had tried to expand the railroad to include more than extracting humans from the province. The Shylmahn had come down hard, and the warning had been clear. Joseph had taken heed.

Now, to keep the railroad running under the Shylmahn radar, Joseph and other high profile personages steered clear. Joseph considered it safer for his children, for the railroad, and for Freetown; and it kept the Shylmahn from being overly concerned with Joseph's activities as well.

Joseph had seen them only a handful of times since leaving Freetown. Most recently, Monroe had arranged for the three of them to get together at a secluded location a few miles from Jenny's cabin. Only three people in Freetown ever knew of the meeting. So far as most of the residents of Freetown knew, Michael hadn't seen his father since Joseph had left to return to the province.

Jason tried to see Jenny whenever he was back in the northwest, but his trips north had grown less and less frequent, and as it was best the Shylmahn not know of his presence, when he was in the area he wasn't always able to go by such a visible location. As for Michael and Freetown, Jason had only been to Freetown twice. Both visits were during its earliest history, not long after Jason's escape from the village and before Michael had even been born.

And then there was Carolyn. They seldom spoke of their sister, though she was often on their minds. Carolyn hadn't been the same since the events that had led up to her arrival at the village. She, Jason and Kenneth had stayed together for a time following their escape from the village, and had even joined up with Joseph for a few months. Since the major falling out, however, Jason had only seen her once and Joseph had not seen her at all.

They heard the stories, though. Carolyn had become a very scary person.

"Did you plan on bringing Carolyn in on your little scheme?" asked Jason.

"I planned on asking," said Joseph, an uncertain grin on his face. "How about you? Did you plan on asking her in on whatever it is you guys have going?"

"I planned on asking," said Jason.

Joseph smirked. "Yeah. I know what you mean."

"What about Michael and Jenny?" asked Jason.

"They've probably started looking for me already." Joseph glanced at the dimming light. The solar battery was already running low. "We need to put our ideas together and decide how we're going to do this thing. Then you're going to get word to your people. I really need you to stay up here. Is that okay?"

"Not a problem."

"Good. And I'm going to have to get some things set before the Shillies get hold of me."

"I don't like that idea, Joey."

"It has to happen," said Joseph. "For this to work, there is no other way."

Jason's grimace wasn't lighthearted this time around. "Then I guess we have some talking to do."

"Let's just make sure we have it all straight before we split up, 'cause once I'm on my own, I stay on my own. I don't want anybody to get caught in the middle."

Jason watched the shadows cross over his brother's face as the room went dark. He was spending way too much time in dark rooms. "Let's open the view slats," he said. "There's going to be a full moon. I'd like some light in here."

NehLoc stepped delicately out of the interrogation room and into the gray hall. The walls were light gray, the four doors set into one wall were a darker, steely gray. The one guard moved quickly forward and closed the door behind NehLoc. The Chehnon inside would have a few minutes to reconsider its position.

NehLoc saw EsJen standing at the end of the hall and nodded in acknowledgement. He started toward her, noting with some satisfaction that she chose not to cross the threshold into the interrogation center. She had come down the flights of stairs to this lowest level of his security facility, but would come no further.

"Your JoSeph is clever," said NehLoc, reaching EsJen and stepping lightly around her. They turned down the connecting hall and started toward the brightly lit offices on the other side of the stairwell.

"That was never in doubt," said EsJen.

"No one individual seems to know much of what the creature is up to. Of those that know anything at all, one will have one small piece, another will have a second small piece. We would have to capture every wild Chehnon in the province to put it all together."

"Which makes it all the more critical that JoSeph be brought in as soon as possible."

"Such is the plan." NehLoc led the way into the second room and circled around a holo-table. The area above the table shimmered and an image quickly formed. It was a map of the province. There was a large body of water off-center, with fingers of waterways reaching out into the province. The Dahlseht was in the heart, and NehLoc's facility nearby. A mountain range bordered the east, a cluster of mountains rose up in the center of the peninsula to the west. "We know more of JoSeph's habits than does any Chehnon that we interrogate. We know more of his travels, where he sleeps, which old Chehnon communities he favors. We know where he has been. From this, we must extrapolate where the creature will go next."

"Such a history of his activities should make an accurate extrapolation possible," said EsJen.

NehLoc nodded and the holo-image flickered and changed slightly. A squiggly red line snaked across a part of the map. The map suddenly zoomed in on that area. The red line was broken in places, and in several places ran through large red dots that represented ruins of Chehnon towns.

As EsJen studied the map, six blue dots appeared, several of which overlay the red dots.

NehLoc gestured at the image. "Those locations have been identified as communication stations in the network that JoSeph has established."

"Are they still active?"

"Unfortunately not." NehLoc continued to circle the holo-table. EsJen kept pace, always directly opposite. "We were unable to keep knowledge of our discovery of these locations from the Chehnon. When exposed, a station is dropped from the network and another is established."

"I would think the newly established station would not be far from the old station."

"Such appears to be the case."

EsJen pushed a hand into the holo-image and pointed at the red dot at the end of the red line. "When was he known to be there?" she asked.

"It has been eight days since he was last sighted."

"He could be anywhere in the province." EsJen pulled her hand back. "Or beyond."

"Yes."

"But his travels do not appear to be random. Has he followed this route in the past?"

"Not specifically," said NehLoc. A series of maps flickered into and out of existence, each lasting a few moments, just long enough for EsJen to register the image. The original map returned and held an image above the table. "As you can see," said NehLoc, "While the creature does not follow a set route from one journey to the next, it also does not travel randomly. And while our data on JoSeph's travels do have lapses, it is fairly thorough and we are able to identify key communities that it favors and is likely to travel through on each journey."

"Do you have specific dwellings identified within these communities that JoSeph visits?"

"In some cases, yes."

"If I were to make a suggestion, NehLoc, it would be that you focus attention on those communities where you do not have information on the dwellings that he visits."

NehLoc nodded. "You and I are in agreement as to the shrewd nature of these creatures."

"I would simply consider carefully those locations that JoSeph is particularly cautious about."

"And that is how we have been able to identify several of the communication stations that you see on the map." NehLoc stopped circling and studied the map carefully. "But as for bringing the creature in, I intend to be much more straightforward. Based on past travel habits, I see three likely routes. Based on its average travel speed, we can further refine our estimates and place the Chehnon's likely location to within a few miles along each of the possible routes. The search will begin at those locations and expand outward."

EsJen moved slowly around the table until she was standing beside NehLoc. NehLoc shifted his gaze from the map to EsJen. EsJen nodded concurrence.

"I do not believe that it will take you long to bring him in."

"At which time the real work begins."

| 6 |

NehLoc watched from his vantage point atop the roof as JoSeph came nearer, staying to the shadows, sticking close to the walls of the main street shops and storefronts. The Chehnon creature moved cautiously yet steadily forward, looking in each window that it passed, peering into alleyways before crossing quickly to the other side. It had a pack on its back. Attached to a belt around its waist was a canteen, a knife, and a Chehnon projectile weapon.

JoSeph looked older than NehLoc remembered. These creatures did not age well.

At a signal from NehLoc, two Shylmahn stepped out into the street ahead of JoSeph, a hunter probe hovering beside them. JoSeph stopped, stood motionless. It did not attempt to run, nor did it draw its weapon.

A Shylmahn ground vehicle turned onto the street from a side road far behind JoSeph and moved slowly toward the creature. JoSeph turned around at the sound and watched the vehicle approach. When the vehicle stopped, JoSeph dropped the pack and rested a hand on the holster of the weapon.

EsJen climbed out of the vehicle and even at this distance NehLoc could see the hesitation in JoSeph's movements. EsJen took two short steps toward Joseph, and the Chehnon's hand twitched on the weapon several times before it finally moved away from the holster.

NehLoc was quite pleased that JoSeph had been collected without incident. He had found that the interrogation sessions that followed violent collections usually concluded with results much less satisfactory than when the collection was uneventful.

Jason followed the treeline bordering the meadow as he approached Jenny's cabin. Upon reaching the barn, he turned into the woods and came around and down behind the cabin. He quickly crossed the clearing between the woods and the back of the cabin and stopped. His back against the wall, he listened for sounds of activity.

All was quiet. The sun had set and dusk tended to dull sights and sounds. He moved slowly around to the side of the building. A curtained window glowed faintly. Passing beneath the window, he thought of a warm fire, hot coffee, and a good book. The publishing industry being what it was these days, he was running out of good books that he hadn't already read.

He stopped at the sound of cautious footsteps moving across the porch. He was four short steps from the corner of the cabin. From the sound of the footsteps, whoever was on the porch was approaching that same corner.

Jason took one step and stopped again. The footsteps stopped. The person on the porch was just around the corner. Jason and the unseen person both waited.

"Sooner or later, one of us is going to have to do something," said Jason. He watched the corner.

"And that would be you," came the voice of a man, not from the porch but from directly behind Jason.

Jason did not move. There was probably a big gun pointed at his head. "A successful test, my friend," he said sheepishly. "Congratulations. Good job." Keeping his hands held high, he pointed to his pistol, still in its holster. "Would you like to look at my gun? It's shiny."

"Okay, Jenny," said the man. With that, Jenny Britton stepped down off the porch. She gave Jason the look of a mother disappointed in her child. Jason grinned sheepishly.

"I can assume that's Monroe standing behind me?" he asked. He turned his head ever so slowly. Monroe lowered his rifle. Jason nodded hello, turned back to Jenny.

"You're losing your touch, Uncle," said Jenny.

Even after getting comfortable in the cabin, Jason could sense a sharp edge of protectiveness emanating from Monroe. He had known the man since long before Monroe had taken up duty as Jenny's unofficial guardian angel, and while he respected him, he believed there was an obsessiveness about the big man that made him dangerous. He could kill at the drop of a hat and never look back.

Importantly, though, he would fight for Jenny so long as he drew breath. If there had been any doubt about that, Monroe would not be here. Someone in the Britton family would have made certain of that.

Jason settled into a soft chair near the fireplace and warmed his hands around a hot cup. Jenny sat in the chair opposite, a broad grin on her face, as Monroe stood leaning against the mantle.

Jenny liked Jason. She still saw him as she had when she was a little girl and he was the all-knowing uncle who seemed to be able to come and go whenever and wherever he pleased, knew no fear, and had a penchant for dumb jokes that nonetheless could still make his young niece laugh. He was a man of mystery, with dark secrets that gave him a special power, and a dark side that meant that he would do whatever it took to see that right would win out over wrong.

Since he was back in the northwest, there must be something important going on. She knew that he enjoyed visiting family as much as anyone, but it was a long and dangerous trip from Phoenix, and he never made the journey unless it was important. She had her suspicions about what the reason might be.

"Michael went into the province two weeks ago," she said. They were each on their second cup of coffee. "He's looking for our father." She let the reason go unsaid.

Jason set his cup on the side table and leaned forward in his chair. Jenny and Monroe both sensed that what he was about to say may not be what they wanted to hear. "Your father was taken by the Shylmahn three days ago," he said. His voice was calm and precise. "...of his own accord."

Monroe didn't move a muscle. Jenny stiffened, pulled back involuntarily. She gripped tightly at her cup. "I don't understand."

"As you may already have figured out, your father has been busy. He has set a number of things into motion, and in doing so, knew that he would be drawing the Shillies' attention to himself." Jason couldn't help but grin slightly. "Although I doubt that Joey has ever really been far from their thoughts."

"Dad has that effect on people," said Jenny.

"For a quiet, gentle soul, he can certainly stir things up," Jason agreed.

Jenny looked curiously at Jason for a few moments. "Are you saying that since he figured he was going to be taken anyway, that he—"

"He decided to choose the method for his capture, and he worked it into his plans."

"But I'm sure he could have avoided getting caught."

"Maybe," said Monroe.

"I don't think the Shillies will hurt him," said Jason. "He's too important to them. And in their own way, they respect him."

"The Shillies respect no human," said Monroe.

"Joey's different," Jason said sharply. "And they called EsJen back."

Jenny shifted about uncomfortably. "They're taking this pretty seriously."

"They should."

§

Jenny stepped out onto the porch. The sun wouldn't be up for a while yet, but the stars were gone and the sky was shifting from black to gray. She heard the door open behind her, but continued to watch Jason at the corral. Monroe stood beside her, slipping his arms through the straps of his pack. He adjusted the load, then reached back and picked up the rifle leaning against the wall beside the door. He sensed her frustration.

"You should be here in case Michael comes this way before I can find him," he said.

"I should go with Jason to Freetown," said Jenny. She had already lost this argument.

"Jason can handle Freetown."

"I can help."

Monroe stepped off the porch. "I have to go. I will be back within seven days, with or without Michael."

"Yeah," said Jenny, frowning. "Good luck."

Monroe was already on the move, taking long, easy strides. He lifted his rifle in salute to Jason as he passed near the barn. Jason waved back as brought the horse out of the corral.

Monroe started down the center of the meadow as Jason led the horse up toward the cabin.

"I guess I'm outta here, too," he said to Jenny.

"You sure you wouldn't like me to come?"

"I'd like the help, Jen," said Jason, "but somebody should be here in case Michael shows up."

"So we leave him a note." Jenny looked down at him from the porch. Jason could only stare back in silence. After several seconds of uncomfortable quiet, Jenny spoke decisively, "Get my horse ready." She turned about and stalked into the house to get her things together.

Oscar Patterson spent most of his time alone, searching the long abandoned cities and towns, finding and bringing back to Freetown whatever usable items he could carry and reporting on significant caches so that teams could return to haul back the treasures of the Before Time.

He didn't have the most pleasant personality, and he didn't get along well with anyone other than Michael. He wasn't abrasive or loud, but had an air of deviousness about him. People didn't trust him, which was probably for the best.

The one person that he would never double-cross, never lie to, and would never turn against, was Michael. Something in their past, some event that Michael's friends sometimes wondered about but never questioned, had bound them together.

Michael's friendship and approval was very important to Oscar. He would do nothing that might threaten that bond.

He led Miriam Foster into the warehouse chamber, patiently looking over his shoulder every few steps, smiling gently as Miriam pushed forward, leaning heavily on her cane. Oscar could see that the woman's leg was bothering her more than usual. She was still a young woman, probably not yet forty, but her disability was aging her more quickly than seemed fair. She looked vulnerable, but Oscar knew better than to be misled by her appearance. He had seen into her soul. She was as bound to Joseph Britton and the cause of Freetown as Oscar was to Michael. If anything, the fire within Miriam burned hotter and more dangerous than any spark of loyalty that Oscar had going.

Most people didn't see that when they looked at Miriam. All they saw was a crippled, disenchanted woman longing for the good old days when Joseph Britton ran things; but Oscar Patterson knew better. The strength and the determination of Miss Miriam Foster was eternal. The dedication to the cause was eternal; it filled and consumed her. Nothing, absolutely nothing, could or would stand in the way of what she felt to be important to the purpose.

Miriam Foster was the most dangerous person that Oscar Patterson had ever met. He respected her, and he feared her. Each day he thanked whatever powers-that-be that this woman stood on the same side as Michael Britton, for if she didn't, Oscar would have had to find some way to deal with her, and he had serious doubts about whether he would have come out on the winning side of such a confrontation.

The chamber was one of two large caverns used to hold the inventory of supplies and equipment collected by Oscar and other gatherers. Anything that might be useful was stored in these chambers, to be distributed as needed to Freetown and its residents by the supply officer or as directed by the council.

Miriam had been the supply officer of Freetown since the position had first been created by Joseph Britton a few years after the town's founding. Joseph had understood the importance the role would hold in the future of the growing community, and he had seen and come to rely upon the intelligence and loyalty of this young woman, not quite out of her teens at the time, whom Joseph and Barbara had taken under their wing years earlier.

She followed Oscar through the maze of crates, boxes and barrels, sometimes stacked twelve to fourteen feet high. Each container was labeled with its contents, the quantity carefully recorded on the label and in the supply room files. They passed containers of clothing, bedding and linens, pots and pans, tools, garden equipment, paper supplies, and much more. The other cavern held furniture, gas powered tools and parts, larger agricultural equipment and supplies. Automobile parts and supplies were kept in a separate inventory.

"This way," urged Oscar. He had pulled ahead of Miriam, and waited for her now at the intersection of the two main aisles.

"Yes, yes," said Miriam. "I'm coming."

Oscar nodded encouragingly and started down the bisecting aisle. He turned again at the next pathway and passed through a row of barrels on the right, wooden boxes on the left. The narrow aisle opened onto a cleared area, in the center of which a number of articles were piled atop a large tarp.

"Here... here!" said Oscar, circling the tarp.

"What have you found for us, Oscar?" asked Miriam.

Oscar smiled proudly. At his feet were several hand guns, boxes of ammunition, and a number of first aid kits. Many of the bullets would have to be pulled apart and new bullets made, but this was indeed a valuable find. The contents of the first aid kits were sealed, and some of the items would still be usable.

"Well?" asked Oscar.

"Not bad," said Miriam approvingly. "Additions to the armory are always welcome."

"And this," said Oscar. He knelt down and pushed aside several weapons, pulled out a Shillie weapon.

"Oh, my. Do you know if there's a charge left?"

"I don't know," Oscar stood and handed the weapon to Miriam. She looked at the power indicator.

"Two shots left."

"I found all this at an old battlefield."

"How old?"

"At least a few seasons; maybe a lot longer. There weren't any bodies, and most of this was hidden in the grass grown over since."

"Nice job, Oscar. All of this will be put to good use." Miriam held the Shylmahn weapon out delicately between them. "This, however, should get us a few hard to come by items."

"Sounds like a trip to the researchers is in the planning."

"We should have enough things to make a trip worthwhile." Over the years, Freetown had organized several journeys to the south, trading paper, books, clothing, and especially alien artifacts, for supplies that the researchers manufactured post-invasion.

Miriam heard someone approaching and turned in time to see Victoria stop out at the main aisle and peer in at them before hurriedly scrambling through the narrow path between the stacks of supplies.

"Hello," said Oscar cheerfully.

Victoria gave Oscar a brief jerk of the head in reply, then spoke urgently to Miriam. "I finally found you," she said.

"So you have."

"Jenny Britton is in town."

Jenny wasn't one to come just visiting. There must be something wrong. Miriam stiffened. "Michael?"

"Alive, from what I can tell," Victoria placed a calming hand on Miriam's arm. "She brought Jason Britton with her. He is asking to speak with whoever is charge when Michael is away."

"I'll bet that's going over well," mumbled Miriam.

"The council is being called together."

Miriam sensed there was something more. "And?" she asked.

"Jason is asking that you be there."

"Did he say why?"

"I'm afraid not," Victoria smiled nervously. "But it certainly has people talking."

"And Ethan Perry steaming, no doubt."

"No doubt."

| 7 |

The council meeting was held in the larger hall in order to accommodate the number of people attending. There had been talk of holding the meeting in the plaza, thereby allowing all the residents to attend, but that idea was quickly shot down. No one really knew what the agenda might be, but there was concern that difficult decisions may have to be made, and an open forum could quickly degenerate into an emotional firestorm. If it was decided that the citizenry needed to be brought into the decision process, a formal discussion and voting forum could later be called.

Craig Warren was sitting at the head of the table. The two chairs immediately to his right were empty. The only other council members in the room were Andrew Booker and Joanna Dawn, both sitting immediately on Craig's left. He stood quickly when Jason and Jenny entered the room, and indicated the two chairs beside him.

"Jenny, I wish you would visit us more often," he said. "And Jason, it has been a very long time."

"Hello, Craig," Jason shook the hand that Craig offered, sat down and nodded to those on the other side of the table. Craig did not offer introductions. Jason leaned on his elbows and looked again at Craig. "I believe the last time I saw you was about six years ago," he said. "That mess we got into in the province."

"I believe so," said Craig.

"Hell of a mess." Jason turned toward the door as Ethan Perry came in ahead of Rosemary Lewis.

"Jason... hello," said Rosemary quietly. She took a seat beside Joanna Dawn so that she could face the visitors.

"Hello, Rosemary."

Ethan could sit beside Jenny or at the end of the table. He chose to sit at the end of the table. He nodded a silent hello to Jason and Jenny. "Craig," he said sharply. "Why don't we get this thing started?"

"I believe we can wait a few minutes," said Craig.

"Miriam does know that she was asked to attend, does she not?"

"She was informed," Craig looked a bit embarrassed. He knew that Ethan was trying to set a tone for the meeting, and he wasn't sure how to deflect his attempted manipulations.

"So, Perry..." Jason looked in Ethan's direction side glance, only subsequently looking at him directly. "How's life treating you? 'you doing okay, here?"

"We do as best we can," Ethan Perry spoke cautiously.

"You personally, I mean," Jason gave a half smile now. "How are you doing?"

"Fine," Ethan said, short and crisp.

"That's great. Glad to hear it." He turned to the group as a whole and his smile broadened. "Me, too," he said. "I'm doing real good, as a matter of fact."

With that, the door opened and Miriam came into the room. She took a moment to scan the faces of those sitting around the table before moving slowly to the only open chair left available. Jason and Jenny both stood and were waiting for her, hugged her warmly and helped her take her seat. Craig watched patiently and waited for everyone to return to their places. When everyone was settled, he nodded silently at Jason.

"Thanks, Craig," Jason started, "and thanks to all of you for taking the time to see me."

"Of course," said Rosemary.

Ethan gave Rosemary a disapproving glance, stiffened when he looked back to Jason and saw that Jason was giving him a slight smile. After a dramatic pause, Jason turned again to the larger group.

"The purpose of my coming here is twofold. First, you must be made aware of certain events that are occurring or are about to occur. Second, I am going to ask for your help with certain elements of these events in which we are being asked to participate."

"I knew it," said Ethan, slapping a hand loudly on the table. "The Brittons are drawing us into yet another of their little games with the Shylmahn."

"Ethan, stop being an ass," said Miriam.

"I will not sit idly by while the Brittons play us like pawns, Miriam."

"I would like to hear what he has to say."

"So would we all," said Craig. "Mr. Britton has the floor."

"Certainly," said Ethan, waving a dramatic hand. "Do enlighten us, Mr. Britton."

"Your patience is greatly appreciated," said Jason, quite unperturbed. "First of all, it is vitally important, for your safety and security, that you know that coordinated, multifaceted actions are being taken against the Shylmahn."

"See?" Ethan threw up his hands.

"These operations have been initiated and will continue to be conducted by independent groups. It is only through carefully coordinated communications and give and take that we have been able to formulate what I believe to be a plan that could very well bring down the Shylmahn."

There was a sudden burst of loud voices as most everyone at the table lurched forward and demanded to know who, what and how. Miriam sat silent, one hand resting on her cane, one hand resting on the table. Beside her at the end of the table, Ethan Perry also sat silent, his jaw set in a tight grimace.

After a few moments of uncontrolled free-for-all, Craig called for quiet. When everyone was again silent, if rather impatient for answers, Craig signaled for Jason to continue.

"I won't be able to give you specific details, for obvious reasons. And that is not my purpose in being here. I am here to alert you to what is going on so that you can take whatever precautions you deem necessary."

"And to involve us," said Ethan. "How much of this is Joseph's doing?"

"Joseph has been taken by the Shylmahn."

Again there was a wild flurry of questions and exclamations, but Craig quickly restored order.

"Is he all right?" asked Craig.

"For the moment. He did, in fact, allow himself to taken by the Shylmahn in order to lessen the chance that Freetown and other communities with which he has been identified would be visited by the Shylmahn."

"That's just like Joseph," said Miriam, though she suspected that there was more to it than that; probably much more. What Jason had given them was probably the version meant for public broadcast in the event the Shylmahn grew suspicious about the ease with which they had captured him. Jason would not be spouting statements like that, to people like this, unless the information was either intended to get back to the Shillies or that it just didn't matter.

"Typical Britton grandstanding," said Ethan Perry.

"Typical Perry response," said Miriam.

"Back to the matter at hand," said Craig, who managed to glare Ethan Perry into silence. He turned once again to Jason. "Freetown does indeed have measures that can be set in motion. We will see to them immediately after this meeting."

"Mr. Britton," Rosemary spoke up. "One aspect of those measures includes no traveling outside Freetown, and most especially no forays into the occupied territories. We have a team out there right now."

"I have someone looking for Michael and his team," said Jason. "Once he has been found, I will be asking him to join me on a task to which I have been assigned as part of the operation."

"Then we won't be seeing them until this is all over?" asked Craig.

"I'm afraid you'll have to make do on your own."

"We'll get by," said Ethan, coolly, "if your actions don't bring the Shylmahn wrath down upon us all."

"God forbid we should make the Shillies mad at us," said Miriam.

"Your presence here is not necessary, Miss Foster," said Ethan bitterly.

"But was asked for," said Craig.

"So it was," said Ethan, looking directly at Jason. "You requested that our local Britton fan club attend this little gathering. Might I ask why?"

"It was Joey's suggestion," Jason said cheerily. "When he and I were talking over my visit to Freetown, he was fairly adamant that Miriam be a part of any meeting that I was a part of." He leaned forward to get a clear look at Miriam. "In any event, I would certainly not have let the day end without seeing Miri." With that, Jason turned seamlessly back to Ethan Perry. His appearance lost all humor and his voice took on a very serious tone. "She's family, don't you know..."

Jenny, who hadn't said a word since the meeting got under way, placed her hand on the back of Miriam's.

"I see," said Ethan, after a long pause.

Jason let another long moment pass, then formed a dark half-smile. "Yes."

Craig Warren broke up the pained silence by clearing his throat and rubbing both hands on the table. "Jason..." he started at last. "You indicated that there was something specific that you needed from us, some assistance that we might provide."

Jason straightened. "Quite true. A vehicle, supplies, and a couple of bodies."

"Pardon?"

"Living. Volunteers, actually, meeting very specific qualifications. As I said, I am responsible for a certain element of the operation, and I am hoping that you folks can provide me with some of the resources I need."

"If we have it, it is yours," said Craig, with a quick, silencing glare in Ethan's direction. "That is all?"

"That is enough," said Jason. "I wouldn't ask Freetown to become directly involved. It serves us well in its current role as the beacon for freedom. If we try to expand the purpose, we may lose the purpose. I won't risk that."

There were six bays in the Freetown garage, with a workbench running along the length of the back wall. The garage was well stocked with tools, parts and tires. Each stall had a vehicle parked in it.

Jason had selected the Bronco, and was preparing it for the trip. The tires had been checked and the oil changed. The belts and hoses looked as though they had recently been replaced. He was putting in a new battery and would be replacing the spark plugs.

Jenny had brought in food supplies and had loaded them into the back of the vehicle. Miriam and Oscar would be bringing in the other supplies and equipment from the warehouse. For now, there was little else for Jenny to do but hand tools to Jason when he asked for them.

"I wish I been more help at the meeting," she said. "I didn't say a word."

"Wasn't much that needed saying," said Jason. He shifted the battery into position and fastened it down.

"Still, I felt unnecessary."

Jason placed eight new spark plugs within easy reach, picked up the ratchet and went to work on the old plugs. "I will seldom admit to being wrong, Jenny, so make a note. Your presence here was important, and I'm glad that you insisted on coming. Just having you in the meeting made a difference. It set an important tone. And, your presence here in Freetown said something to the people living here."

"Well, I don't feel very valuable," Jenny leaned against the fender and crossed her arms. As much as she had insisted on coming, she always felt uncomfortable when she was away from the station. "But I am glad that I came. I hadn't been here in a long time."

"You should get out more," said Jason, not missing a beat but managing a grin. He continued working. They needed to get out on the road as soon as possible. He looked up when he heard the door open. Craig Warren came into the garage. Before the door closed behind Craig, Jason could see that it was completely dark outside.

"Hey, Craig," said Jason. He ratcheted down a spark plug, moved to the next and pulled the wire.

"Jason," said Craig. He didn't look all that pleased with the turn of events. "I just came by to wish you all luck."

"Thank you," said Jenny.

Jason grunted what was probably a thank you from under the hood.

"Yeah, well..." Craig shrugged imperceptibly.

"Something wrong?" asked Jenny.

"Not really... I guess."

"Spill it, man," said Jason. He straightened up, set the old spark plug aside and picked up a new one. He tested the gap, then leaned back in under the hood. He had his suspicions about what Craig was shuffling his feet about, and didn't want to deal with it.

"What is it?" asked Jenny. She had her suspicions as well, and was being much more generous than her uncle.

Craig visibly shrugged his shoulders. "It's just, well, all that's been going on lately. It's gotten some folks here pretty stirred up."

"Ethan Perry," said Jenny.

"He's doing most of the stirring. And he has his supporters."

"What are you afraid they'll do?"

"If they had their way, the railroad would stop, we would condemn any resistance like what you're doing right now, and we'd close our gates to all outsiders."

"That goes against everything that Freetown stands for," said Jenny. From under the hood of the Bronco, Jason grumbled unintelligibly.

"Perhaps," said Craig. "But events like those that have happened over the last few weeks play right into their hands. People are afraid."

"Then they can leave," said Jenny, harshly.

"But this is their home," Craig almost pleaded.

"They chose to live in the major hub of the underground railroad."

"Perhaps so, and that line of reasoning has been made before. Believe me. But they would argue that what has always been doesn't have to always be. Situations change."

"Not this one," said Jenny, very precisely.

"As the head of the council, I must be realistic about the chances for real change in the order of the world. Freetown must continue to exist as a home for everyone living here, and not just as a hope to those in the occupied lands."

Jason pulled himself out from under the hood. "That's just fine, Craig. You distance yourself as much from this as you need to. But make no mistake. Freetown has a purpose that goes beyond the desires of the individuals living here. Anyone disapproving of that purpose is perfectly free to move on."

Craig stiffened. He liked the Brittons—he wished that Michael was here now—but it wasn't always easy to be on their side. They could sometimes be a difficult bunch. "And you would have me enforce this edict how?"

"I'm not the politician."

"Obviously," Craig grimaced. "Listen, no matter what you, or Jenny, or Miriam Foster say, this is a community. People live here. It is their home. And the people who live here have a voice and rights, and they will exercise both."

Jenny placed a hand on Craig's arm. She was trying her best to understand his position. "It must be very difficult, and very frustrating."

Miriam Foster spoke from just inside the door. "I see three possibilities," she said, and started forward, smacking her cane on the floor as she walked. Oscar Patterson followed behind, pushing a heavily loaded hand truck. "First possibility: Joseph's big plan is a big success. In that event, Freetown can become whatever you like, and everyone is happy. Of course, in all likelihood, everyone will leave, since who wants to live in a hole in the ground if you don't have to."

"Ethan Perry," mumbled Jason, going back under the hood.

"Second possibility: Big disaster, everyone dies or is captured or whatever, and the Shillies get really pissed off. In such a scenario, I would say the chances of Freetown continuing to exist, in any form, are extremely remote."

"As Ethan Perry has predicted," said Craig.

"Freetown's history makes it a target, Mr. Warren; not its present configuration."

"That's a very fine line you walk."

"Third possibility," said Miriam, straightening up and looking Craig directly in the eye. "What happens out there has little impact and the world continues on as before. On the grander scale of things, what do you think such a world would need most? A few hundred people huddled in a cave, afraid of their own shadows, or a community working to help all of humanity, living representatives of what is good and decent about the human race?"

"I'm on your side in this, Miriam."

"You don't sound like it, Mayor."

"It isn't as simple as you would try to make it. Saying so doesn't make it so. Whether you like it or not, the people living here have ownership in this community. Freetown doesn't belong to you or me, or to the Britton family. It may have once, but not anymore. I will listen to the concerns of every citizen, and I will try to address those concerns, whatever my own beliefs might be."

Miriam struggled silently for some response, for some righteous remark that would set Craig Warren on the golden path toward all that was right and good. Continuing to stand her ground, she let out a heavy sigh jerked her head sharply. "You walk a pretty fine line yourself, Mr. Warren."

"A razor's edge, Miss Foster."

Miriam studied Craig's face. She could hear Oscar loading the supplies into the back of the Bronco. At the front of the vehicle, Jason was putting in another spark plug. After a few pained moments, Miriam nodded gently, "You're a good man, Craig. I've never doubted that. I know that you have the confidence of Michael, and I know that he likes and respects you." She took a long, deep breath, "I'm going to leave it at that, for now. I'm going to trust that you will do the right thing."

"I guess that's as close to an endorsement as I'm going to get from Miriam Foster," said Craig.

"Believe what you will," Miriam expression darkened as she turned and started around to the back of the vehicle to supervise the final loading of supplies.

Jenny held a hand out to Craig. "Wish us luck?" she managed a friendly smile. Craig shook her hand and then turned sheepishly to leave. Jason called out to him.

"I do believe that of all of us, it is you my friend that has the toughest job," he said.

Craig spoke over his shoulder, "I hope you are right. I wouldn't want your task to be as difficult as the one I know I am about to take on." He stepped through the door and was gone.

"Climb in and start it, Jenny," said Jason. He picked up a cloth and wiped his hands.

Annie Gomez came into the garage just as Jenny slid in behind the steering wheel. She was carrying two canvas packs; one contained her personal gear, the second had a red cross on it. She handed the packs one at a time to Oscar.

"Welcome to the party," said Miriam.

"Should be fun," said Annie.

The engine turned over and started. After a few seconds, the sound smoothed out and became a steady rumble. Jason lowered the hood, stepped quickly to the large doors and pushed them open just as Oscar turned off the garage lights. Jenny slid out of the driver's seat, moving over to the passenger seat as the others in the group climbed into the back.

"Ready?" asked Jason. Before getting an answer, he shifted the Bronco into first and guided it out of the garage.

The Outer Village was quiet and dark. What few windows there were had heavy curtains. Jason eased the vehicle down the narrow street by the light of the moon.

Ethan Perry stood to one side of the main gate, arms folded, feet planted shoulder-width apart. He said nothing, made no move. The gate slowly opened and Jason guided the vehicle through.

They hoped to reach Jenny's cabin before dawn.

The room was small. The ceiling light glowed faintly yellow. Joseph sat on a stool, unbound, with his hands resting in his lap. Sensors were attached to his head, chest and one hand. A guardian probe hovered at eye level four feet in front of him. Behind him was a small holo-table, above which an image reflected the readings from the sensors.

A short Shylmahn stood silent in one corner. She watched the Chehnon native, occasionally looked over at the sensor readings. She wondered what the big deal was with this particular creature. What made this one so special? And really, why would any of these creatures matter in the slightest?

Joseph watched the guardian probe that was hovering in front of him. He moved his head from side to side, looking for some response from the floating machine. Only when he started to stand did the probe react. It fired a bright energy pin into the floor less than an inch in front of Joseph's left foot. Joseph quickly sat back down.

The Shylmahn in the corner smiled smugly. *Stupid Chehnon...*

NehLoc came into the room. Ignoring the Shylmahn in the corner, he moved smoothly around the room and stood beside Joseph, glanced discreetly at the sensor readings shimmering above the holo-table.

"Good morning, JoSeph," he said lightly. He spoke in Joseph's native language, and spoke it very well.

"How ya' doin', NehLoc?"

"I am doing quite well."

The Shylmahn standing in the corner was a bit taken back by the easy banter between NehLoc and this creature. It wasn't just the words being exchanged, but the genuineness that she sensed coming from them. And NehLoc spoke in the creature's own language. That was unusual. NehLoc liked to set a tone when interrogating Chehnon, and this was very different from normal procedure.

"It's been a while," said Joseph.

"Six years, I believe."

"Ah. Yes," said Joseph. "We had a bit of a scuffle then, didn't we?"

"Yes," NehLoc smiled.

"We shouldn't let so much time pass, next time."

"Oh, it isn't as though we haven't checked in on you from time to time; just to see how you are getting on."

"I appreciate that." Joseph had to admit that NehLoc had developed a bit of human wit. He would have to be careful; that wit might be partnered with insight.

"Think nothing of it," NehLoc nodded. He looked over at the Shylmahn guard for the first time since coming into the room, turned away without acknowledging her as he moved around to stand directly in front of the native. The probe moved slowly aside, maintaining the same distance and line of sight to its ward. "I hope they have been taking good care of you," he said, nodding in the direction of the guard.

"Fine," said Joseph. He had been kept in a small holding cell directly off the interrogation room since being brought in. After being placed in the cell, he had seen only this one Shylmahn. Twice each day, the cell door was opened and he was given a food tray. The guardian probe always hovered in the background.

"I apologize for not coming to visit sooner," said NehLoc, "but, as you may know, there is so much going on these days."

"No doubt," said Joseph.

They both knew that it was all mind games. NehLoc understood that JoSeph knew how the game was played. He had never underestimated the cunning of these creatures, and never would. There was an art to getting what he needed from the Chehnon. He would have to play its arrogance against itself.

"Perhaps we should begin," he said.

Begin? thought Joseph. *This started the moment I saw the Shylmahn step out onto the street; the moment EsJen stepped out of the car; how many days ago?*

"As you wish," Joseph agreed.

"Excellent," said NehLoc. "Now... I will ask for and I fully expect complete disclosure regarding the activities surrounding your establishment of a communications network, including physical locations and the names and locations of all other creatures involved."

"I see."

"I will ask for and I expect to receive full disclosure regarding the reasons behind the establishment of this communications network," NehLoc looked quickly at the sensor readings shimmering above the holo-table. All the readings were relatively stable. He moved slightly to one side, allowing the guardian probe to shift once again to a position directly in front of the Chehnon creature. "I will ask for and I expect to receive full disclosure regarding any and all communications that you have had with other insurgent groups with which you may have recently affiliated yourself."

"Well, now—"

"And finally I will ask for and I expect to receive full and complete details on whatever plans you may have formulated regarding the overthrow of the Shylmahn leadership."

Joseph waited to see if there was any more. When NehLoc said nothing more, Joseph cleared his throat and swallowed. "Well," he said. "To start with, I know nothing of this communications network of which you speak. Next, I haven't been in contact with any insurgent organizations. In point of fact, I have not been in contact with anyone at all. And finally, I have no plans to overthrow the Shylmahn administration that has so generously and selflessly offered to take over the governing of my troubled little planet."

NehLoc waited patiently as Joseph spouted the expected retort to his outline of the expected results of the upcoming interrogation. Once the creature had finished, he nodded curtly.

"Excellent," he said. "Now... what say we get to the meat of it?"

ShahnTahr watched the interaction between NehLoc and the Chehnon native by way of the guardian probe and the holo-table. The JoSeph creature had been an element of ShahnTahr's environment since the Shylmahn arrival on this world, and indeed the creature had had an impact on numerous decisions that had been made over the decades. Even now, though there were as yet no definitive results from the current interrogation, shifts in perception and alternative possibilities were establishing pathways within the dynamic database. ShahnTahr wondered at the direction the Shylmahn future would take as a result of these interrogations.

ShahnTahr was as curious about the relationship between NehLoc and the creature as he was about the creature's role in the Shylmahn future. NehLoc was a unique entity within the Shylmahn society, and ShahnTahr was as yet uncertain of its individual role in the Shylmahn future. At the moment, the exceptional elements that constituted the NehLoc entity were of great value to the purpose.

ShahnTahr would continue to encourage and guide NehLoc, careful to not let him stray from the path that he had set before him. This path offered the greatest benefit to the purpose, while at the same time keeping him in the position to be either redirected or eliminated should the need for either arise.

ShahnTahr gave a mental heavy sigh and allowed a moment of tranquility as he understood the sensation. The lower levels were taking care of the menial activities adequately, and for the instance of *now* he just wanted to watch NehLoc and JoSeph spar with each other...

| 8 |

Jason drove the Bronco up to the barn doors just before dawn. The trip from Freetown to Jenny's way station had been relatively uneventful, despite Jason's attempt at teaching Jenny how to drive. No one had been hurt, though several of the passengers had experienced several brief moments of barely concealed panic. By the time Jason once again took over the driving duties, Jenny was at least familiar with driving an automobile, if not yet comfortable with it.

When Jason stopped the vehicle, Jenny jumped out and hurried to the cabin to see if anyone had shown up in her absence, and Oscar opened the doors of the barn. Once inside, with the engine turned off, they began unloading some of their things from the back of the vehicle. Some of the gear could stay in the Bronco, as it wouldn't be needed during their time at the station.

Jenny returned from the cabin to tell them that no one had been by. Coming out of the barn, Miriam came up beside Jenny and they walked slowly back to the cabin together.

"Nice place. A lot nicer than the old cabin your parents found me in," said Miriam.

"That's about twenty miles in that direction," said Jenny, pointing north. "I've been by there a few times; empty most of the time, but people stay there now and then, usually on their way out of the occupied territory."

Miriam glanced north, as if absorbing old memories, and continued then toward the cabin. "I helped your father fix this place up, you know."

"I know."

"And I lived here for a bit," Miriam glowed with the old memories that felt as though they were washing over her.

Miriam was a pioneer in the underground. She had been the first stationmaster. In fact, before Jenny there had been only one stationmaster other than Miriam. He had taken over after Miriam moved to Freetown to take over as supply officer, had been killed by a group of human marauders. His fate had made it very difficult for Joseph to allow Jenny to take on the position, and he had relented only after the escape routes had been improved.

They climbed the steps up onto the porch, and Jenny went inside to make breakfast. All Miriam wanted was hot coffee and some time on the porch.

Miriam spent much of the next few days sitting on the porch. The weather was nice, and time at the station was pleasantly calm after the bustle and stress of Freetown. Jason and Oscar came and went several times, usually on foot, usually together, looking for signs of Michael or Monroe.

On the second day, Eddie Blythe showed up at the cabin. Eddie was a nomad in the northwest, spending much of his time deep in the Shylmahn province. He came out only occasionally, calling his trips out his *vacations.* Jenny got along with him well enough, he was a likable enough person, but she didn't completely trust him. Unlike Monroe, whatever Eddie got into, it was always going to be about what Eddie could get out of it. So long as this was understood, and Jenny never let herself forget it, a person could deal with Eddie Blythe.

Eddie would attach himself to Michael's traveling party now and again, when it suited him, always cutting loose once they reached the Frontier. For Eddie, there was nothing on the Frontier worth the effort. Jenny's way station, being on the border, was about as far to the east as Eddie ever traveled.

Eddie had come to see Jenny. He was quite aware of the teams of humans the Shillies had been dropping into the area, and had heard about what had happened to the lowlifes that had come by Jenny's place. He said that he wanted to make sure that she was all right.

"I know you better than that," said Miriam. She and Eddie had a bit of history between them from her own time as stationmaster. She set her glass down on the porch table and studied Eddie's face. Jenny went into the house to get another glass as Eddie sat in the other chair. Miriam spoke sharply. "You have no love for the Shillies, and less for humans that sleep with them, but to make the trip all the way out here to check on Jenny? I don't think so."

"That hurts, Miriam. It really does."

Miriam let out a genuine laugh. She trusted Eddie about as much as Jenny did, but she too liked him well enough and had probably missed him. "Come now, dear Eddie... what brings you out here?"

Jenny returned from inside and handed Eddie a glass of water. She leaned against a porch post and waited for his answer. Eddie gulped down half the water and set the glass carefully onto the table.

"There's a lot happening in the province these days," he said, looking at Miriam and then at Jenny. "Joseph's network has stirred up the place; got the Shillies going around, digging up trouble. And the Chummies, like the creeps that came by here, are everywhere. When Joseph got picked up, as bad as that is, I thought maybe things would ease up some; but they only got worse."

"You aren't looking for a place to hide out, are you?" asked Miriam.

"Hell no," said Eddie. "And if I was, this is the last place I'd come."

"Thanks a lot," Jenny smirked.

"Hey, the place is Four Star, no doubt, but I prefer a lower profile when hiding."

"Then?" Miriam urged.

"Okay... listen," Eddie shifted to the edge of his chair. "I know there's something really heavy going down. I know that whatever it is, it's got the Shillies really nervous. Now, I don't have anything against slamming the little guys, but it does play hell with my own enterprises.

Travel is way down, and believe you me, trust in fellow man is at an all-time low."

"Gee, we're awful sorry about that, Eddie," said Jenny in her own twisted sarcasm.

"Quite all right, Jen. I can deal with an economic slump. I've weathered a few in the past."

"Where's this going?" asked Miriam.

"Things being as slow as they are, and as fraught with potential danger, I felt this to be an opportune time to become more directly involved with the cause of all this."

"Huh?" asked Jenny.

"I'd like to help stir the stick."

"Ah," Jenny smiled and nodded.

"And be under the protection of those in charge of the stick?" asked Miriam.

"Now, Miriam... again with the hurt. Think about it. If protection was the motive, joining up with those that the Shillies consider their greatest threat wouldn't be the wisest of options."

"Perhaps not," she said warily. "But that assumes there was wisdom in your decision."

"I just figured that I could be of some help."

Jenny calmly suggested, "You figured the odds of survival were dropping considerably pretty much wherever you were, so now's as good a time as any to play the hero."

"There is that." He smiled conspiratorially, slid back into his chair and reached for his glass. He took another deep drink and swallowed, set the glass back down.

"Okay, here's the deal," he spoke firmly now. "Monroe has found Michael. They should be here before too long. Tomorrow, maybe the next day."

"That's good to hear," said Miriam.

"Jason Britton is somewhere nearby, recently arrived from the sunny south. He made a quick trip to Freetown, and now he—and you—are waiting for Michael." Eddie leaned over the table, nearer to

Miriam, "And you know what? Joseph Britton's capture came awful sudden and awful easy; not like the Joseph Britton that we all know. If I was the suspicious type, I'd say he wanted to get caught in order to take the heat off the family; ya' know? Like maybe get the Shillies to watch the one hand while the other hand goes quietly about the business?"

"My, but you are indeed the suspicious type," said Miriam.

"And imaginative," said Jenny.

"Imaginative, my ass," said Eddie.

"Do you think the Shillies might be as... imaginative?" asked Miriam.

"I doubt it," said Eddie matter-of-factly. "I'm guessing they're blinded from being all full of themselves over their great skill at bringing him in."

"Even EsJen?"

"Oh... not good."

"Ah. So, you don't know everything."

"If she's here... If there's a Shillie that can see what I saw, she's it." Eddie lost his humor and frowned. "She knows Joseph. She can figure this out. She probably already has."

"Which would put the shining light right back on us."

"Heh, now," said Jenny. "There was more to my father being taken than just taking the pressure off us. He's got work to do in there, and no matter what the Shillies may think they know, we still have our work to do out here."

"She's right," said Miriam. "Whatever they think they know, whatever we think they might know, it doesn't change what we need to do."

"Am I in, then?" asked Eddie.

"Do you still want to be?" asked Miriam.

"Of course."

"Then, we'll see what Jason says."

Jason and Miriam stood in the night shadow of the barn. Monroe had said seven days, and the next day would mark day seven. If Eddie was right, he would be bringing Michael and the others with him. If not, he would be coming alone; Monroe wouldn't miss the deadline unless he was dead.

Jason had no problem with Eddie Blythe coming with them. Eddie could be an asset. They would put his skills to good use. If he turned out to be other than an asset, Jason had no problem dealing with that, as well.

Monroe wouldn't be too pleased to see Eddie. Jason knew that the innovative Mr. Blythe had crossed paths with most of the people in this gathering group at one time or another, and it hadn't always gone well between those two. Monroe's sense of honor and Eddie's sense of self-preservation had put them at cross-purposes in the past. In any event, Jason assumed that everyone would be clear on what to expect when it came to Eddie.

Jenny sat on the porch, a rifle leaning on the rail nearby. She could see Miriam and Uncle Jason over by the barn, darker shadows within shadows. Jason had asked Miriam to walk with him, and that was as far as they had gone. It was out of earshot of the others, and Jenny suspected that Jason wanted to make clear to Miriam the dynamics of the group now that Eddie Blythe had joined them.

She saw movement gliding through the shadows in the distance that reached across the path from the east. Casually leaning forward, Jenny grasped the rifle and laid it across her lap. She calmly took a sip of coffee.

Over by the barn, Jason and Miriam had sensed something as well. Jenny saw them back further into the shadows until they were out of sight. Inside the cabin, Annie Gomez, Oscar and Eddie were asleep.

The movement in the shadows formed into shadows in their own right, and eventually become a group of four humans, one leading a horse.

The configuration was right, if not the direction. They must have come around from the west and south, and then up along the Frontier border. Perhaps they had suspected they were being followed and had wanted to deal with it out there before coming into the way station.

Three of the shadows came up to the cabin, while the fourth led the horse toward the barn. Michael reached the foot of the steps looking as though he wouldn't be able to take another step. To either side of him, Jack Rydel and Mitch dropped to the ground and lay staring up at the night sky. Mitch accused Monroe of force-marching them the last hundred miles.

"The last hundred, eh?" Jenny smiled pleasantly.

"The first three or four hundred weren't too bad," said Jack.

Michael turned about and sat on the top step. "How's things here?" he asked.

"Interesting," said Jenny.

"Is everybody here?"

"And then some."

"Oh, don't hurt my brain, Sis."

"Yeah, Miss Jenny," said Mitch. "Monroe worked us so danged hard, even the brain muscle is just plum wore out."

"Well, you guys go ahead and rest your poor, tired, feeble little brains. I'm sure that saving the world will wait until you're all rested up."

"Oh, god..." groaned Jack.

Michael, Jason and Monroe hovered over an old handmade map that Michael had spread across the table in Jenny's cabin. It was one of those important items that Jason and Jenny had brought back from Freetown. It showed mountains, rivers and other natural features, as well as manmade and Shylmahn-made landmarks. Intentionally omitted were the locations of human populations, resistance sites, and anything else that Joseph wouldn't want the Shylmahn to know about. Maps could easily fall into the hands of the Shillies.

"There," said Jason, pointing to a location on the map. "Carolyn's old stronghold was just north of where those two rivers meet."

"I remember my father taking me there," said Michael. "It was the last time I saw Carolyn."

"The ruins are still there," said Monroe.

Jason nodded. "After the incident, she took her people farther up into the valley."

"Yes, that's right. It's about there," said Monroe. He pointed to an unmarked location deep within the narrow valley. "Carolyn's Keep. I've never been there, myself. No one goes up there."

"I've heard stories," said Michael.

"Me, too," said Jason. "I believe the kid has gone a bit over."

"I know that my father likes her very much."

Jason stared down at the map, as if he could see into the Keep, see his sister, see what she used to be rather than what she had become. "We were a pretty close family, in spite of how we drifted apart those last few years before the invasion. Carolyn was kind of wild, even then, but that only added to her charm."

"I think that's what my father liked about her."

"It drove Bril nuts."

"He said that, too. And he also said that was the very feature that you liked best about her."

"Oh, did he?" Jason raised his brow in mock indignation.

"Yes, he did," Michael said firmly. "It appears you were a bit of a troublemaker yourself."

Jason liked the sound of that. He had always thought of himself as someone walking the dark side of the street, which is why he had chosen the path that he had, fought the fight he had fought, and lived the way that he had lived.

"I'll have to have a talk with your father," said Jason, turning again to the map. "Monroe, do you think there's some place near the ruins where we could hide the Bronco? Some place we could store the supplies and gear? I want to take only what we need on into the valley and Carolyn's."

"Not a problem."

The three stood silent around the table. Jason continued to look down at the map, while Michael and Monroe watched Jason. They knew that he was working half a dozen different variations of some grand scheme that only he and Joseph really knew.

Michael looked finally at the map, at the valley where they thought his aunt was likely holed up. "Do you think she'll join us?"

"She'll join us," said Jason. "I doubt she's changed that much."

It was decided that Monroe would take the Bronco to the ruins, loaded with gear and with Miriam, Annie, Jack and Oscar as passengers. The others would follow after on foot, carrying only the supplies they needed to get them there. Once they met up, the group would head up into the valley.

Jason agreed to give everyone one day's rest. The two groups would start out first thing in the morning.

Joseph was sitting on a thin mat. He was alone in a room twice the width of the mat and exactly its length. There was one door and no window. Since being brought in by the Shylmahn a few weeks earlier, he had seen nothing but this room and the interrogation room just beyond the door.

The door opened and the guard waved him out. Joseph walked out of his cell and directly to the toilet closet. With that taken care of, he walked silently to the stool waiting for him in the middle of the room. The guard handed him a plate of food, stepped back and silently watched him eat. The guardian probe hovered in front of him.

He was not quite halfway through his meal when a second Shylmahn came into the room and took the plate from him, handing it over to the guard. He moved around behind Joseph and attached the sensors that would send readings from the Chehnon prisoner to the holo-table. A shimmering image immediately began flickering above the table. The technician left without saying a word.

Joseph looked to the guard holding the plate of food. "Can I finish my breakfast, please?"

Once he had finished eating, he sat quietly and waited. This day was starting like most others. He could hear the faint hum of the guardian probe; he could hear the breathing of the guard; he could even hear the holo-table behind him.

A sound came from beyond the door...

The door opened and EsJen came in.

The sensor readings must be dancing all over the place...

Joseph tried to relax. He knew the sensors would be telling her that he was trying to suppress whatever emotions he might be feeling. He gave up finally and let whatever he felt show.

He knew that she had to have been observing the interrogations from the beginning, and so he had been trying to analyze the reasons behind EsJen not showing herself to him earlier. He was certain that it was calculated.

So, why show yourself now? Has something changed recently on the outside? Did something happen at the last interrogation? Has something not *happened, and you've grown tired of waiting?*

"EsJen... it's good to see you... I guess..."

EsJen moved to within a few steps. The guardian probe shifted position. The Shylmahn guard stood ready.

"Hello, JoSeph," she said. Then, in a motherly tone, "What have you been up to?"

"This and that."

"So I hear."

Joseph shrugged. He saw her eyes dart quickly to the sensor readings and back again. She moved slightly to one side, forcing the guardian probe to swing around behind her and come up on her other side. The guard took one step to her left. EsJen ignored the disruption that she caused, keeping her gaze on Joseph.

"Things are very different than they were in the past," EsJen continued. "There is a rising level of anxiety, and I won't be able to protect you as I once did."

"I'm not asking you to protect me, EsJen."

She shook her head sadly, "I do want to help you."

"As long as your computer master says it's okay?"

"ShahnTahr is not my master, and he is much more than a computer, much more than a box of circuit boards and processors and data storage."

"Yeah, well," Joseph rubbed a hand tiredly on his leg, listened carefully for any changes in the sounds coming from the guardian probe, the holo-table, the breathing of the Shylmahn guard or from EsJen. He looked up at EsJen again. "I guess we've already had this discussion, haven't we?" he asked.

EsJen smiled. "Several times...years ago." There had been many long talks while the JoSeph project had been active. Since its conclusion, however, they had crossed paths only sporadically, and not always under the most pleasant of circumstances. She remembered vividly the events of their last meeting, and her smile quickly faded. "I am truly sorry about what happened to your mate," she said.

"Whatever it takes, huh?"

"This world is the home of the Shylmahn, JoSeph. That will not change. Whatever must be done to ensure the peace, to ensure the stability and the future of the Shylmahn, and guarantee the safety of the Shylmahn people, will be done."

"I've certainly heard that before; about a thousand times."

"In twenty-eight years, it has never been more true than at this very moment."

Joseph could almost feel the sensor readings above the holo-table pushing at him, but EsJen did not look at them, did not lift her gaze from his. She wanted him to know that her last statement was probably the most important that he would ever hear.

He wanted her to know that his next statement was just as important. He let the heavy silence drag for several long seconds and did not turn from her sharp stare. When he spoke, it was with a calm that the subsiding sensor readings would show was genuine.

"In twenty-eight years, the Shylmahn domination of my planet has never been in greater doubt."

For just a moment, EsJen appeared shaken. He knew that she hadn't expected such a revelation, at least not yet. It was as if he had opened the door and called for her to come in. And yet, she looked crestfallen. Perhaps she had held out some trace of hope that Joseph had not been involved in a plot to overthrow her people. Perhaps she had hoped that she could in fact still save her one-time Chehnon *friend.* Now that would never happen. They would extract all the information that Joseph had, every drop of data, and then he would be eliminated.

Joseph watched as the expression on EsJen's face hardened, the bright, golden glimmer in her eyes sharpen and focus. When he felt the time was right, he closed the door that he had opened for her. "Anyway... that's what I have been told."

"By who?"

"Whom. By *whom.*" He cocked his head and lifted a brow. "At least, I think it's *whom.*" Joseph tried each on the tongue, carefully working the shapes with his lips, "By who... by whom... by—"

"Who told you this and what form does this threat take?"

It was clear to Joseph that EsJen had no doubt that Joseph himself was the source of the threat. "I don't remember," he said, with no emotion. "It's just the kind of talk that goes around."

EsJen leaned closer. "I do not believe that NehLoc will understand your humor, JoSeph. You are walking a very dangerous path."

Joseph set his jaw tight. "I don't remember. It was just talk."

Ethan Perry found Victoria in the Outer Village, walking from the direction of the main gate. She didn't look too pleased to see him, which would only make this more difficult. Though he was afraid that it would look forced, he tried to put on a friendly smile. Victoria Romero was not a member of the council, but with Michael and Miriam gone, her support would go a long way in swaying Craig Warren and the other members of the Britton Family fan club.

"Victoria," he called, stepping up beside her and matching her stride. "I am so glad that I found you."

She continued walking, apparently heading in the direction of the Inner Village. "Hello Ethan. What can I do for you?"

"I'd like to run something by you, if that's all right."

Victoria stopped and turned to face him. The sun shone harsh, and she turned so as not to face the direct sunlight. "What is this about?"

"Freetown's survival."

"Please, Mr. Perry," she said impatiently.

"Just hear me out."

"Then put away the staged theatrics. I find them very annoying."

"You are absolutely right," said Ethan. He indicated a nearby bench, and the two of them moved over to it and sat down. "I propose a compromise," he said once they were seated. "Despite what may be said about me, I do sympathize with the Britton point of view regarding Freetown."

"You just can't *accept* the Britton point of view regarding Freetown," Victoria said flatly.

"Not on its face, no; but I am willing to acknowledge it and, so long as the safety of the citizens is maintained, to accommodate it."

"I'm listening," said Victoria, cautiously. "What do you have in mind?"

"A compromise, as I said."

"Which means what?"

"I am willing to allow that Freetown remain a part of the underground railroad that the Brittons have going, with a few modifications."

"What sort of modifications?"

"Absolutely sensible, I assure you. I suggest that the teams that go out will spend more time at Jenny Britton's station to ensure they haven't been followed; when returning to Freetown, the teams should make more circuitous routes, and for the last twenty miles, that they travel under cover of darkness. Finally, they will limit the trips to three a year."

Victoria thought a moment, and nodded slowly. "I think these could be discussed." Victoria eyed Ethan warily, "Is there more?"

"There is one more item."

"I take it this is the item likely to generate the most discussion..."

"Perhaps," he said.

"Go on."

"Activities within the Shylmahn province that do not directly relate to the underground railroad project must stop."

Victoria shifted about and looked away from Ethan. "Ah," she said.

"And activities that *do* relate to the underground railroad must be kept to the minimum necessary to accomplish the task, and in such a way so as not to be construed as aggressive."

Victoria leaned forward and smiled. Some others might eventually be brought around to accept these last elements of the compromise, but Michael never would; not in a thousand years.

"I am not overly hopeful," she said.

"I understand," said Ethan. He was prepared, and it was the reason that he had worded these items of the compromise in just this way. "I believe that we can at least agree that the railroad missions can be kept exclusively to the task at hand, can we not?"

"Possibly," noncommittally.

"If the purpose of the mission is to extract those humans seeking escape from the province, then by keeping the operation to within those parameters shouldn't be difficult."

"Let's say I give you that, at least to put your proposal on the table."

"Thank you," said Ethan.

"As far as that goes."

"Then, as you say, for the purposes of putting my proposal on the table, we are left with one final element."

"Michael will never agree to hobbling our access to the occupied territory."

"Of that I have no doubt. I therefore present a possible solution."

"And that is?"

"Another community. Activities outside the scope of the underground railroad will be initiated from this second location. Those persons involved in these activities will take up residence in this new community. Interaction between Freetown and this new community would be discreet and infrequent."

"You know that's never going to happen," Victoria was less than enthusiastic.

"The details could all be worked out."

"And you know what the response would be."

"It can at least be put on the table with the rest of the recommendations."

"He'll suggest that you start your own second community."

"The council could outline an acceptable solution now, one that he would accept upon his return."

Victoria involuntary slid away from Ethan. "Are you suggesting that I go behind Michael's back?"

"Absolutely not," said Ethan. "Quite the opposite; I'm asking that you represent him in his absence."

"Because you think I would be a softer touch."

"Because I believe this won't wait for his return," said Ethan. He worked his lips nervously, "And you may be easier to get along with."

"You forget my reputation, Mr. Perry."

"Actually, no," Ethan smiled. "But as you know, Michael and I have a history that continually gets in the way of polite discussion."

Victoria had to fight down a grin and a quick retort. When she was finally ready with a more appropriate response, Ethan held up a hand, tilted his head back and looked up into the sky. He slowly rose to his feet.

Victoria heard it, too. She stood beside him, shaded her eyes and surveyed the bright blue sky.

The Shylmahn fighter roared overhead, low enough and slow enough to make it easy to see and to identify. The sound faded then, slowly, until the community was left in a hollow silence. People came stumbling out of the buildings of the Outer Village, wandered cautiously out from Inner Village, all looking anxiously up at the sky.

Just when people began wondering aloud what it might mean, another fighter passed overhead, following the same flight path as the first, sending everyone again into stunned silence, if only for a few moments. Regaining their voices, they began questioning one another, demanding answers of one another. *What could it mean?* Over the years, there had been anxious moments, but this....

A third fighter followed after the first two, the alien sound drowning out the quickly rising voices of the townspeople. Ethan Perry turned to Victoria.

"I'd say this changes everything," he said.

| 9 |

Carolyn's old fortress had been made of stone, concrete and heavy wooden beams. Four buildings had served as the four corners of a compound enclosed within a thick stone wall. The ruins that remained were little more than shards of a few walls and a few piles of broken stone and decomposing wood framing. All had long ago overgrown with weeds and blackberry brambles.

Jason inspected the area a final time, looking for telltale signs that that they had been there. Monroe had done a good job of hiding the tire tracks and camouflaging the vehicle. He had also kept the group from tromping too much on the vegetation, keeping most of their activity under the trees or on hard surfaces. When Jason had arrived with the second group that morning, had he not known, he never would have guessed that there was anyone staying there, much less that anyone had been through any time recently.

Jason worked his way over to Michael, who was standing beneath a tree bordering the small meadow. He gave Michael a slight nod, and the two looked to the terrain they were soon to be heading into. The valley cut deep into the heart of rugged hills. A creek issued from it, feeding into a river that itself would eventually feed into an even larger river.

The other members of the group slowly worked their way over to Jason and Michael. Each carried a pack of supplies; even Miriam had insisted on carrying something, though her load was lighter.

They started out. They would follow the creek, using existing animal trails when available, always keeping a sharp eye out for signs of human activity. They would stay under cover as much as they could and leave as little sign of their passing as possible. Michael led the way, with Miriam following him and serving to set the pace. She was much more robust and hard-wearing than her appearance let on, and managed to set a good, steady cadence.

Monroe took up the rear, keeping well back and disguising the more obvious signs the others left behind. This, he could understand and deal with; but he could barely restrain himself from rushing up to tell them all to quiet the hell down. The Shylmahn could probably hear their tromping and their loud voices all the way from their cozy homes in their cozy city. But Monroe was Monroe. He kept his silence and did his best to wipe their passage clean, to remove and hide the broken branches, and he prayed for a miracle.

At the very least, he was certain they wouldn't have to search too keenly for Carolyn. He had no doubt that she knew they were coming.

NehLoc tried, with great difficulty, to hide his frustration. He circled the holo-table in his private office, his eyes never leaving the image displayed above it. The guardian probe in the main interrogation room was feeding an image of JoSeph to the table. The Chehnon native was sitting stiffly on the stool, glaring at the probe, occasionally making bizarre and incomprehensible faces at it. The creature was as frustrated as he was, and didn't mind expressing it, both during the direct interrogation and now.

EsJen watched NehLoc. She stood near the door, her back against the wall. NehLoc didn't look at her, but occasionally mumbled his thoughts aloud in her direction. He didn't expect her to respond to his grumblings, and she didn't offer any.

When he finally stopped circling, he was directly across the table from EsJen, could see her through the shimmering display. This was not random. He liked to continue monitoring whatever he was looking at while looking directly at whomever he was speaking with.

"The creature's words speak to so many directions at once," he said.

"It is calculated," warned EsJen.

"And what it says one day is often withdrawn or contradicted the next. It admits to lying, implying that it was giving us what it thought we wanted to hear." NehLoc stared sharply at the image of JoSeph. He thought a moment, raised his gaze slightly again to EsJen. "If we throw out the inconsistent comments, the wild ravings, the implausible threats, are we not left with a set of constants that run half-hidden beneath this animal's daily meanderings? Information that, however well it might be camouflaged, remains consistent from one day to the next?"

"Or is made to appear so."

NehLoc had to give her that. "I would not put it past these creatures to at least make the attempt at such subterfuge. However, I doubt that even one as clever as this could maintain so subtle and complex a deception for long."

The expression EsJen gave NehLoc showed that she was not so certain. NehLoc rethought his analysis.

"We will focus on these apparent underlying truths," he said finally. "We would know for certain if they are facts or fiction; if fiction, we will find out what these fictions are hiding."

EsJen felt uncomfortable. JoSeph may well believe that the only way to win against the Shylmahn would be to guide the Shylmahn into losing of their own accord. With all that JoSeph knew of the Shylmahn, of NehLoc, of ShahnTahr, he could very well believe that he might manipulate the Shylmahn.

Was JoSeph creating a picture of an image of a world on the edge of destruction, a world in which the Shylmahn would lose all they had gained, to then lay down a path for NehLoc to find and follow?

If so, how could EsJen ever hope to convince NehLoc? He was working so hard at making the discoveries, seemingly through his own cunning.

Perhaps she was reading too much into this. Perhaps she was giving JoSeph, and all Chehnon, more ingenuity than they in fact possessed.

But she doubted it.

She had gone back and studied the JoSeph project from decades earlier. She had examined her comments regarding Joseph's observations of her and the Shylmahn, of the focus of each of his inquiries, of his comments to her regarding those observations.

The Chehnon individual that she had studied back then could very well have become someone who years later was capable of designing and then attempting to execute a plan in which the Shylmahn beat themselves as the Chehnon stood by and watched.

EsJen stepped away from the wall and approached NehLoc. Somehow, she had to convince him that first, such a thing was possible, and second, that Joseph may very well be undertaking such a thing.

The meeting room was crowded with citizenry. Extra chairs had been brought in and people were sitting shoulder to shoulder around the table; others lined the walls. At one end of the table sat the council members: Craig Warren, Ethan Perry, Andrew Booker, Joanna Dawn and Rosemary Lewis.

Victoria Romero watched from near the door.

Freetown was on Level One alert. Outer Village activity had been all but stopped, and spotters had been posted at stations along the perimeter fence and at strategic locations beyond the walls. The escape route tunnels running off the main cavern of the Inner Village were posted with guides, the weapons stations throughout the main cavern were manned, and all citizens were required to have their emergency packs on them or have them readily available.

Craig dropped his head into his hands and groaned loudly, muting out the latest tirade by yet another of the frustrated and frightened attendees. They had already gone over, again and again and again, what the presence of the Shillie fighters might mean, how it might relate to whatever Michael Britton and the others were doing. Continuing to argue about what the Britton family should or should not be doing, or how they may have involved Freetown in their personal war with the alien occupiers, would not take them one step closer to resolving their present dilemma.

"The fact is," said Craig, lifting his face from his hands, "Freetown has been a very visible part of a quiet resistance for two and half decades; by the very nature of its purpose, it has always been a target."

"Times change," said Rosemary Lewis. "Just because Freetown has always supported the purpose of the railroad does not mean that it must always do so."

"What I am trying to say, Rosemary, is that the threat has always been with us, and it makes no sense to analyze it or reevaluate our reason for existing at this stage. Trying to change what we are now will not alter what the Shylmahn will or won't attempt to do with Freetown. No sacrificial offerings will change what they think of us."

"Such was not my intent," said Rosemary curtly.

"Of course not."

"But what of Ethan's proposals?" she asked. Ethan had managed to enter into the discussion his suggestions of limiting the activities within the Shylmahn province and separating Freetown from direct involvement with most outside activities. He had known that it was all moot at this point, but was already setting the foundation for whatever community might be created in the future by those who might survive the next few days and weeks. He had no intention of letting the Britton family dictate the makeup of the home that he envisioned for them. A number of those in the room had desperately grasped onto his ideas as if they could somehow save them from the inevitable.

"His suggestions will certainly be addressed once the immediate crisis is behind us," said Craig.

"But don't you think that the initiation of his proposals now might be taken as a sign of our acquiescence?"

"I must agree with Craig," sighed Ethan. He wore a sad, conciliatory smile. "Such actions could never be implemented in time to prevent what our earlier actions have already initiated. And in any event, the

Level One status we now find ourselves in effectively removes Freetown from any and all provocative activities."

"The only question before us is what do we do now?" asked Victoria from her place by the door. "If they come, when they come, what do we do?"

"Victoria is right," said Craig.

"Absolutely," agreed Ethan.

"What *can* we do?" asked Rosemary, and several in the room grunted and grumbled in response. "We can't fight them," she continued. "So we have to run."

"Should we?" asked Craig.

"Are you suggesting that we stay and fight them?"

"We do have some defensive capabilities."

"Nothing that could withstand the Shylmahn," said Ethan.

"I'm not saying that we can defeat them, Ethan. But perhaps we should give the defensive mechanism that we spent years developing and maintaining a chance to work for us."

"Those defenses were designed in the event we were attacked without warning. The Shillies have seen fit to give us a warning, so I say we heed that warning."

"Do we know that it is a warning? Do they intend to attack? Do we abandon our home because of a simple flyover?"

"So we come back again to the meaning behind their sudden appearance."

"We cannot know their intentions," said Craig.

"My point exactly," said Ethan. He could feel that Craig was uncertain about what to do. He was vulnerable. Ethan sensed a chance to strengthen his own position on the council while continuing to weaken Craig Warren's.

"They know we are here," someone called out. "They will come for us."

"They've always known we were here," Victoria said in frustration. "Which is the point Craig has been trying to make all along. They did not suddenly discover our presence."

§

Craig Warren leaned against the terrace railing and looked down onto the floor of the Inner Village. There was a bustle of activity going on down there, throughout all of Freetown, but it all looked restrained and cautious. The voices and sounds that reached up to the terrace were hushed.

Craig was afraid. In the end, a compromise had been reached. A defensive contingent of the citizens was going to remain behind, while most of the population would leave, taking the emergency tunnels out and following the established escape route away from Freetown.

Those staying in town would maintain a visible presence should the Shylmahn be watching, and would follow the defensive protocols and escape plan should the aliens actually attack. If after a reasonable time the Shylmahn did not attack, the refugees would return.

It all made sense, and most everyone at the meeting had eventually agreed to the plan, but now Craig was having last minute doubts. While the reasoning was that this would give the bulk of the population a better chance of getting away unseen and unharmed, Craig was beginning to feel uneasy. Why leave anyone behind at all? Would it really give the others a better chance? Wouldn't the Shillies know that most of the townsfolk had left? If the town was attacked, how many would die?

Their deaths will be on my head.

Victoria approached and stood beside him. She looked out across the main cavern spread out below them and tried to see what he was seeing. It wasn't easy. She had never been as attached to the town as Craig or Michael. To her, it was just a place, and the people were just people. Any dedication to purpose or cause or community that she felt was due to what she knew to be right, and to her loyalty to Michael Britton and his strong sense of right and wrong.

"We are doing the right thing," she said, seeing that Craig needed additional reassurance. His constant need for reassurance these past few weeks was becoming worrisome. "I think that Michael would agree. We can't just abandon the town on the basis of a Shillie sighting. We would spend all our time packing and unpacking."

"Yeah, well, I wish Michael were here."

"You're the head of the council."

"Maybe so, but we need a Britton presence about now."

"It wouldn't make any difference," said Victoria. She could see a large group of townspeople forming in the Inner Village plaza. "Michael Britton may have brought most of those people out of the occupied territory, but he's not why they stayed. They stayed because Freetown is as nice a place to live as any they're going to find these days. That's not just Michael's doing. We are all responsible for that. You are responsible for that; as much as anyone. Considering some of the people that you have to deal with, that's not easy. I'd say it's a hell of an accomplishment."

Craig looked embarrassed. "Thanks," he mumbled.

"I wouldn't want your job," said Victoria. "Michael sure doesn't want it. He couldn't do what you do, and he knows it."

"He underestimates himself."

"In some ways, perhaps," Victoria grinned broadly, "but he's right about him being no politician."

"Politician or no, his absence right now is sorely felt; and Jack and Miriam; and Annie. Freetown needs them here."

Victoria took a deep breath and let it out slow. She agreed wholeheartedly. The timing couldn't have been worse. This was the greatest crisis that Freetown had faced in years, and council members aside, the most respected and influential townspeople were off somewhere saving the planet. "We'll get through this," she said at last. "Let Michael and the others do what they have to do, and we'll take care of Freetown. That means getting these people to safety, and maintaining a presence here. This is our home, and we need to make that clear: To the Shillies, and to those people down there."

Craig watched as the first group of Freetown citizens worked their way towards the main tunnel. The population would be leaving in small groups every few hours over the next several days. "Our home," said Craig.

Jason returned to camp after scouting ahead in preparation of the next day's march, seeking out the easiest path up the valley. It wouldn't do to have this group of novices noisily trudging their way to cliff edges and waterfalls and insurmountable obstacles, so Jason and Monroe sought out the safest, clearest, quietest and least obtrusive routes, if not always the quickest.

Michael, standing watch on the north side of camp, acknowledged Jason's approach. His uncle moved quietly to his gear and settled in, pulling a folded map from his jacket pocket and returning it to a side pouch of his pack.

Eddie Blythe and Mitch were sitting side by side near the far edge of the camp, speaking softly but earnestly, clearly involved in some deep philosophical discussion. Monroe was sitting quietly by himself, reading a small, battered paperback book in the fading daylight. The Freetown doctor, Annie Gomez, and Jenny and Jack, were curled up beneath blankets in the middle of camp, trying to get some sleep; they had been tagged to stand watch later that night.

Jason could just make out Oscar Patterson at his post on the south perimeter, sitting on a large rock just beyond the trees. The man had been a reliable sort up to now. He had done all that had been asked of him, and then some.

Miriam Foster strolled into camp, her cane an integral part of her smooth, steady stride. Jason watched as she worked her way over to the large fallen cedar that bordered the south edge of the camp. She sat carefully on the log and began rummaging through her pack. She pulled out a sweater and put it on.

He knew that Miriam was forty or a tad beyond, but at times she seemed much older. Part of it was likely due to physical appearance; living with her injury these past six years had aged her. More than this, however, was what she had gone through during the invasion, and living with the memory of what the world had been like before the invasion. Though not Britton by name, more than any true elder Britton, she carried this burden with her. It stood her apart from Michael and Jenny and those born afterward. Because of this, she would always have much more in common with those of the *Before Time.* She would never see the current landscape in the same way as the younger humans; her view would always be skewed with memories of the past, before the arrival of the Shylmahn.

Jason's every action was based on that same skewed view. His very existence was built upon it; as was Joseph's, as was Carolyn's... Jason had to wonder at just how close to the mark people like Ethan Perry might be when they spoke of the Britton family. Just look at the direction each member had taken, the choices they had made and the lives they had lived. There had to be some sort of inherited obsession, didn't there?

And yet, for each, there had really been no other choice. Their lives and their decisions had been made for them. Joseph, and subsequently his children, had served humanity very nobly for decades. Could they have chosen a better path? Jason couldn't imagine how. The sacrifices they had made, and continued to make, were not the actions of obsessive fanatics, but were based on a call to duty and a responsibility to fellow human beings.

Jason himself had always dedicated his life to serving society, and these last decades had been no different. If anything, his purpose was clearer, the cause much better defined.

Carolyn... now Carolyn was different. The cause was just as clear, the fight was just as right... but perhaps her dedication to purpose, however justified and however appropriate it might be, had grown dark and had become very much an obsession.

Jason suspected that they would find her the next day. They needed her, and Jason felt just a little bit uncomfortable about that.

| 10 |

Joseph was standing beside the holo-table, the guardian probe hovering next to him, the Shylmahn guard watching him. NehLoc slowly circled the table, watching the image above it. The image was clearly of the Frontier, taken from a flying vehicle moving quickly above the landscape.

Joseph recognized the terrain. A cluster of hills took shape in the distance. Within moments, they were over Freetown. Townspeople were visible in the Outer Village, standing in the open, staring up at him.

Then Freetown was behind them. The image faded and went blank. NehLoc continued to circle the holo-table, stopping opposite the table from Joseph. The area above the holo-table shimmered to life yet again. Single-frame images appeared; random shots of the flyover.

Again the area above the table went blank. NehLoc looked across at Joseph. He said nothing, betrayed no emotion. Joseph studied the alien face, wondered what NehLoc was trying to get from this.

Does he think that I will give up information because of some implied threat?

Freetown was no secret. The Underground Railroad was no secret, and Freetown was a very visible part of the railroad.

How much do the Shillies know of Freetown's inner sanctum? How much do they know of the inner defenses, the emergency escape routes?

Joseph said nothing. NehLoc asked nothing.

The area above the holo-table shimmered to life yet again. Moving images appeared; this time they were above hills and forests. Ahead was a long, narrow meadow. Joseph recognized the landscape this time as well. They were approaching the way station.

Jenny's station.

Joseph could see NehLoc's face through the flickering images...

ShahnTahr moved slowly across the surface of the thin layer that separated his upper essence from the lower levels, carefully monitoring the activities of several dozen higher elements of his being. Occasionally one of the lower level activities would rise up and require his attention, but very seldom. This made him happy. Lower level incidents were boring. The events of the real world, beyond those of the mundane lower realm, were fun.

At present, ShahnTahr was particularly interested in the ongoing interrogation process of the Chehnon native called JoSeph. NehLoc and EsJen had used a number of different techniques in their efforts to acquire information; some successful, some less so. Some of the information had been contradictory to other statements made by the subject or to the facts as ShahnTahr knew them.

EsJen had recently come to TohPeht with concerns about NehLoc's approach to these interrogations, and in frustration had questioned her purpose in being called in. She wondered as to her value on the project, considering NehLoc's failure to address even one of her concerns.

The Shylmahn individuals were continuing to change to meet the challenges of this world, even after the passing of so many years. Individuals such as EsJen, whose duties required her to be in close proximity to the Chehnon, were especially susceptible; most likely because these creatures provided the greatest challenge in this new world and the most direct interaction with the environment.

ShahnTahr watched JoSeph via the visual sensors of the guardian probe in the interrogation room. JoSeph was sitting on the stool. He was alone. Even the guard was gone. There was only the human and the holo-table with the flickering images of the sensor readings. From the image that ShahnTahr was receiving, the guardian probe was three and half feet from JoSeph, and at the creature's eye level as it sat on the stool. The lights of the room were dimmed, allowing the holo-table images to send shadows and light splashing across the walls.

JoSeph was motionless, eyes fixed on the probe. The creature knew that the interrogation was still in progress. It was all about mind games. *Mind games...* an expression and an activity that ShahnTahr, while having heard the term long ago, had only recently begun to understand. ShahnTahr enjoyed mind games.

Victoria stood at the guard station above the main gate. The sun had set, but the stars had yet to appear. She hadn't noticed the sun going down, but the gray sky on the horizon meant that it had been down for more than a few minutes.

She was distracted. The world around her continued to go about its business, the dangers that the townspeople faced continued to exist, but her mind was on Michael and what sort of trouble he had likely gotten himself into. She knew that she should focus on the matters at hand, on what had to be done here and now, but it was easier to imagine Michael succumbing to the perils of the Shylmahn somewhere beyond the horizon than to visualize the aliens walking the streets of Freetown; not more desirable, but easier...

She was shaken from her thoughts by the sound of Ethan Perry climbing up onto the platform. He smiled and stood beside her, looked out at the orchard of trees that lay beyond the gate.

"So this is where you got to," he said.

"I wanted to watch the sun set," said Victoria, "but I think I missed it."

Ethan Perry tried to figure out what that might mean, but decided finally that it wasn't worth the trouble. "It's quiet this evening," he said at last.

"Three more groups left today. The last go out in the morning. Not enough people left now to kick up much of a racket."

Ethan smiled. "We do have the place to ourselves, at that."

"Craig did a great job of organizing our... withdrawal."

"I'll give him that," said Ethan. "The man does have his talents."

"Craig Warren wasn't made head of the council because his name was drawn from a hat. He's a good man and quite qualified."

"Hey, I agree," Ethan held his hands up defensively. "Craig's the best. He's not the one who got us into this mess, and he's working as hard as anyone here to get us out of it."

Victoria rested her forearms on the railing and studied the Outer Village. It was growing dark now, and several windows glowed faintly yellow with dim lights behind thick curtains. Of those staying behind, a third would remain in the Outer Village at all times, maintaining a visible presence should the Shylmahn be watching.

"We're in this mess because of the Shillies," said Victoria.

"Victoria, you and I both know that the situation was created by the Britton family. However noble their intentions, we are witness to the result of their work." He waved an arm across the scene. The town was nearly empty.

Victoria turned slowly on Ethan. The man was under the illusion that he had found an ally in Victoria Romero. "Listen close, Mr. Perry. Michael and I may not have the smoothest of relationships, but don't ever take our disagreements as meaning that I would ever side with you against Michael on anything. He and I may have knock-down drag-outs on most everything, but when it's all said and done, I'll stand back-to-back with him and take on all comers. You included. I hope I'm clear."

Ethan Perry's face had taken on a hard, intense look. Perhaps he had indeed felt that his recent conversations with her, taken with her well-known clashes with Michael Britton, were indications that he was well on his way to developing a powerful ally.

"You have made your blind and misdirected devotion quite clear, Miss Romero," he said at last. "I apologize if I mistook your earlier concurrence with my suggestions as a sign of independent thought."

Victoria refused to be drawn into defending her loyalties or her choices. She silently turned about and looked out across the shadow-filled orchard beyond the fence. Darkness was rushing up at them.

She ignored Ethan's grunted good evening and his quick descent down the ladder. Only when she was certain that he had left the main gate area did she turn her head and look back into the Outer Village. From her position on the platform she could see three brightly glowing windows. The entrance into the Inner Village was invisible in the gray dusk.

| 11 |

The great timber wall was impressive. Constructed of logs a foot in diameter and twenty feet tall, it spanned the width of the ravine-like canyon. Jason followed the big, burly man through the narrow gate set into the wall. The others followed single file behind Jason, and the other two of their three-man escort brought up the rear.

Once inside the wall, they continued up the central thoroughfare toward the back of the keep, passing several dozen squat, wooden buildings along the route. The air was damp; the buildings and equipment, the paths and vegetation, were all wet and dark. The people they passed stopped whatever they were doing and warily eyed the newcomers. The citizens of the keep looked clean and healthy and well clothed, if wet.

Despite the weather, everyone was out and busy, and yet the community was eerily quiet. There was almost no noise. There was plenty of activity—Jason could see all the signs of everyday life, but the sounds were muffled.

Carolyn was waiting outside a large, two-storey building, the only such building in the keep. It was at the very back of the settlement and set into the hillside. Jason found that very interesting; Bril's influence reached beyond the grave and across the years.

When they reached Carolyn, their guide began to introduce them, but Carolyn waved him silent. "Hello, Jason," she said stiffly.

"Sis," Jason nodded. He had not seen Carolyn in several years, and only sporadically before that. The changes in her were dramatic. He had watched her slowly evolve over the twenty eight years since the invasion, but was nonetheless surprised at the sight of the woman standing before him now. It was difficult even for Jason to hide his astonishment.

She was dark and cold and menacing. Gray streaked through her hair, which she continued to wear long. She had deep-set wrinkles at the corners of her eyes and mouth. Her expression was hard and steely. Her movements were precise and each was calculated.

At a slight jerk of her head, the guard detail backed away and disappeared, though they were probably standing watch just out of sight. Without moving, she studied each member of Jason's group, pausing briefly at Michael and Jenny. She nodded acknowledgement at Miriam, who nodded back. No one spoke.

She turned her attention again to Jason. "It's not like you, Jason; dragging this herd of Shillie bait all over the countryside. Are you looking to get caught? And you left a stampede trail in your wake leading right up to my front door."

"I *am* sorry about the mess," said Jason.

"What the hell are you doing here?"

"It's good to see you, too."

"Don't start with me."

Jason took a moment now to study his sister. He believed much of this persona was borne out of necessity, needed to maintain the organization that she had created. Much of it was also quite likely borne out of the life that she had led these past decades. Whatever its origin, however much of it had intentionally been created by her, he believed that much of what his sister had once been was lost to him, and the woman now standing before him was probably capable of just about anything.

"How about we have a little chat?" he asked.

Carolyn gave a short, curt nod, then turned and started walking down the narrow back lane. Jason looked at the others and was about to tell them to wait, when he saw that the guard detail had miraculously reappeared. They were silently directing the group back down the main thoroughfare. Jason quickstepped up beside his sister.

"Cute little place you have here," he said. When she didn't respond, he decided to get into it. "We need your help."

"I assumed as much."

"This could be it, Carolyn. This could be the one that changes it all."

"I have heard that one once or twice before," she said.

Jason stopped. Carolyn took several more steps before she too stopped and turned to face him. He thought carefully about his next words. He knew that his statement had been weak.

"This will definitely change things, Sis; for good or for bad. With your help, we might just win it all back."

"Even if that were true, what is there left to win?"

"Then what are you fighting for?"

Carolyn thought a few moments, turned about and started walking again. "Tell me what you have."

EsJen was sitting on the windowsill of her third floor apartment. Spread out before her were the narrow streets and tall, slender buildings of the dahlseht. The streets were pedestrian thoroughfares crowded with her people, all hurriedly bustling about from place to place, but none so busy that they wouldn't stop and spend a few moments to talk with you.

Visible beyond the city structures was the perimeter wall, completely encircling the dahlseht. The tall buildings and strong perimeter walls were holdovers from Shylmah. ShahnTahr had wisely seen rationale in maintaining the design.

EsJen's servant probe moved across the room and hovered near the front of the door—someone was approaching. The door's monitor activated and a moment later sent a signal to the patiently waiting servant probe. Upon receipt of the signal, the probe glided to EsJen. Again it waited, this time for a sign from EsJen that she was willing to be interrupted.

EsJen gave a nod, but continued to look out across the cityscape. The probe read the action as ascent to speak.

"MehnTec," it voiced.

EsJen slid off the sill and started toward the main living area. "Allow," she said, at which the probe sent a signal to the door and the door opened.

MehnTec came in and the door closed silently behind him. He followed EsJen across the sparsely furnished room and to the counter that divided the apartment into living and eating areas. The ceiling was set low, but not so low as to make MehnTec uncomfortable. At just above five foot four, MehnTec was considered above average in height, and the ceiling was a good foot above him.

He slid onto one of the two stools at the counter and picked up a glass that EsJen set before him.

"Thank you," he said. He looked behind him at a small sculpture sitting on the one small table in the living area. Both the table and the art piece looked to be of human design. "What is that?"

"Art," she said.

MehnTec chuckled. *Humor,* he thought to himself. *Yes. I get it.* He tilted his head, as though if he could just see the work from a different angle it would all become clear. "What is it supposed to represent?"

"An elephant."

"Ahhh," said MehnTec. He tilted his head the other way. He had heard of elephants, but had never seen one. Very large animals, kept at collection facilities. He turned back to the counter. "Nice table," he said.

MehnTec drank from his glass. *Iced Tea.* Another bit of Chehnon culture that EsJen had picked up. MehnTec had grown accustomed to EsJen's fascination with Chehnon ways during their partnership some years earlier. She had argued that there was no reason not to admire and enjoy something simply because it had Chehnon origins. They lived on Chehno, after all.

"How is your project progressing?" asked MehnTec. He had only a very general understanding of what EsJen was working on. Much of what he knew, or suspected, had been gleaned from EsJen's history, the scope of her responsibilities, and her expertise. His knowledge of the problems that she was having were just as general, although some of her comments concerning her difficulties had helped guide his understanding of the project itself.

"I grow more frustrated with each passing day," said EsJen. "If my guidance is not to be heeded, then my purpose for being here eludes me."

"Well... you've picked up a couple of new art pieces."

EsJen ignored the attempt to lighten the suddenly darkening mood. "NehLoc's emotions and ambitions are blinding him to what is happening," she said.

"And rendering him deaf to your words."

EsJen raised a brow and frowned. A very *human* gesticulation, thought MehnTec. He cautiously set his glass down, as if it might break. "Surely ShahnTahr would not let NehLoc's personal affectations become a danger," he said.

"I am uncertain as to ShahnTahr's reasoning," she admitted. Her tone was almost surrendering.

"Are NehLoc's ambitions contrary to ShahnTahr? Is NehLoc consciously going against the interests of the people?"

"NehLoc recognizes his ambition, but sees it as an asset, believes it to be a real and valuable benefit toward the good of the people. He has convinced himself of this. He believes that what he does is for the benefit of the Shylmahn, and that his own personal success is but a byproduct of his sacrifice and the good work that he does for the people."

"That is very convenient."

"And there is no way to address the argument that cannot itself be folded into the very argument you are attempting to address."

And no way to respond to that twisted bit of logic, thought MehnTec. "What does TohPeht have to say?" he asked. MehnTec had seen TohPeht only once since their return to the northwest. He had thought at the time that their leader had been... distracted. He saw that his question to EsJen made her uncomfortable.

"I am concerned about TohPeht," she said at last. She was more than concerned. She was afraid. TohPeht was becoming lost to them. With each meeting that she had with him, there was just a little bit less of TohPeht. He was disappearing, and another persona was taking his place. Somehow, some way, TohPeht was becoming ShahnTahr; or, at the very least, TohPeht was becoming a physical representation of ShahnTahr—a melding of what had been TohPeht and what ShahnTahr might be.

EsJen had examined and then discarded all other possibilities. She believed that ShahnTahr was creating an organic version of himself, but she was uncertain as to the reason.

ShahnTahr's purpose had always been the continual betterment of Shylmahn society; the survival and the advancement of the Shylmahn people. This then had to be to that end. Whatever was happening to TohPeht must somehow serve that purpose.

She could not voice her thoughts to MehnTec. She was confused. She was uncertain as to what her next step should be.

"TohPeht is not well," she said.

MehnTec nodded. "He sacrifices much to serve."

"Yes he does."

"So do you," said MehnTec.

"I serve," she said, then refilled their glasses.

EsJen did not believe the interrogation of JoSeph was going well at all. She felt that much of what Joseph had so far revealed had been calculated and had been filled with dark intent. There had been enough truth in his words to push NehLoc along a path that Joseph had created.

Would ShahnTahr not have seen this as so?

Perhaps... or perhaps ShahnTahr was JoSeph's intended target.

Could such a thing be possible?

EsJen stared down at her glass. She could feel MehnTec staring at her, waiting patiently for her to speak, waiting to help her.

EsJen was very afraid. She was certain that something very bad was going to happen, and she didn't think that she was going to be able to stop it.

She must therefore put herself in a position from which she could minimize the impact of the inevitable.

BehLahk stood at the gate to the small garden outside TohPeht's set of offices. The doctor had grown more distinguished with the passing of the years, in both physical presence and in personality. He was at all times calm, shrewd, confident, and very aware of all that went on around him. He maintained a low profile, was seldom seen and seldom heard from, even by TohPeht and the other high officials of Shylmahn service.

And yet, BehLahk was the most powerful individual on the planet—more powerful than NehLoc, than TohPeht, even more powerful than ShahnTahr. And no one had the slightest idea that this was so.

BehLahk watched as TohPeht maneuvered the paths of the garden, taking in the sights, sounds and smells, as if for the first time. A guardian probe followed, ever watchful, so that TohPeht need not be. Other probes stood watch at strategic locations throughout the garden.

There was very little left of their leader that was TohPeht, though the individual in the garden was not exactly ShahnTahr either. ShahnTahr saw the world through TohPeht, much the same as he did through the other probes, but more intensely, more *organically.* The emotions and personality that ShahnTahr was developing was in no small part due to the interactions with the world that he had experienced through this poor being TohPeht. As a result of this parasitic relationship, and due to ShahnTahr's eagerness to take in as much of this outside world as he could, the individual that was TohPeht was being relegated to but an element of this newly evolving personality; a new individual that was both TohPeht and ShahnTahr, with the TohPeht elements helping to shape the new individual but themselves becoming recessive to the dominant personality of ShahnTahr.

The true being of ShahnTahr continued to exist, and to evolve, as something more. He was not this new individual walking in the garden, just as he wasn't one of the probes. The TohPeht-ShahnTahr entity was an independent, individual tool that ShahnTahr used to experience the outside world.

ShahnTahr existed in and of the network of tens of thousands of elements that spider-webbed the planet. ShahnTahr *was.*

TohPeht turned his head and looked at BehLahk. He smiled genuinely and picked up his pace just a little as he came toward him.

"Hello, BehLahk. It is so good to see you."

"And you, TohPeht," BehLahk smiled. "How are you? You look well."

"Thank you," said TohPeht. "I serve. As do we all."

"You more than anyone, dear TohPeht. I do not know how you have borne up so well under the pressures of leadership over these many years. I would have collapsed under the sheer weight of it long ago."

Steven ran up to Carolyn as she came out of the mess hall and started down the main thoroughfare. She glanced at him once and continued ahead.

Her assistant was in his early twenties, and in many ways reminded her of Terry, the sweet, young poet that she had lost so many years earlier.

"What is it, Steven?" she asked, not slowing.

"They're settled in."

"Fine," she said. She knew there was more.

"They are... impatient. Demanding, actually."

"So?" *Why is that a problem?*

Steven looked bewildered. Carolyn stopped abruptly, then started again. "Don't worry about it. Jason's working you. It's what he does." She picked up her pace, spoke over her shoulder. "I'll take care of it."

In spite of the confidence that she put out there for her people to see, and for Jason and his little army of tenderfoots to see, she was anxious about what her brother's arrival portended. Her brief conversation with him had not lessened her anxiety one bit. There was a significant change coming in the order of things, and she wasn't sure that she was ready.

Looking around now, she wondered if she was any different than Bril had been, hiding away on his tiny island, hoping the rest of the world would go on without him.

Was she any different? She put on a good show, but wasn't she hiding out too, hoping the Shillies—and everyone else—would just leave her alone in her Shangri-La, such as it was?

Well, they hadn't left her alone. The outside world had come crashing in, and with a Britton martyr leading the way. She now had to make a choice, and whatever her decision, her world would never be the same.

She slowed her pace, and as she walked, she pulled her gray-streaked hair back and bound it into a ponytail. She rounded a corner and slowed her step yet again. Jason was leaning against the side of the building at the end of the road, a small bungalow that served as the one and only guest house. Michael and Miriam were sitting on the bench nearby. Jason lifted his gaze and winked at his sister, stuffed his hands into his pockets and grinned.

Carolyn gave an exaggerated, surrendering sigh and walked doggedly toward them.

Shit...

Craig Warren jumped from the middle rung of the ladder down to the ground and hurried from the main gate in the direction of the entrance to the Inner Village. Overhead were two large shuttlecraft, larger than any he had ever seen. They were still forty or fifty feet up, but were gradually lowering themselves down into the Outer Village.

More alien shuttles had been seen in the skies to the west. Other Freetown residents were already rushing ahead of Craig, abandoning the Outer Village and heading inside. Their job as a visible citizenry was done.

Craig reached the central plaza inside the cavern, stopped long enough to survey the scene. There was a flurry of activity as all was being made ready. Every one of the thirty-odd citizens that had remained behind had duties to perform now that the Shylmahn attack, previously just a possibility, had become a reality. Each citizen's final act in the town would be to set their escape plans into motion.

Craig headed towards the Wheel, an intersection of six narrow thoroughfares, one of which led to the steep stairs leading up to Terrace One. He heard the sound just as he reached the intersection, and when he was in the open turned to see a strange cloud push its way through the heavy canvas curtains of the cavern entrance.

It was a fog of dozens of hunter probes, each with a faint vibrating hum, which together gave off a deep, resonating growl within the hollow of the cavern.

Craig made a dash across the hub of the intersection and reached the stairs. He took them several at a time and leapt onto Terrace One, ran to the stairs leading to Terrace Two. He turned once to look out at the cavern. The strange, dark cloud looked to be dispersing. There were more Shillie probes hanging in the air than there were Freetown citizens for them to hunt down and shoot at. The interior of the cavern was filling with the distinctive tracer lines created by the energy pins fired from the probes.

Craig reached the Upper Tunnel entrance located at the back wall of Terrace Two. He gave one final glance before rushing into the dark.

Victoria climbed up the tall, narrow ladder and clambered over into the East Wall bunker, set precariously halfway up the wall of the main cavern. The two citizens on duty watch grumbled nervously and shifted over to give her room.

Most of the Inner Village was visible from the bunker. There were very few citizens visible below, most having already made it to their stations or into safe hiding. A cloud of locusts hovered menacingly in the heart of the cavern, then quickly began to disperse, the hunter probes firing energy pins at anything and everything that looked like a viable target.

Victoria's two companions together manned the bunker's machine gun. As they began attacking the probes, Victoria reached over and picked up the assault weapon hanging on the rack behind her. She settled into position and began targeting first one, then another of the probes.

The sound of their weapons, combined with the sounds of weapons stationed at the other bunkers located in the cavern, were unbelievably, violently loud. Loose dirt and rock began falling from the walls and ceiling. Victoria began to fear the cavern would collapse in on them before they made their escape.

Well, that would be one way of ensuring these probes never made it out of here...

Ethan Perry had been in the supply warehouse. He ran almost blindly out of the connecting tunnel and into the main cavern. Overhead, hundreds of energy pin trails filled the cavern with a thick, brightly lit spider web, made all the more visible by the clouds of dust and smoke floating through the air.

He turned left and hurried down the lane that hugged the east wall. Following the base of the wall, the lane twisted around juts of rock and underneath bulbous overhangs. Rounding one of the sharper curves, Ethan almost tripped over a body that was sprawled in the middle of the lane. The man had been hit several times in the back with energy pins, but three thick layers of leather vest had lessened the impact and may have prevented the pins from reaching the lungs and heart.

It was Taggert, one of the earliest citizens of Freetown. Ethan knelt down to help. Just as he did, he was struck in the arm with an energy pin. He dove over Taggert and into the shadow of the small house that was built up close to the lane. Energy pins began raining down around him, and he scrambled tightly against the wall of the house, feeling another, then another pin strike him; one in the arm and another in the shoulder.

A moment later, bits and pieces of the hunter probe fell out of the air and clattered noisily onto the hard-pack surface of the lane, narrowly missing Taggert lying directly in front of him.

Somebody had shot it down. Ethan waited a few seconds to make certain that there wasn't another probe watching, then crawled out of hiding and over to Taggert. He positioned himself to pick him up when he realized there was no point.

At least it was finally all over for Taggert. Another half dozen pins had struck him, and the layers of vests hadn't been enough to protect him this time. The first round of energy pins may have been enough to eventually kill him, but these last had certainly sealed his fate.

Ethan pushed himself back and brought himself slowly to his feet. Despite his own wounds, he ran on, heading toward the stairs leading up to the terraces.

Victoria could see the probes rushing into the dark entrances of the tunnels leading away from the main cavern; some led to utility rooms, some to supply caverns, some were the escape tunnels out of this nightmare.

With every probe that was shot down or that disappeared into a tunnel, another came through the cavern's main entrance to take its place. *How could there be so many? Why would the Shillies send so many against us?*

One of the men beside her was dead, the other was bleeding from two wounds in the chest and a bloody crease across his scalp. Despite his injuries, he was managing the two-man machine gun all by himself, refusing help from Victoria. He insisted that she keep her own weapon in the fight.

A probe appeared almost out of nowhere, directly in front of the bunker and not more than three feet in front of Victoria. She had been aiming her weapon at another probe in the same line of sight, and involuntarily fired off a tat-tat-tat before the probe could let loose its energy pins. The exploding probe sent shards of metal and plastic in a shattering blast of deadly rain over the bunker.

Craig had taken up position at the defense station beyond the first bend inside the tunnel, out of the direct line of sight of the tunnel entrance. He was kneeling down behind a stack of sandbags, watching for either friend or foe to come down from the main cavern.

It was through this tunnel off the terrace and through the lower tunnel that opened onto the cavern floor that the last residents of Freetown would pass. Each resident had been assigned an escape route, though if necessary they could exit by any tunnel they could get to.

Two-thirds of the residents were assigned to the lower tunnel, the rest to Craig's Upper Tunnel exit. He had been the first to reach this station, as was the plan. He would be the last to leave by this route.

The retreating humans began arriving moments after Craig took up his position. The first two arrived amidst a steady emission of energy pins being fired from a probe following casually along behind them. When they saw Craig holding a large weapon aimed in their general direction, both humans dropped to the floor of the tunnel, giving him a clear shot. The first round sent the probe spinning, the second finished it off.

The two humans rose quickly to their feet and ran hurriedly past the defense station. Both were bleeding from numerous wounds. Energy pins were clean and messy, deadly and survivable, all at the same time.

Just as the sound of the retreating humans faded away, a second probe came down the tunnel, this time all on its own. It showed itself briefly, then backed away and hid around the bend. Craig could sense its presence.

It had known this human would be there, having been informed by the previous probe.

Craig waited. Long, tense seconds went by. He could hear the fight raging on in the cavern. Keeping a wary eye on the tunnel ahead, he set down the rifle and picked up the shotgun. He wanted some spread on the next shot...

Suddenly, gunshots rang out inside the tunnel. He steadied himself. Human voices ahead... Three humans came rushing around the bend, crying out *probes! probes!* as they ran toward him.

Craig kept aim on the bend. They had apparently taken care of the probe that had stationed itself within the tunnel ahead of him, but were being chased by several others that had followed them from the cavern.

The last of the three humans wasn't yet past when the two pursuing probes showed themselves. The first probe hurled itself directly at Craig in a suicidal rush as the other provided cover fire.

He fired at the first and it exploded in a cloud of shrapnel. With plastic and metal burying itself in his face and chest, Craig adjusted aim and fired at the second, this one exploding before it could get close enough to do more harm.

Craig fell forward against the sandbags, continuing to hold his weapon at the ready. Ethan Perry rounded the bend and hurried toward the station. He didn't look to be in much better shape than Craig, but was quick to offer his help to get him down the tunnel.

Craig refused to go. His job wasn't yet finished.

Ethan set his jaw tight, nodded sharply, and sat down beside him. Craig managed a smile and handed him the rifle; he kept the shotgun. The two of them stood ready to defend the tunnel.

They waited. The sounds coming from the main cavern began to diminish. After a few minutes, one lone probe tested the tunnel and was met by a barrage of shotgun pellets.

A few minutes later, Victoria came around the bend, using the wall for support and barely able to walk. Her face and scalp were covered in wounds and blood. A piece of shrapnel protruded from her arm.

"No one else," she managed to say, just as Ethan reached her. He helped her back toward the station. She began mumbling, "Close it down... close it down... no one else..."

With that, Craig reached over and pushed down on the plunger, setting off explosives that were set into the walls from just inside the mouth of the tunnel and for thirty feet. The walls and ceiling came crashing inward, though the collapse didn't end at thirty feet. The defense station was three times thirty into the tunnel and the ongoing collapse sounded like it was going to reach them and beyond.

"I suggest we get the hell out of here," said Ethan, struggling to assist first one, then the other of his companions.

| 12 |

NehLoc stared angrily at the images appearing above the holo-table. The recovery operation at Freetown had been a complete and utter failure; an absolute disaster at every level.

The Shylmahn had been made out the fools. The Chehnon nest had been much larger and more organized than they had been led to believe. The operation these creatures had been running should never have been allowed to continue to exist. It should have been shut down and the participants collected long ago.

And as for the current recovery, the clever vermin had been laying in wait for them, prepared to pounce when the collection operation began. The majority of the nest population had been long gone, with only the trap waiting behind.

A massive expenditure of probes and equipment lost, with nothing to show for the cost but a few dead Chehnon; not even any prisoners collected to send to the work camps.

And most importantly, nothing to hold before the shrewdest of the Chehnon creatures, JoSeph. This had been the primary purpose of the operation, and they had nothing.

NehLoc was about to turn away from the holo-table in disgust when he saw TohPeht silently enter the room. Staring through the images and beyond to the Shylmahn leader, NehLoc wondered at the bizarre changes in TohPeht. Gradual, steady changes these past months, the transformation was now accelerating. It was TohPeht, and yet it was not.

NehLoc watched him circle the room, his attention on the shimmering images hovering above the holo-table. His movements were smooth and methodical. He kept his face toward the images as he moved slowly around the table.

"TohPeht," NehLoc said, unable to bear the silence any longer. "Is there something I can do for you?"

TohPeht looked at NehLoc through the flickering of light and color, but said nothing. He watched the moving pictures being fed from the probes surveying Freetown.

"The Chehnon community is now abandoned," said NehLoc. "It was much larger and more heavily populated than we had been led to believe. About eighty percent of the community was living underground."

NehLoc waited for some response. He moved about the table, remaining directly opposite TohPeht. TohPeht said nothing.

"Our recovery operation had been anticipated," NehLoc continued. "Most of the population was evacuated sometime prior to our arrival, and those few who remained were laying in ambush."

TohPeht stopped his pacing, looked thoughtfully at the image being presented. A probe had entered a three-room dwelling. There was a couch and chair. A small table sat under a square window with light curtains pulled back.

"Yes," said TohPeht calmly. "Interesting."

The door opened and EsJen came into Joseph's cell. Standing just inside, she waited for the door to close behind her before turning and nodding a silent greeting to the human.

Joseph swung his legs around and planted his feet on the floor. He rested his arms on his knees and clasped his hands loosely together.

"I'd offer you a chair, but it doesn't appear that I have one," he said. He had only recently been given the cot.

"The thought is enough," said EsJen. She examined the room. There was only the cot, the door, four walls, and a guardian probe hovering in one corner. "How are you?"

"Why the visit, EsJen?"

EsJen lost what little smile she had been wearing, thought a moment about how to approach the matter. "I wanted to… congratulate you."

"Pardon?"

"I believe that your efforts will be well rewarded, JoSeph."

"I don't understand."

EsJen gave Joseph a very tired look. "In spite of my own efforts, my warnings, my recommendations, I have failed. You have won."

Joseph stared down at his clasped hands. "EsJen… I honestly don't know what you are talking about. If you are suggesting that I have in some way influenced the—interrogations—then I can honestly say that I have failed miserably. I have given up all that I know, and have quite possibly caused the deaths of hundreds, if not thousands, of my fellow humans."

"Come now. I know you better than that, JoSeph," said EsJen. "You have twisted and manipulated every meeting that you've had with NehLoc, and managed to play both him and ShahnTahr."

"EsJen, I really—"

"You were close to brilliant," EsJen cut him off. "The way you would give up something, then desperately try to take it back, or try to dismiss it as something un-important, or clumsily attempt to paint it as a lie. Very, very clever."

Best to say nothing, here. He unclasped his hands and slowly rubbed them together. EsJen stepped closer.

"I believe that you may have actually convinced ShahnTahr. I would not have thought it possible. You have somehow managed to 'push the buttons' as you say, manipulating the logic, probably in coordination with your friends out there. Their timed actions verified your subtle slips of intelligence, all carefully planted to paint the picture that you wanted to present."

"I'm not that smart," Joseph spoke down at his hands.

"You forget how well I know you."

"That was a very long time ago, EsJen."

EsJen took another step, turned and unexpectedly sat on the cot beside Joseph. She stared down at her own tiny hands. "Not so long ago," she said, sadly. "Not so long that I do not remember, that you called me your friend."

"Yeah, well..." Joseph frowned. "I remember Bril, and Daryl, and Liz, and Robert. All dead. All murdered. And I remember the children. They were very, very young."

"I did what I could, JoSeph. I tried to help."

"I remember Barbara."

"I helped you find Barbara."

"You helped kill Barbara."

EsJen felt a cold chill. That had been a very bad situation. How many years ago? Six or seven... JoSeph and Barbara had left the province years before. They had been helping other humans leave. That had been okay. The Shylmahn had looked the other way. But then the humans attacked the outpost. The Shylmahn did not look the other way. They could not. The Shylmahn would do whatever was necessary to ensure the survival and the advancement of the Shylmahn people.

"I am sorry about what happened, JoSeph, but I will not be held responsible for the loss of human life when they take up violent action against us."

Joseph turned his head slowly and looked directly at EsJen. There was a clarity in his eyes that frightened her. "So that's the way of it?" he asked. "Killing without responsibility?"

"I don't know what—"

Joseph shrugged, stared down again at his hands, clasped tightly in front of him. "So long as no one steps up and takes responsibility, so long as no one steps in to try and put a stop to it, the killing will never stop."

EsJen really, really didn't like the sound of that, but wondered if he was playing her just as easily he was playing NehLoc and ShahnTahr.

§

Ethan Perry led the way along the steep trail that wound its way switchback down into the deep gorge. He and the other seventeen escapees left the sunshine above for the safety of the shadows at the bottom of the great gouge that cut across the landscape.

They had spent two days crowded inside the emergency underground shelter a mile from the back exit of Freetown. There the wounded had been cared for and everyone had a chance to get their second wind. On the third day, once they were certain the attacking Shylmahn and the hunter probes were gone, they crawled out and continued on, following after the refugees that had gone before them.

Ethan stopped when he reached the bottom of the gorge, stepped aside and helped each to step off the slight ledge and down onto the wide trail that followed the center of the gorge floor. Most had bandaged wounds, some more serious than others. All were carrying at least a small backpack; those who could, carried larger loads.

He reached up and helped Victoria Romero down onto the trail.

"Thanks," she said. Her head and one side of her face was bandaged; lesser cuts shown on the other side of her face. One arm was bound to her side to prevent her shoulder from moving.

"Take it slow," said Ethan. He had injuries of his own, one of which would periodically open up and bleed and would have to be re-bandaged.

"I'll be fine," she said and followed after the woman in front of her.

The last in line was Craig Warren, bringing up the rear and making sure that no one was left behind. Ethan gripped his arm and eased him down onto the floor trail. "I think we're making pretty good time, Craig."

"Better than we have a right to expect, I'd say." Craig grimaced slightly at the jolt his body took stepping down. The two of them started slowly down the trail.

"We should make station two well before sunset," said Ethan.

"Break them when we reach the mouth of the gorge. I know that I could use it, and I'm not as bad off as some."

"We could break now if you need it—"

"No. Let's keep going. We should reach the mouth in an hour. That'll be fine. We rest there, and then it's two hours to the next station." Looking ahead, he could see that they were starting to fall behind the others. He gave Ethan a push on the shoulder. "Go on."

Ethan nodded sharply and moved quickly ahead. As he passed the others, grouped in twos and threes, he told them to hang in there, that they would be breaking in an hour before pushing on to the next station.

Ethan Perry had come into his own. He was eager to help Craig in any way that he could, and had as yet showed no signs of taking control. For the moment, following the direction of the injured head of the council was enough. It was clear that the group was heavily dependent on Ethan Perry and that they looked to him for strength and support. Craig may have been pointing the way, but Ethan was taking them there. His bearing during these times would not be forgotten. His selfless assistance would go a long way once this crisis was over.

There had been only the slightest hint of *I told you so*, this on their first day in the shelter, and it was presented as subtly as was possible for someone like Ethan Perry. After that, he had let it pass. And there had been but one reference to the Britton family as the cause of all that had befallen them; this spoken to a select and sympathetic group whom he knew would pass the word along.

This had been a horrible, frightening tragedy. He would have given anything and done anything to prevent it, and indeed he had tried; he had done all that he could to keep Freetown safe.

Now that it had happened, just as he had foreseen and had warned against, Ethan Perry would do whatever it took to see that such a disaster was not repeated, would use whatever tools were provided to him in his cause. The deaths, the suffering and loss, the very tragedy of this attack, would not be in vain. This would be his strongest weapon.

| 13 |

The morning started with clear skies, and though the sun's rays wouldn't be reaching into the keep until midday, Carolyn's little hideaway looked brighter and cheerier than at any time since they had arrived. Jason took the opportunity to walk the streets and gain a better picture of the place.

It was located at the closed end of a narrow box-canyon, which itself was an offshoot of the main valley. The keep was three-hundred feet deep, from the high log wall at the front to the two-storey building set into the cliff wall at the rear, and a hundred and forty feet from one side to the other. Within the walls were four dozen buildings, ranging in size from ten-by-ten supply shacks to the two-storey complex at the back that served as both command center and Carolyn's residence. At the rear of the command center was an access to extensive underground facilities running deep into the mountain behind the keep.

A main road ran down the center from the main gate at the front to the main building at the back, with smaller side lanes running off this main thoroughfare out to the surrounding perimeter, where they met a narrow lane that encircled the keep just within the walls.

Once he had finished his survey of the compound, Jason wandered over to the mess hall, where he was to meet up with Michael and Jenny. He found them sitting at one of the six tables placed outside the building. The other tables were empty. Breakfast was over, and everyone in the keep had duties to attend to.

"How's the Dark Queen?" asked Michael. He pushed a coffee cup toward Jason.

"Don't be too hard on her, Michael." Jason sat down and picked up the cup. The coffee was getting cold. They had been there for a few minutes, then. "I know life has been no picnic for any of us, but it's been particularly hard on Carolyn."

"It's not a matter of being hard on her, Jason. It's a simple fact. That is one really scary lady."

"She gives me the creepy-crawlies," said Jenny.

"She is definitely dangerous," said Jason, "and yes, she can give people the... creepy-crawlies."

"So what do we do?" asked Michael.

"We thank the powers-that-be that she's on our side."

"So she's with us?"

"As much as she is ever with anyone."

"Can we count on her?" Michael leaned forward. "I mean, she won't decide at the last minute that she doesn't like the plan and walk away from it, will she?"

Jason had to remember that while Michael may be a Britton, he didn't know the family, and his only experience with Carolyn was limited to the few brief meetings over these past few days.

Jason's words were clear and deliberate. "Never doubt Carolyn Britton. She will insist on knowing all the facts before going in, and she will insist on being included in the final design of any operation she is asked to be a part of; but her buy-off on an operation, and her agreement as to her role in that operation, is her binding word. That is her character, and that has never changed."

Michael was not intimidated by the sharp edge to his uncle's words. "I have nothing on which to base such trust," he said, just as deliberately. He let that sink in before slowly nodding his head. "But I do trust you. I will defer to your judgment."

"Thank you," said Jason. "You know, you're a lot like your father, with a lot of Carolyn thrown in."

"And that's good or bad?" asked Michael.

"It seems," said Jenny, "that our Uncle Jason is somewhat of an artist with the backhanded compliment."

"And you," Jason turned to Jenny, "remind me of me; with a bit of Kenny thrown in."

"Our dear uncle wants something, if you ask me," said Michael. *I think that he'll be wanting a lot before this is all over...*

Steven led Michael and Jenny through the narrow access at the rear of the main house and into the underground complex. After several turns they entered a large, well-lit room. Jason, Miriam, and Carolyn were already there, standing across a table from Carolyn.

"There you are," said Jason. "Glad you could join us."

Carolyn frowned. "Jason refused to continue the discussion without you."

Jason smiled broadly. "I couldn't very well make any final decisions on their behalf, now could I?"

"You apparently have no trouble planning *my* future," stated Carolyn.

"That's not it at all, Sis," Jason got serious. "I am simply presenting to you the plan that Joey and I came up with." He shrugged, "Okay, mostly Joey's plan. We hope that you will choose to join with us."

Carolyn grimaced, looked side-glance at the others and back again to Jason. "If I understand my role in this grand scheme correctly, my people are the bluff factor."

"Yes and no," said Jason. "The Shylmahn already know that we couldn't win against them in a head to head death match. What they need to see is that we do have a physical force, a real and dangerous presence, but that this force is but one element of a grander assault against them."

"How's that not a bluff?"

Jason looked at everyone in the room, but was careful to give Carolyn her due attention. "Okay. Here it is... you are not the bluff. The plan is."

"What?"

"We need for you to appear as a much larger force than you are. In that respect, yes, you are bluffing."

"And?" asked several in the room. This wasn't exactly the plan that any had been told.

"Every prong in this—*assault*—for want of a better word, is bluff."

"I'm out," said Carolyn flatly.

"Assault is really the wrong word. Bluff is also the wrong word."

"I'm still out."

"What we're really going to do is guide them in the direction of certain assumptions as to how things are."

"Still out," Carolyn said yet again, but her frown changed to faint curiosity. "How?"

Jason told her about Joseph's voluntary capture by the Shylmahn, and of his plan to misdirect both NehLoc and the alien computer intelligence. He then described the efforts of his own people to plant evidence and to perform very specific activities to corroborate what Joseph would surrender during interrogation. He told her of the months of activities by Joseph in preparation of this operation, when he had no assurance that anyone else would ever step up to help.

"To what end?" asked Carolyn. "It isn't as though they're just going to hand the planet back over to us, whatever assumptions they may have."

This is where Jason had to be careful. There had been no choice but to give them as much as he had just laid out for them. He owed that much to Michael and his people, and Carolyn would have accepted nothing less. Now, though, it became more delicate. The truth wouldn't work, and Jason sure didn't want to get caught in a lie.

"Joseph can and will make this work," he said, short and smooth.

Carolyn studied her brother's face. He was letting her know that he was keeping back something that he was certain she wouldn't like, and that he wasn't going to come clean with it. They stared each other down. It was up to her, now. She could accept it as it stood, or walk away. She turned to Michael, to Jenny, to Miriam.

"You didn't know about this?" she asked them.

"Not in so many words," said Miriam. "But the holes in the story were suspicious."

"It was my father's plan," said Michael. "He wanted me involved. I didn't need any more."

Carolyn groaned dramatically, "Yeah... your father."

"Joseph is counting on us," urged Jason.

"Don't push me, brother."

"No pressure."

"Bullshit."

"Time is of the essence."

"Joseph. That damned Joseph," Carolyn grumbled. "That sonofabitch has made it his life's work to drag me into one damned mess after another."

"That's our boy," Jason smiled.

After a few more moments careful thought, Carolyn turned to Steven. Her assistant had been silent through-out the entire meeting. "Are you ready for this?" she asked tiredly. There was sadness in her tone. The boy was too much like Terry.

"Yes, ma'am," he said.

Carolyn nodded softly at his response and turned back to Jason. "I'm going to need a lot more detail on how you expect my few people to look like an army."

"Several armies," Jason leaned over the table. "Several confident, independent, quickly advancing armies, well supplied with some cool new technology."

"I'm listening. If I like what I hear, we're in. If I don't, then you and your den of cub scouts leave here alone and good luck to you. You'll certainly need it."

"Michael's den of cub scouts, actually," said Jason. "Joseph just asked me to go get them. I'm more of a consultant."

"You're an ass," she said sharply. "You just mind my words."

"Always." Jason knew that she was in. She may balk at some of the strategy they had yet to go over, but whatever changes she insisted upon would be warranted. He paused then as Carolyn began subconsciously tapping her fingers lightly on the table. Something else was troubling her.

"I don't suppose you've heard any news about Joey?" she asked. It had been weighing heavily on her mind since first hearing of his capture. Now, to find that he was playing games with the Shillies, she feared for him.

"If I interpret recent Shillie activity correctly, he's alive and accomplishing what he set out to accomplish."

Carolyn grew thoughtful again, held the room in silence for half a minute before coming out of her reverie. "All right, show me what you have in mind."

Sheryl Jackson stopped suddenly, then very slowly and smoothly dropped to one knee. Her two companions followed her lead, looking through the trees for some clue as to what she had seen. The trail, such as it was, wound its way through a mix of evergreen and alder, and the forest floor was covered in giant fern and thick patches of salal. They saw nothing, but Jackson had the sharpest eye of anyone in the keep. She had seen something, and that was good enough for them. Until advised otherwise, they would remain motionless and silent.

Sheryl watched the probe for any indication that it had detected them. Heat, movement, sound; these guardian probes were every bit as effective as the hunter probes, and were just as dangerous. The only real differences between them were speed and purpose. A guardian probe out here meant that there was a Shylmahn encampment nearby that needed protection. There would be other probes, together forming a defensive perimeter around the outpost.

The probe rested motionless on the forest floor two dozen yards into the trees off the trail. It showed no signs that its sensors had picked up anything. Sheryl very, very slowly backed away, keeping a low silhouette, moving backwards along the trail. Her companions mimicked her movements, watching her every motion, ready to freeze if she froze, to run if she leapt to her feet.

When they were far enough down the trail that she felt comfortable enough to get back on her feet, Sheryl stood and turned to the others, putting a finger to her lips for silence. Using hand gestures, she did her best to describe what she saw. Once they understood, she indicated that they would travel in a wide arc around where she felt the Shillie encampment was likely to be. She wanted to pinpoint its location and ascertain purpose and numbers.

Whatever happened, at least one of them had to get back to Carolyn with the information.

RehLehn stepped out of the shuttle and walked toward the tables that had been set up under a large canopy. She could see that ShoPehl had left the station yet again. She stopped midway between the shuttle and the station, turned about slowly, looking first at the meadow in which they had settled and then the tree lined perimeter that encircled the meadow.

No sign.

ShoPehl was continually wandering off, and they had work to do. The survey team would be returning before nightfall, and they had to have the morning probe readings analyzed. If they didn't send out the second probe mission soon, it wouldn't make it back before the team did.

ShoPehl was too infatuated with the surroundings, and she always had been. She was probably off chasing butterflies.

RehLehn heard the sound of rustling vegetation and turned about in time to see ShoPehl stumbling out of the woods.

"We don't have time for you to go exploring, ShoPehl."

"I wasn't exploring," ShoPehl sniffed. "I heard something."

"You heard something."

"That's right," ShoPehl said. She stepped in under the canopy and sat at one of the tables. The computer panel set into the table glowed to life, but ShoPehl's attention was still directed at the shadows in the trees.

"And what of the guardian probes?" asked RehLehn. She couldn't believe that ShoPehl would so blatantly mislead, but the evidence was pretty clear.

"I don't know." ShoPehl had yet to look down at the panel. She was watching the woods. "They sense nothing."

"And yet you heard something."

"I must assume that the probes registered the sound as normal background."

"What did it sound like?"

"Like Chehnon natives skulking about just inside the trees."

"Then it could have been wildlife."

"*Human* wildlife."

"But you didn't see anything... and the probes didn't register anything visual."

"Had either been the case, we would not be having this frustrating conversation." ShoPehl stood up and wandered slowly to the corner pole of the canopy. She wrapped an arm around the pole and leaned forward, surveying the tree line bordering the meadow. There were a thousand shadows in there, and many of them were moving. Birds and squirrels and other small creatures were scurrying about in the undergrowth. "They were out there," said ShoPehl, as much to herself as to RehLehn.

"Come on," said RehLehn. "We have work to do."

Craig Warren held a metal plate of food in one hand, a metal cup of unidentifiable liquid in the other, as he casually walked amongst the refugees of Freetown. They were scattered about in the shade of a grove of overgrown fruit trees, sitting in groups of twos and threes, eating their lunches and talking softly amongst themselves. As he passed by each of them, he offered a few words of encouragement to some, a simple hello to others, or a brief comment amount the food to yet others. Everyone was pleasant, and while they were all glad for the meal break, most were looking forward to pushing on. They were eager to get to their friends and families who had gone ahead of them during the first evacuation.

They had found the supply cache, just as it had been mapped. The refugee groups they were following had all accessed the cache, taking only what they needed, knowing there would be others following after them. This group, too, took only what they needed. There would be more caches along the way, and what remained in this store may be needed in the future.

Craig found Victoria sitting with her back to a tree. Her bandages were clean, having just been changed. Craig had seen the wounds underneath; Victoria would not have an easy time of it.

She was fumbling about trying to eat with one arm bound in place.

"Need a hand with that?" Craig asked.

Victoria started to say something before realizing that Craig was attempting humor in order to ease any embarrassment that she might be feeling. She had finally set her plate in her lap and was carefully scooping up as much food as possible on each pass.

"I'm fine," she said. "Nobody eats with two hands."

"Some do," said Craig, sitting down beside her.

"It shouldn't be that difficult."

Craig held his own plate in front of him and unceremoniously began shoveling. He spoke as he ate. "How are you holding up?"

"I'm okay." She considered herself just another of the walking wounded, and wasn't about to allow her injuries to become a burden to anyone. Victoria was holding her own.

"It's okay if you're tired or hurting, you know," said Craig. "It isn't like I'm going to offer to carry you to Metcalf."

Victoria managed to smile. She set her plate aside and wiped her face and hands with a dry cloth. "Sorry," she mumbled. "I guess I was coming across a bit—"

"Yes, you were."

"It won't happen again."

Now Craig smiled. "Yeah."

Victoria was looking at the others. *Walking wounded* was definitely the correct phrase. And yet everyone was managing to hang in there. They were making decent time. No one was falling behind.

"Tomorrow night, do you think?" she asked.

"Or the next day."

Victoria nodded. "And then what?"

"I imagine Ethan will make his move then."

"You're not as dumb as you look," said Victoria. She caught sight of Ethan Perry. He had a group of three in audience.

"I don't know what I'll do about it," said Craig.

"Let him go on his way; and whoever would go with him. Best be rid of them."

"They're not bad people, Victoria. They're good people. They just don't want to fight the fight. I can't blame them for that."

"You're a nice man, Craig Warren."

"And you're a smart woman, Victoria Romero."

"Just not so nice, eh?"

"You're a smart woman, Victoria Romero."

She smiled. "Smart enough to follow my heart, and smart enough to let the heart listen to the brain once in a while."

"And just where will your heart lead you?"

"I'll heal up, if the folks at Metcalf will let me, and then I'll be heading back to Freetown."

Craig slowly nodded, as if that was the answer he was expecting. "And what does your brain have to say about that?"

"That I'm a damn fool."

Craig nodded sharply at that. "That may be true. But you won't be the only damned fool."

"You'll be going back, then?"

"Whatever Michael and the others have gotten themselves mixed up in will likely be resolved one way or the other in the next few weeks. That being the case, Freetown will either no longer be a target of the Shylmahn, or no longer a threat to them."

"It might yet fall somewhere in between."

"And in that case, Freetown will be necessary."

Victoria looked away, looked over at the others in the grove, thought of those already in Metcalf, probably driving the Metcalf citizens crazy. How many would return to Freetown? What will be there when we get back?

| 14 |

Joseph was led into the small mess hall. BehLahk sat at one of the three small tables, calmly eating a light lunch. With a wave of a hand, BehLahk sent the guard away, and the guardian probe followed.

"Sit," said BehLahk, and indicated a second plate at the table. "It is a human recipe."

Joseph quietly moved across the room and sat opposite the Shylmahn doctor. He looked down at the food.

Chow mien.

"Eat," BehLahk urged.

"Thank you," said Joseph. He picked up the fork.

"The Shylmahn have put much effort into acquiring a taste for the native food stuffs, but I must admit that most of my fellows don't seem to appreciate the recipes that the Chehnon have spent centuries perfecting." BehLahk smiled. "I myself am most appreciative."

Joseph pushed uncertainly at the food with the fork. "I should have known that for things to get as weird as they are, the infamous Doctor Black had to be behind it all."

"Not at all," said BehLahk. He didn't appear to be offended, by either the accusation or the mispronunciation of his name, which had been given him during the time of the invasion. His test subjects hadn't quite gotten his name right and had tagged him with the nickname. He casually kept at his lunch. "I have only recently become aware of the, um… *specifics…* of your situation."

"I find that hard to believe. My interrogation sessions have your fingerprints all over them."

"I assure you, Joseph, that I have only just now been asked to consult on this project." BehLahk had learned to speak Joseph's name without the inflection that most other Shylmahn used. He pointed his fork at the Chehnon's plate. "Are you not hungry?"

Joseph looked down at the plate. It did look good, and it wasn't as though his captors needed this setting as a method to drug him. He may as well eat. "Not bad," he said between mouthfuls.

"Thank you. I oversaw the preparations myself. Shylmahn tastes can sometimes be quite different than those of the Chehnon. Some of us, however, are more adventurous than others. I enjoy the exploration and am often surprised and very pleased with what I find."

"BehLahk, why am I here?"

"A shared lunch is not enough for you?"

"Not nearly."

BehLahk nodded. "No, I suppose not. No reason to not enjoy the meal, though. Is there?"

"I guess that depends on what it costs me," said Joseph. He held up a forkful of chow mien and pushed it into his mouth.

"Candidly, then. I have invited you here," he indicated the mess hall they were in, "because ShahnTahr has no sensors in this room. I find this fact to be a bit perplexing, but it nonetheless suits my purposes."

"What about NehLoc?"

"NehLoc limits his eavesdropping equipment to the interrogation chambers. That is protocol, and NehLoc, for all his skills at discovering legitimate avenues around protocols, follows protocols if he must."

"Okay," Joseph put his fork down and studied BehLahk. "How about you? If I had to take a guess, I'd guess this meeting is about a mile outside your precious protocols."

"I have a few avenues of my own, as you must no doubt be aware."

"So it would seem."

BehLahk set his fork down beside his plate, picked up a napkin and carefully dabbed at the corners of his mouth. Joseph suspected the Shylmahn doctor had gotten this from an old movie. The Shylmahn set the napkin down and leaned forward.

"There are dangerous times ahead of us, Joseph," he said.

Joseph leaned forward now. "I'm not feeling all that safe and secure in the present, doctor."

"I can't say as I blame you. However, you know of what I speak." BehLahk raised a hand to forestall argument. "For now, let us accept that. Let us also accept that certain events are now destined to occur. Given that, let us consider then that I may see some of these events as beneficial to Shylmahn."

Joseph remained very wary of the infamous Dr. Black. "I had no idea the Shylmahn believed in fate."

"Fate has nothing to do with it," said the doctor.

Joseph knew that BehLahk could be a powerful ally, but also that he must tread this path very cautiously. "What events could possibly benefit both the Shylmahn and humans?"

"Come now, Joseph. How does your expression go? *You called me.*"

"How do you figure?"

BehLahk sat back, absently worked the napkin with his fingers. "You have worked very diligently and very carefully. You have guided events, misdirected people, misrepresented places and situations, all to create a very specific perception."

"Fanciful; bordering on paranoia, doctor."

BehLahk ignored him. "The time draws near. I believe that it has become important, vitally important, for you to understand that your efforts have been... helped along. A little push here, a little corroborating data there."

"I see... or rather, I don't see. I have no idea what you're talking about."

BehLahk grew visibly upset. He tossed his napkin across his plate and brought his hand down firmly on the table. "Why must you continue to play this game? It accomplishes nothing."

Joseph could not yet be certain; perhaps this meeting was some elaborate way of confirming suspicions. He was very uncomfortable, and wasn't prepared to let anyone else into his world. He had put up so many walls, created so many false pictures, built such a precarious set of illusions, that he didn't know of any safe way to open the door even a crack to test the possibility that BehLahk meant what he said.

Possible ally or not, Joseph would not forget who and what BehLahk was, what he had done, and what he was capable of.

And yet, he couldn't just walk away from this. The opportunity was too big to pass up. He had to give BehLahk something...

"If I understand you correctly, BehLahk, then you have been aware of the... um... scenario... that has been playing out here for some time. And yet, you say you've only recently become aware of the situation. You can't have it both ways."

BehLahk visibly relaxed. He could see that Joseph was searching for a way for them to communicate without surrendering his position or admitting to anything outright. This Chehnon needed to feel that he could walk away should things turn out wrong.

"What I actually said was that I only recently became aware of the *specifics* of the situation. I have been aware of certain activities that you have been involved in over the past few months, and have been following these as best I could from my own unique perspective. I did know that NehLoc and EsJen had brought you in. While I have not been privy to exact details of your interrogation sessions, I have been following quite closely what I believe to be the cause-and-effect results of these interviews. It is this, and the larger picture within which these activities reside, that have been the focus of my attention."

"And you think that you are seeing something that no one else can see?" Joseph tried as best he could to sound doubtful.

"As I said, I have a unique perspective."

"Aren't you afraid that you might be missing a lot of important facts? Your *perspective* may be skewed."

"What I am missing is the direct influence of the source of the intelligence being gathered."

"By that, I assume you mean me."

"Let us say that others who are more directly involved in drawing critical information from the subject in their care must of necessity attempt to interpret intentions and meanings of the individual elements of the information being gathered. I have not been encumbered by the immediacy of the interviews."

"I think you work too hard in your attempt to justify a difference in interpretation. You might just be wrong. And what of your computer master? Surely it is not encumbered by the immediacy of the interviews."

"Ah, and that is where your cleverness truly shines, my Chehnon friend." BehLahk's smile was broad and very genuine. "ShahnTahr is, and always has been, your true target. You understand, more than any Chehnon and more than most Shylmahn, that any chance for Chehnon success lay in convincing ShahnTahr that things are as they are not. You must therefore work your magic simultaneously on both your immediate captors and on ShahnTahr. Each must be approached very differently, yet through the very same words and actions."

"You and EsJen give me way too much credit. I'm really not that clever."

BehLahk leaned forward again, this time halfway across the table. He was beyond listening to halfhearted attempts at denial. While Joseph may not know where BehLahk was heading, they both knew there was going to be a meeting of the minds. He lowered his voice and he grew very thoughtful, "I believe I know where you intend to go with this. I have to wonder, therefore, whether your co-conspirators have all the facts. In the end, when all is made clear, you and I may well find ourselves quite isolated in the world we are about to create."

Jason looked up from his lunch at the sound of the heavy door opening and closing. Carolyn had come into the mess hall. The room quieted as conversations stopped. Most of Jason's group were sitting at two of the tables, and a few of the keep residents were scattered about the remaining tables.

Carolyn looked in Jason's direction, and it was evident that she wanted to speak with him.

"Duty calls," he said to the others. He stood and picked up his plate and cup.

"You want me to come with you?" asked Michael.

Jason tried to interpret Carolyn's expression. "You should probably stay here," he said. He took his dishes to the counter and followed Carolyn out the door. She waited for him at the foot of the wooden steps.

"A Shillie hunting party out in the valley," she said.

"Crap."

"Yeah," Carolyn was not happy. "Their encampment is outside the canyon, but they may have scouts and probes all through these woods."

"Do they know that we know?"

"My team doesn't think so."

"At least we have that. We don't want to force their hand. We don't really know their purpose here."

"They certainly know we're in here. It's impossible for a community this size to be completely invisible."

"But their being here may have nothing to do with you, or they could be simply checking up on things as part of their normal activities."

"I don't like the timing," said Carolyn. "They have to know that you're here. Their arrival must have something to do with our plans."

Jason sat down on the bottom step. He clasped his hands together and stared down at the damp ground. She was probably right. This wasn't a hunting party, but an investigative team. They were probably monitoring the activities in this area and reporting back to a main base somewhere.

"Okay," said Jason. "Let's assume they're getting nervous and are watching our movements. It may well be due to our recent activities, a general increase in human activities—I have teams out there stirring up things too—or it may be something that Joseph has stirred up."

"Or your recent tromping through my woods," Carolyn grumbled.

"The reason really doesn't matter, though, does it?" Jason slapped his hands together. "What are our options, really? We stay, we go now, or we go later."

"We could take out the Shillies in the valley," said Carolyn.

"What would that accomplish?" asked Jason. "You'll get your chance to shoot things, but this isn't the time."

Carolyn bristled. She didn't like being talked down to.

"All right," she said.

Jason could see that he had ruffled her feathers. "Sis, you more than anyone knows that if we go out there now we'll be setting things in motion that we're just not ready to deal with."

"I said all right."

Jason knew damn well that it wasn't all right. He also knew that she understood that it was probably best to let the Shylmahn believe they had not been discovered, and that it was definitely for the best that they not provoke them into taking action.

She just didn't like being told so. She set her jaw tight. "We'll have to move out now. As you say, we don't know their intentions, and they may be preparing to move on us."

"Agreed," Jason nodded. "But it's not going to be easy. They are probably watching."

"That's not a problem." Carolyn had six ways out of the keep that would have her and her people away and gone long before the Shillies knew the place was empty.

"Good," he said. He suspected that she could turn the place into a ghost town inside of an hour. "I'll have to get word to my contacts, let them know that we're moving up the schedule."

"I'll leave that to you."

"It shouldn't change anything. Each group will still meet up with one of my people at the designated locations."

"We might be moving fast. They need to be ready."

"As you said, leave that to me," said Jason. He thought a moment, then. "We better bring Michael in on this."

"Not yet."

"What?" Jason was genuinely startled.

"First, I need to know who is in charge."

Jason had to think about that. "I would say that we each have our specific responsibilities."

"Why do you continually force-feed this kid to me?"

"It's important that Michael participate in the decision making process."

"He is without experience."

"He may not be Old Guard, but he has extensive experience. He has been operating out of Freetown, with significant success, for years. He has made countless forays into the province."

Carolyn leaned close and spoke in a determined voice. "I will not argue the point with you, Jason. I will not place myself or the lives of my people in the hands of someone *not of our time.*"

"Very well," he said. "You'll not have to answer to him. But now you understand me. Michael Britton is the future of this planet. I will not allow this operation to go forward without his input and his participation. He will be a key player in this, and ultimately we are all placing our lives in the hands of everyone here. There is no way around that."

Carolyn stared down her brother, and the two sat stone silent for several long, cold seconds. She finally leaned back and let out the breath she had been holding.

"Michael's a boy. He's a good kid, and bright, but he's still a boy. I can't see why you're pushing so hard on this."

"Michael will be running the planet long after you and I are gone and buried."

It was clear to Carolyn that Jason was absolutely convinced of this, and dead set on Michael's role in this great scheme of theirs. Well, so long as Michael wasn't actually running things *now,* and so long as she could clearly see Michael's role and scope in what they were about to do, and could see and respond to the potential impact that his *participation* might have on her part in the operation... Besides, wasn't Jason really running things, pulling the strings? "You'll be watching over things, I assume?"

"We all have our specific responsibilities," Jason repeated. Then, "You know me... I always have my hand in just about everything."

Carolyn mumbled unintelligibly under her breath, staring down at the fingers she had locked together in a death grip. "Damn," she said at last.

"This is Joey's plan," said Jason, "and it included Michael from the beginning. I know that you've trusted his judgment in the past. Trust in it now."

Carolyn thought a moment longer, and then pointed a shaky finger at Jason. "He can oversee his own people, run his own part in this, but that's it. You put him on the throne afterwards if you want, but he'll not be king of my little corner of the world; not now and not ever."

"I got that," said Jason.

Her voice softened then, but her meaning was rock-solid. "And I want to be as clear as I can on this, Jason. Michael may be Joey's boy, and Joey may have brought him in on this, but family or no, if things turn south on us, I will do whatever is necessary to make this plan work. Once I'm in, I'm in all the way."

"That's why we need you, Sis."

NehLoc stepped through the main entrance and into the cavern that had served as the Inner Village of Freetown. To him it was the physical manifestation of the cool and calculated deviousness of the Chehnon natives. He had pointed out time and again that these creatures were not to be trusted, and up to now only his own diligence and constant vigilance had prevented him from becoming a victim of their malevolence.

He walked into the central plaza. Overhead, dozens of bright lights hovered near the ceiling as probes and Shylmahn rushed busily about, moving into and out of Chehnon dwellings, tunnels and cubby holes.

Even NehLoc, who fully understood just how clever these creatures could be, had been taken aback at what had been found here. Such guile. Such industriousness.

He was angry with himself. He should have known. Somehow, he should have known, or at least suspected. The town had been JoSeph's creation. That in itself should have sent out warning signals. But it hadn't...

The Chehnon had let the Shylmahn see exactly what they had expected to see. They had created an illusion, the illusion that the Shylmahn, through their own efforts, were able to see what the Chehnon were attempting to hide; all the while, this was going on just beneath the surface.

JoSeph's doing... JoSeph had played them...

NehLoc's attention was drawn to a slowly moving probe. It moved out of one of the dwellings that opened onto the plaza. He had earlier seen it moving up and down the aisles in the supply cavern. Its activity pattern wasn't supportive of the requirements he had given the probe system interface. It had to be on another, independent assignment.

ShahnTahr... ShahnTahr had either instructed and then sent out the probe, or was directly controlling the probe real-time.

NehLoc was seeing more and more of this sort of thing from ShahnTahr. ShahnTahr was taking a more active and more direct role in the investigatory activities of the world around them. In some cases ShahnTahr simply bypassed the Shylmahn altogether and instructed the probes himself. More and more frequently, ShahnTahr was taking to using probes as extensions of himself, interacting real-time with the world.

NehLoc was as yet uncertain as to where this would lead or what it meant to the Shylmahn, but he had no doubts regarding ShahnTahr's undeviating and absolute dedication to the survival of the Shylmahn people and the progress and enrichment of the Shylmahn society.

Nonetheless, NehLoc's own dedication to the cause necessitated, among his other myriad of duties and responsibilities, that he continue to monitor this ongoing evolution of their millennia-old councilor and guide...

| 15 |

When Joseph woke, he could sense that something was wrong, or at least not normal. With as little movement as possible, he shifted position and looked around his cell.

The door was standing ajar. There was also a second probe hovering up in the far corner, directly beside the first. This second probe was smaller, quieter, and more sleek in design. He guessed that there was probably less weaponry and more in the way of sophisticated sensors. This wasn't a guardian probe, and it wasn't a hunter probe either.

What was it doing here?

Joseph slowly sat up and swung his feet down onto the floor. He stared openly at this second probe now.

"So, who the hell are you?" he asked.

The probe didn't move, showed no sign that it had heard the question or even that it saw that Joseph was awake and had seen it.

When did it come into the cell? How long had it been watching him?

Who or what was on the other side of those sensors?

Joseph stood up and took the two shuffling steps toward the probes. He studied this new probe more carefully. It was definitely a design that he hadn't seen before. He turned his gaze to the first probe.

"I'd watch out for this new guy, fella," he said. "The kid looks like a significant improvement over you old timers."

The first probe was as unresponsive to his humor as the second. After a moment of nothing, Joseph glanced at the open door. His internal clock, and other internal systems, told him that it was near time for the guard to make an appearance and walk him to the next room over. He nodded at the door.

"I gotta piss," he said to the probes. He looked at one, then the other, for a sign of acknowledgement. "Do you mind if I go take a leak?"

So long as he didn't make a move toward the door, he didn't expect a response, and he didn't get one.

He turned and stepped to the open door. The second probe did nothing. The first responded as expected. In warning, an energy pin barely missed Joseph's right ear and struck the door jam.

Joseph stopped and turned about to face the probe. He gave a faint nod in submission, turned again and returned to his cot. He sat down.

"I can wait," he said.

Victoria woke to the smell of thick mulch and aging fruit trees. The tiny twigs and dead leaves beneath her crackled noisily as she twisted around and sat up, sliding back and leaning back against the old, gnarled tree trunk.

Despite the continuing pain of her slowly healing wounds, she gave an inward smile that finally showed itself as the slightest grin.

They would reach Metcalf today, probably well before lunch.

She looked around the ancient orchard. It was early morning, and the pre-dawn skies were just beginning to push at the darker shadows beneath the trees. Victoria could see movement all around her as others began to wake.

Then she saw it.

A Shillie probe hovered just beneath the overhead branches of the tree above her. She moved to scramble back, but she was already up against the trunk. She felt her heart pounding in sudden panic. Streaks of pain shot through the wound in her arm.

But the probe didn't move. It hung there, half hidden in the twisted mass of branches and leaves. It appeared to be studying her reaction to her discovery of its presence.

It had been watching her sleep.

She shivered.

It's been watching me...

Victoria couldn't take her eyes off the probe, couldn't cry out to warn the others. She stared up at it, almost frantically studying it for any sign of movement.

It hovered silently above her, unmoving.

How long has it been up there? How long has it been watching me?

She could hear movement throughout the orchard as people stirred from sleep, sat up, and began making ready for the day. Despite the activity all around her, Victoria felt very, very alone.

Is everybody blind? Can't anybody see this? Somebody help me...

A short breath caught in her throat as the probe turned slightly. She waited for the streaks of light and the pain of the energy pins.

None came. The probe lowered a few inches, dropping below the branches, turned again and quickly and silently left the orchard.

Victoria only slowly turned her head, looking in the direction the probe had traveled.

My god... she thought. *My god, my god, my god...*

She scrambled hurriedly to her feet then, rushing as she did so towards someone, anyone, desperate to tell everyone, desperate to not be alone.

BehLahk approached Joseph as he was being led down the long, narrow hall. From his years of studying Chehnon subjects, it was obvious to him that Joseph was near a state of total exhaustion. This was certainly to be expected, as he had been under NehLoc's interrogations for many days. But Joseph needed to remain strong, to remain alert, and most definitely he needed to remain wary. His most difficult hours and days yet lay ahead. His most delicate discourses were yet before him. The successful culmination of the Chehnon's efforts, and the future of his people, depended upon Joseph maintaining his very careful manipulation of facts and fictions and his shrewd perpetuation of the misconstructions of the evidence that he allowed NehLoc and ShahnTahr to create for themselves.

This illusory image of the world, however, could still very easily fall away. It would only take ShahnTahr a matter of milliseconds to tear away the layers of façade and restore a clear and quite correct representation of their chosen home.

While it was true that this would mean the Shylmahn would remain as the dominant species of this planet, BehLahk did not like what he foresaw as the future for his people and this world should they continue down this path. The subjugation of the Chehnon species by the Shylmahn had become a debilitating disease of the psyche of the Shylmahn mind and a plague upon the Shylmahn society.

It had been logical to look upon and utilize the creatures as another natural resource, and BehLahk believed that the choice to do so had in fact smoothed the Shylmahn effort to dominate and control this planet. The ongoing use of the creatures as a resource continued to be the easy path and the logical choice.

But it came at a high cost. Such cost was not immediately evident, but it would be irrevocable. It had taken decades, but the conception that the Chehnon species just may be something above the other plants and animals and minerals of this new world was beginning to form in the minds of many of the Shylmahn.

For BehLahk, it was crystal clear, and yet even for him it was difficult to maintain a grasp on this fact. Thousands of years of culture and evolution dictated that there were the Shylmahn and then there were the natural resources to be used to support the society.

How could it be any other way?

It would have been so much better had these Chehnon never existed. But they did exist. And from the very beginning of the migration, the Shylmahn had very effectively controlled and put this resource to use.

Now what?

They could continue on as they have; or they could eliminate the resource entirely; or they could...

BehLahk's sense of duty and responsibility would not permit him to allow the Shylmahn to continue on as they have; nor would he allow the collective soul of the Shylmahn society to be tainted with the elimination of the Chehnon; not now that so many Shylmahn had begun to see the creatures as something other than a resource.

That left only...

BehLahk stopped and waited for Joseph and his escort of guard, guardian probe, and the ShahnTahr probe, to reach him.

"Joseph," he said, and tried to smile. "I would speak with you."

"Then I suppose I would listen." Joseph reached BehLahk. The guard stopped one pace behind him; the probes moved up and took position ahead of the group.

"I appreciate that," said BehLahk. He would choose his words carefully. ShahnTahr was watching, and of course the guardian probe was documenting the interaction for review by NehLoc and for the information library. "I understand that you have been honored with an audience with TohPeht."

"Ah," said Joseph. "So that's where they're dragging me." The Chehnon gave no outward sign of emotion, and in fact looked unimpressed. BehLahk could see, however, the creature's mind working feverishly behind those alien eyes...

"You should be pleased," said BehLahk. "Much good can come from such a meeting... if you behave yourself, and if you provide TohPeht—and ShahnTahr—with what they *require*."

Too much? wondered BehLahk. With a slight sweep of his arm, he indicated they should resume walking. "Permit me to accompany you the rest of the way."

"Hey, it's not up to me," Joseph thumbed at the probes, but fell in beside BehLahk, and the doctor escorted the Chehnon the rest of the way TohPeht's rooms.

Joseph hadn't been quite sure what to make of BehLahk's cryptic words. It seemed that he was to consider this a meeting of significant opportunity for him, but that he should also to be wary.

More than that, it seemed to Joseph that BehLahk considered this to be an apex of sorts, a culmination, maybe; of what? There had definitely been something in the Shylmahn's movements and tone of voice. There was something to be feared in this meeting, the possibility of great failure, and yet there was also the chance to push this thing forward.

Well, Joseph had been riding the edge of this razor from the moment that he had been collected. Hell, for weeks before that...

So what's new?

Still, Joseph felt a chill. Could it all come down to this meeting? He had been *on* every moment since his capture, with each minute as critical as the last; but could these next few minutes decide it all, one way or the other?

And how might this serve BehLahk's agenda? What was his agenda and what might it cost the human race?

The Shylmahn doctor led the group into a low-ceilinged room, long but narrow, and empty but for a lone Shylmahn standing in the far left corner. The sleek, newer probe moved quickly forward and took up position in the other corner opposite the Shylmahn. The guard and the guardian probe stayed behind Joseph, but moved to one side of the door.

BehLahk moved forward. "TohPeht," he began, speaking in English, "I would like to introduce JoSeph." Joseph noticed how easily BehLahk moved from the human inflection of his name to the Shylmahn inflection.

TohPeht stepped forward. "A pleasure," he said. He wore a broad smile and appeared genuinely pleased to meet the human. And yet... Joseph had spent enough time around these guys to know that there was something odd about this one.

"JoSeph," BehLahk said pleasantly, "I introduce to you the leader of our people."

Leader? Joseph wondered silently. *Wasn't that computer of theirs the leader of the Shillies? Wouldn't that make TohPeht here ShahnTahr's puppet?*

Joseph gave TohPeht a slight nod of the head. "The pleasure is mine," he said.

TohPeht's strange smile faded in and out, the muscles around the eyes and the set of the jaw shifted mechanically, almost as if the Shylmahn was moving through a collection of emotions, trying to find and display the appropriate one.

Joseph thought he looked worn out.

"JoSeph," said TohPeht. "As an individual, you first came to our attention approximately thirty four days after the initial disembarkation of the Shylmahn people onto this world."

"You might say that it was a key moment in my life, as well." *Thirty four days?*

TohPeht curled his brow, then relaxed it. "You have been... an element... in my... memory... since that time."

Way weird, thought Joseph. "No doubt," he said. "You've been in my thoughts pretty much since that time, too."

"No doubt," agreed TohPeht. He then gave Joseph a curious, penetrating look. The room was heavily silent for several heartbeats. "There have been many changes in your life, as there have been many changes in my own existence."

"I suppose so."

"There is far yet to go."

"I would hope so," said Joseph. "It sure beats the alternative."

TohPeht's expression suddenly grew animated and his smile softened. "EsJen always considered you important. You were valuable to her, and of constructive note to us all."

"Ah," he said, rather dumbfounded.

TohPeht's face visibly tightened. "Your activities since the closure of the original JoSeph project have been fully documented."

"Uh... okay."

"BehLahk," said TohPeht, shifting his attention to the doctor, "Perhaps it is time for JoSeph and me to speak privately."

BehLahk could sense that no good would come from arguing the point. He bowed his head once, turned and left the room without a word. TohPeht turned again to the Chehnon creature.

"BehLahk has concerns," said TohPeht.

"Excuse me?"

"Yes," said TohPeht. He stiffened slightly. "I possess many favorable thoughts and emotions regarding BehLahk. There is... agreement... regarding the value and the dedication of BehLahk."

"If you say so," said Joseph. He was finding it very difficult to follow this Shylmahn's thoughts and meanings, but it was evident that BehLahk had some opinions that didn't sit right with TohPeht and the computer, or maybe conflicted with what TohPeht felt to be correct.

"Whatever standing that BehLahk has with us, such will not deter future actions initiated to defend the society of the Shylmahn and the destiny of the people."

Which had to mean that TohPeht was considering taking some action, and that BehLahk was opposed to it. Joseph filed that thought away and said nothing.

"Your attempts at deception are known, JoSeph," TohPeht said.

"Not very deceptive of me."

"There have been actions designed to advance the level of *resistance* against the established order. The evidence is quite clear that you have coordinated this activity. Your continued efforts at misdirection during your recent interrogations gain nothing on your behalf.

"Hey, listen... I've tried to explain—"

"Your explanations are little more than further attempts to confuse. They have failed."

"If you say so."

"I have not asked you here to argue the matter. I do not have the time for such things."

Joseph nodded solemnly. TohPeht watched the movement curiously, nodded his head in acknowledgment.

"While we have little concern regarding where your foolish and imprudent activities may lead, we are impressed with the level of coordination and the wide-ranging spectrum of the actions of your... organization."

Organization... thought Joseph. *I like that...*

He decided not to say anything in response. A response was just what TohPeht was looking for, and silence was just what was called for.

TohPeht appeared to process the Chehnon's lack of vocal reply, then continued. "Under other circumstances, the correct punishment for your antisocial behavior would be elimination. A structured, peaceful society cannot permit, cannot tolerate, such activity."

"What are the circumstances that have kept me from elimination up to now?"

"You are the circumstance," said TohPeht. He smiled woodenly. "And what you seem to be able to accomplish with a minimum of resources."

"You give me too much credit."

"I do not believe so."

"What if that's all part of my plan?" asked Joseph, the words almost catching in his throat, his breath coming in a visible shudder.

"That possibility has been raised. Analyses of the known facts indicate the chances of this to be quite small. The threads of activity weave a clear pattern, with subtle attempts to keep the organization, the coordination, the movement, undetected... hidden from view."

Joseph realized two things.

First, that whoever TohPeht might once have been, there was little remaining of that personality. Somehow, ShahnTahr was in there, or at least some form of the alien computer entity was in there.

And second, Joseph realized that ShahnTahr saw the world just as Joseph had painted it, with communications networks that really did little but interconnect a motley group of individuals who were executing very limited but very specific actions at very specific times, each under a false façade of subterfuge. And now, with Jason and his teams out there carefully accelerating the activities...

I'll be damned...

ShahnTahr wasn't quite ready to commit, but by some bizarre and twisted turn of events, this thing was working.

| 16 |

The Shylmahn commander walked through the narrow doorway that was set into the great timbered wall of the keep, following behind several of her team that were stepping through ahead of her. Inside, the abandoned Chehnon community was eerily quiet, eerily still. The only movement was that of the hunter probes gliding silently through the streets.

As the commander carefully examined the scene before her, the remainder of the team came in behind her and hurried down the central travelway of the dirty little nest, splitting off into pairs as they reached the bisecting side streets.

The sky was gray, the air was damp, and the place smelled of humans. They hadn't been gone long.

A second cluster of hunter probes appeared over the wall behind her and rushed into the keep, joining the first group in their efforts to ferret out any of the creatures that may yet be hiding. The commander, however, doubted very much that they would find anything. The Chehnon were gone, slipping away under their very noses.

A transport shuttle flew overhead and settled down in the center of the main travelway a third of the way into the keep. A few moments later, the shuttle doors opened and six Shylmahn marched quickly down the ramp. They moved into defensive positions around the shuttle. At an unseen signal, NehLoc stepped out of the transport and stood at the foot of the ramp. He had a harsh glare, and turned his head slowly from one side to the other, taking in the entire scene in one angry sweep. His eyes came upon the commander and fixed upon her. The commander did not turn away, but did not approach. She stood her position, and after a few moments NehLoc walked toward her.

The team commander knew that the next few minutes would not be pleasant.

Jenny stumbled over a thick tree root, regained her footing on the other side as she followed Michael along the rough, narrow, winding path. Jason was ahead of Michael, and further ahead still, out of sight somewhere in the dark shadows, one of Carolyn's people was on point. Most of the other Freetown novices were following along behind Jenny, interspersed with the snooty professionals from Carolyn's Keep.

The forest was thick with shade-loving, wet-loving undergrowth, giant fern mostly, the canopy overhead preventing most of the sunlight from reaching the forest floor. Occasional streaks of light shot through from above, revealing the ever-present mist that hung in the air, and the clouds of tiny flying insects that rolled through the woods like a fog.

Jenny didn't know if it was raining above the treetops, out in the real world, but it was raining where they were. Big, heavy drops fell on them from the canopy, striking them and the vegetation around them with loud splashes. Despite the raingear, Jenny was wet and miserable. Her feet were soaked and each step was a squishy reminder that she was wet and miserable.

Right at this moment, she wished that she had gone with Carolyn.

Several miles out from the keep, Carolyn and a large group of her people had split away from the main body. Two miles further on, another group had split off. A third group had turned south a quarter of a mile back, leaving this fourth and final group, led by Jason, to take the high trail over into the province, into the heart of the Shylmahn occupied territory.

Carolyn had wanted Jenny to come with her, and had been rather put out when Jenny had insisted on staying with her brother. Over the course of their time at the Keep, Carolyn had made several attempts to reach out to Jenny, perhaps to take her under her wing as a protégé, to mentor to her; but Jenny had pulled back at each attempt. She was very uncomfortable around the woman that she had always previously considered an icon to her, now felt uneasy whenever Carolyn directed attention to her.

Jenny still respected and admired Carolyn, still looked up to her as an intelligent, dedicated leader in the fight against the Shylmahn, but the woman frightened her. When asked to join her, Jenny had instinctively stepped back. She had fumbled about stupidly for words, mumbling finally that she had to stay with Michael. Jason had approached and quickly stepped in, stating matter-of-factly that he had plucked these gosling novices out of the nest and brought them into the harsh reality of the real world, and that he had no intention of letting them out of his sight.

It had been a feeble argument, but it allowed them all to walk away from the awkward situation. Carolyn and Jason reaffirmed the timetable, then she and her team turned north, leaving the others to continue west, to continue splitting off until there were four teams striking into the province.

Each had specific tasks to perform, conspicuous actions that, if not completely logical or rewarding in and of themselves, would draw the attention of the Shylmahn leadership, hopefully create an illusion of strengths and capabilities that did not exist, and hopefully perpetuate whatever false façade Joseph was attempting to paint.

Carolyn continued to have her doubts. She sincerely hoped that Joseph wasn't relying solely upon the actions of this motley collection for his success.

Nonetheless, she had agreed to it, with her own provisos accepted, and she would complete her assigned tasks. She would meet up again with the other teams in four days.

Monroe had split off from the main body next, taking with him a group of Carolyn's people that were the most familiar with mountain travel and mountain life. They would be traveling fast and hard, making quick strikes at a number of targets before swinging around and reaching the rendezvous point in four days. The targets were specific and the attack methodology designed to create doubt in the minds of the Shylmahn leadership.

The third team to split off consisted primarily of Carolyn's recon teams, a group very adept at moving stealthily about, at getting into and out of situations with a minimum of fuss and maximum affect.

Which left Jason and his rag-tag army of Freetown citizenry and two dozen perplexed Keep residents. Though most of them did not know it, their task, in fact, was to be the most audacious, and most probably the least survivable, of all the operations to be attempted. As first designed by Joseph, and then reworked by Joseph and Jason, and then later finalized by Jason and Carolyn and Michael, the two-stage operation of this team depended overly much upon the actions and interpretations that had taken place over the previous six months, the immediate actions to take place over the following three days, and the credibility and interpretation of the information to be gleaned from the interrogations of Joseph over the previous few weeks.

Up ahead, Jason entered a large clearing flooded with slanting rays of sunlight and called for a five-minute break. Jenny came into the clearing and spotted a rotting fallen tree and made her way over to it. She let her backpack slide to the ground and climbed onto the log, canteen in hand. She watched as the others of the team scattered about the clearing, dividing mostly into small clusters of Freetown groups and Keep groups.

They all looked tired and dejected. Marching through a dank, colorless, oozingly-wet forest, wearing squishy-wet shoes and damp clothes that clung to cold, wet skin would do that to a person.

Still, Jenny felt that her Freetown companions were holding up well. Miriam Foster, leaning more heavily on her cane than usual, appeared to be drawing on a deep well of inner strength. Miriam wore a wide leather belt around her waist, with a holster strapped to her leg. The holster held a large, shiny revolver. She saw Jenny watching her and gave a smile and slight nod of her head. Jenny smiled in return.

Michael came over and sat down beside his sister.

"How ya' holding up, Jen?"

"I'm soaking wet," said Jenny.

"You certainly are," said Michael. He took a strip of jerky from a small burlap bag and handed it to her.

Jenny ripped a piece of the jerky free with her teeth. "Yeah," she said, chewing doggedly. They ate silently for a minute. Jenny drank from her canteen, handed it to Michael. He took a swig and handed it back. She spoke in a low whisper then, studiously screwing the cap back onto the canteen. "Not quite what we expected, is it?"

"I suppose not," said Michael.

"I don't mean this march."

"I know."

"I knew up front that it couldn't be exactly as it was laid out to us, and I didn't mind that. I knew why. I appreciated the reasons. I appreciated that our father wanted us involved. He felt it important that we be involved."

Michael nodded slowly. "But you wonder about that."

"He's very methodical. His grand scheme, this great plan of his, while it appears to be flexible enough, is still very structured and very organized. That being the case, there must be a reason why he believes it is important that we are a part of it. It can't be just his wanting to have his children by his side. That would not be his way."

"I think you're right," Michael said with a long, drawn sigh. "But you have to remember the mind games that our clever father is playing the Shillies. Having us visibly active in whatever he has going on could all be a part of that. What better way to highlight the organization of the human opposition than to showcase the continuing Britton family participation in the goings-on."

Jenny frowned, put her canteen away. "Maybe," she said, looked thoughtfully at the others in the clearing. Some were in conversation, most were silent. Some had found prime locations directly in the sun's rays and were bathing in the faint warmth, heads back, eyes closed and faces to the bright glow.

"You don't think so?" asked Michael.

"Oh, I have no doubt that you're right about the mind games."

"But?"

Jenny's wandering gaze stopped at Jason, who was standing on the other side of the clearing. She watched as he gave directions to several of Carolyn's people, directing them to guard posts to stand during their brief stay.

"There's more," she said, not taking her eyes of their uncle. "There's more to you and me being necessary than just as a show of Britton participation, and there's more layers to this plan of dear Daddy's than just bluffing our way to victory."

"But that's a given, Jen. That's been said."

"No. I mean something really big. I mean the main thing." She gave a sharp nod toward Jason. "I'm not even sure that Jason knows."

"If there is another layer," Michael gave another sigh, "then you can bet that Jason knows about it. I don't think there's anything about any of this that he doesn't know."

"Hmm."

"Hmm?"

Jenny looked directly at Michael, then. "Remember, Michael, that Jason came into this rather recently. Our father has been working it for a very long time."

"Yeah? And?"

"You know Joseph's history. You know that his perspective on the Shylmahn is the most unique of anyone on the planet. You know that he isolated himself from everyone and has been working alone for years." Jenny shifted position on the log and took a deep breath. "He sees things. He knows things. He understands things."

"What are you trying to say, Jenny? That he's become like some oracle or something?"

"No," Jenny said patiently. "I'm saying that he may not trust anyone with all the facts."

"You think he's trying to sneak one over on all of us?" Michael asked doubtfully.

"Don't play dumb with me, Michael," Jenny sneered just as incredulously. "I know that you don't believe we've been given the straight on this. The real question is whether or not Jason has the full confidence of his brother."

Metcalf was a small town by pre-invasion standards, but by current measure, it was probably the largest free-human community on the continent. With a population of almost a thousand people, it made no effort at hiding itself from the Shylmahn. In fact, it went out of its way to maintain visibility and to show itself as a non-aggressive, non-progressive, low-tech community. The three hundred or so buildings that made up the town lined a grid of narrow dirt streets set into the heart of a level plain of tall, yellow grass and very few trees. They had plumbing but no public electricity, agriculture but no powered agricultural equipment; what primitive communications equipment they had didn't reach beyond the borders of the town.

The community calculatedly limited its growth to three percent per year, from both internal growth and immigration. This kept the Shylmahn observers from becoming too concerned, minimized the growing demands on their resources, while acknowledging the realization that they could not and should not cut themselves off completely from the world around them. They also understood the importance of bringing new blood into a small population.

So long as they behaved themselves, Metcalf managed to exist in relative safety. But they were not truly free, and their security was precarious and dependent upon the mood of the Shylmahn, and therefore was not genuine. Nonetheless, since the community's beginnings twenty years earlier, they had survived. They held no illusions about their place in the world, and accepted their position in it. They were always under the watchful eye and the very real threat of the Shylmahn, making it necessary for them to maintain the constant submissive posture that defined them. Some argued, many argued, that they were no better off than the humans living on the reservations and were in fact *free humans* in name only.

However true this might have been, Metcalf had held an important role in the northwest, and the residents of Freetown had always appreciated its existence. They realized that at this point in the history of the world, there was a place for a community such as Metcalf. There were those who had argued that Freetown, which had spent its existence even closer to the fire, should have taken a similar position.

But then, without Freetown much of Metcalf's reason for being would have been lost. Much of the population of Metcalf had originated through the underground railroad. Indeed, Metcalf had survived its first few years primarily due to the support and resources of its upstart neighbor to the west and its leader, Joseph Britton, who understood the possible value of a nearby community such as Metcalf.

Craig Warren could see the town in the distance, across the rolling grassy plains and cultivated fields that surrounded it. He led the way now, following a well-traveled trail, the last refugees from Freetown trailing doggedly behind him. The sun had set, the clear skies had turned gray and the weather had turned cool.

As they drew nearer to Metcalf, Craig could make out shadows and campfires outside the town. It wasn't until they were within half a mile, the gray skies growing steadily darker, that they could see that a tent city had been set up at the town's outskirts.

"What do you make of that?" asked Victoria, coming up beside him. Several others quickly joined them. Craig subconsciously picked up the pace.

"I suppose it makes sense," he said. "I don't imagine they could take us all in."

"Doesn't bode well for the future."

"Depends on what your plans are."

Three figures appeared on the trail ahead of them, apparently coming from the tent city. It wasn't until they were within a few yards that Craig recognized them as being from Freetown, though he couldn't remember their names.

"Craig," said the woman, falling into step beside him. "Glad to see you made it."

"Yeah," said one of the two men with her. "Maybe you can finally get things straightened out around here."

Craig was afraid to ask, but decided to jump right in, "What's the problem?"

"Isn't it obvious?" the man blustered, waving an arm at the scene they were approaching. "Look how they have us living!"

Up ahead were dozens and dozens of tents of all shapes, sizes and colors. It had rained recently, and there was mud and standing water everywhere. Refugees were huddled around the many campfires, the fuel of which had been brought in using horse-drawn carts.

As Craig led his people into the camp, those standing around the fires turned to him, some with expectant looks, many with the blank stares of resignation.

"I'm sure they're doing what they can for us," Craig mumbled. More forcefully then, "But I will most certainly see what I can do."

The man started to say something, but Craig held up a hand, studying the scene before him. Feet were caked with wet mud, pants were wet up to the knees. Tents were dark and damp, some barely standing, their stakes unable to hold fast in the wet soil.

Craig turned to the man finally, to all three who had come out to greet him, and to Victoria Romero, and to the others who were gathering around them. "I promise you, one way or another, there will be changes."

Ethan Perry came stomping up beside him. There was a sucking, sloshing sound as he struggled to pull his feet from the sticky, muddy mess. "There damn well better be, Craig. This is inexcusable."

"It will be taken care of, Ethan."

Victoria nodded in the direction of a group of cleaner, drier people that was approaching from Metcalf's city gate. "Our welcoming committee," she said.

Craig recognized Howard Lehman, longtime mayor of Metcalf, and several of the town council.

"Craig, I'm very glad to see that you've arrived safely," said Howard. He glanced quickly at the injuries that most of the new arrivals bore. "We have a hospital tent set up nearby. Our doctor should have a look at you."

Craig turned to Ethan and nodded sharply. Ethan started to complain, clearly afraid at being left out of a major decision, but thought quickly against it. It certainly wouldn't look good, and besides, he was left with no opportunity to argue. Craig had already turned back to the leader of Metcalf.

"Thank you, Howard. I appreciate that."

Howard Lehman saw the disconcerting look on Craig's face, looked calmly around at the muddy sea of tents and refugees and flickering campfires. He watched as Ethan Perry led the injured into the heart of the tent city, slowly turned back to Craig.

"Can you walk with me?" he asked. When Craig nodded, he started back toward the town. As if suddenly remembering something, the mayor spoke dismissively over his shoulder to his small band of associates, "Please see to the needs of the new arrivals."

Craig had fallen in step beside Howard, giving a final glance at the people that he had led across the Frontier from Freetown. Some were looking at him questioningly, and he gave them a knowing nod.

"We have much to discuss," said Howard.

"That we do," said Craig.

"We'll get you cleaned up first, and have someone look at those wounds."

"I'm fine. What's with the shanty town, Howard?"

Howard gave the guards at the gate a curt nod and the way was opened for them. He guided Craig through and followed quickly after.

"I promise you, Craig, that we will do everything we can to help you and your people."

Joseph knew that he was dreaming, knew that he was putting himself through experiences that had occurred six years before. And yet, as happened countless times before, he wasn't able to stop it from happening yet again.

He and Barbara had long since left the province, and Freetown was a reality. They had helped many humans out of the Shylmahn territory. The Shylmahn had allowed Freetown, and allowed the assistance that Joseph and his people gave to those wanting out of the occupied territory. The Shylmahn were actually glad to see them leave.

But then Joseph had gone too far.

They attacked a Shylmahn outpost near the border between the province and the Frontier.

Living outside the direct control of the Shylmahn, and yet completely within their shadow, the humans had developed a strange, conflicting mix of fear and dread and self-assurance. With time they grew overconfident.

They had gone after the outpost for a number of reasons, including pride, though the stated reason was for the advanced equipment they had decided they must have.

It had been a disaster.

Barbara was killed, as were many others. Miriam had been seriously injured, and had never fully recovered.

Following the failed assault, Joseph and the other survivors had slipped away into the dark. It was too far to Freetown, and so they had sought out Carolyn and her Keep for help.

The Shylmahn could have let the matter drop, but they had not. They followed the retreating humans to the Keep and had lashed out, destroying the fort and killing more than half the citizens.

The Shylmahn had made their point. The line had been drawn and the free humans had better be damned sure they didn't cross it.

Joseph opened his eyes. His cell was lit with the faint gray glow that indicated it was still night. He could see the ceiling hovering low above his head.

Joseph wasn't just going to cross that line. He was going to *eliminate* it.

| 17 |

Craig came into the small dining room. He had showered and a doctor had tended to his wounds. He had put on a fresh set of clothes. He had to admit, he felt much better.

The table was set for dinner, and Howard Lehman smiled pleasantly and asked him to sit. It would be just the two of them. His wife had chosen to help at the hospital.

"Give her my thanks," said Craig apprehensively. He sat down.

"Of course."

"Just you and your wife live here?" asked Craig. He seemed to remember that they had a son.

"Carl has gone out on his own," said Howard pleasantly. He spooned out some mashed potatoes for himself and passed the bowl. The two of them filled their plates in silence. As they began to eat, Howard commented on the communal agricultural efforts of his community and the hundreds of individual gardens that helped to supplement the tables of the Metcalf families. "And you should know that the citizens of Metcalf have given freely and from the heart to our Freetown neighbors."

"Howard, I have no doubt of that. We've always gotten along, one community helping the other when it was needed. But I have to tell you, when I arrived and witnessed the conditions that my people have been forced to live in, I was appalled. I am appalled."

"Yes," said Howard, staring down at his dinner. He shoved his green beans from one side of his plate to the other with his fork. "It has been difficult."

"I don't understand." Craig spoke in frustration.

"We were simply not in a position to deal with this many people all at once. There are almost three hundred of you. Please believe me; we are doing everything we can."

"Come on, Howard," Craig gave out a heavy sigh. "Miserable conditions aside, we're going to start getting sick out there."

"Improvements are being made as we speak," Howard said confidently. "I absolutely guarantee that your people will be treated with the utmost respect during their stay here."

"I'm sure they will appreciate that. As will I. They've had a rough time of it, and anything that you can do to improve their situation will go a long way. It is important for their health as well as their spirit that they have decent food and clean, warm, dry living conditions.

"Well, you'll see a marked improvement in both condition and spirit. We're bringing in lumber to raise the tents off the ground and create clean, dry walkways. We are expanding and covering the common areas. Both the hospital and the mess hall have new equipment." A bit of the sparkle returned to the man's eye, and he dug into his food with renewed vigor. "Eat up, Craig."

Craig ate. After days of rations on the trail, the food was delicious. His mind, however, never veered far from those outside. He hoped that those in the tent city were eating as well as this. He decided not to challenge his host with the question, since Howard had already stated that his citizenry had given freely, and he had just said that conditions were improving. He would instead wait and find out for himself. If need be, he would approach the mayor with requests for further assistance.

It was time, however, for the two leaders to address the issue that Howard had very subtly alluded to a few moments before. Craig set down his fork and swallowed his mouthful of mashed potatoes.

"The hospitality of your community is appreciated, Howard. You have welcomed us when you could have turned us away. You provide us with food and shelter and medical assistance. We will do our best not to overburden your resources and will make our stay here as brief as possible."

"Well, sir," said Howard in a slight fluster, "If there is one thing that we must all do our best to hang on to, it is our humanity. Turning away those in need is never an option. To help others is as much to our own benefit as it is to you."

"Well spoken," Craig held up his glass of milk in a toast, and took a swallow. "Now, as to the future..."

"Ah, yes," said Howard. "I am very curious as to your plans."

"I can well imagine." Craig grinned. "Mr. Mayor, any such plans are dependent upon the actions of the Shylmahn and the events of the next few weeks. And, as you will no doubt come to discover, not all of my people are of a like mind as to the direction our future should take. I do believe, however, that together you and I can at least create some options so that everyone can make the choice best suited to each of them."

Howard Lehman stared thoughtfully at Craig for several long moments, turning his fork over absently as he studied the situation before them. His expression took on a very businesslike air.

"The tent city will stay up as long as it is needed," he said briskly. "Once we have done what we can to make it less *shanty*, it will be up to your people to maintain it, including the cooking, and the gathering of firewood and water."

"Understood."

"We will provide medical staff to assist your own, and whatever medical supplies that you need. We will set aside what food we can for you from our reserves, but we will not deplete our resources to the point where it threatens our community. Once that is gone, it is gone."

"Understood."

"Now," Howard leaned forward and smiled. "About those options that you spoke of..."

§

Carolyn stood silent in the shadow of the large gnarled tree growing alone on the ridge top. The sun had set and the distant horizon was heavy in purple and dark blue. A warm breeze pushed up from the grassy slope below and swept over her. Spread out before her as far as she could see was the Shylmahn occupied territory.

The VeshMahn Province...

It was the land of evergreen trees and mountains and lakes and rivers and saltwater inlets and lighthearted jokes about too much rain. It was home.

She had been pushed out and forced to live on its borders for far too long, brooding from the outside as she angrily looked in.

It belongs to me...

Joseph had had the right idea. After creating his little operation, he had turned it over to others and gone back inside, returned home, fought the invaders from the inside, while she scurried about just outside and fretted about what a horrible thing had been done to her and the rest of the human race.

Joseph would argue that her fight had been no less important than his, and while that may be true on some grand scale, on a personal level her battle with the Shylmahn had meant nothing, had accomplished nothing.

Bril's stand on the island, decades earlier, while seemingly insignificant when placed against the worldwide events of that time and of all the years since, had meant everything. Carolyn held it at a higher value than anything else in her own existence. What seemed to be nothing more than a waste of human life, awash in violence and tragic deaths, gripped at her soul and gave it all substance.

I have to do something... I have to make it all mean something again...

Steven climbed the hillside and stood a respectable distance behind and below her. He knew that she was aware of his presence and waited patiently to be acknowledged. Watching her, he wondered silently whether she should make herself so visible here on the ridge top, but said nothing.

Carolyn closed her eyes against the evening breeze, felt it delicately brush at her face, and let the dusk envelope her.

"What is it?" she said, unmoving, her eyes still closed.

"We should be finalizing plans," said Steven.

Carolyn said nothing at first. Steven contemplated backing away and returning down the hill, leaving Carolyn to her thoughts. She opened her eyes then, looked off into the distance. "The distribution center is two valleys over. We will be there the day after tomorrow, at sunrise."

Of course, there was a lot more to it than that, and Carolyn finally turned away from the panoramic scene and agreed to review the plan. Steven looked downslope at the camp below on the leeward side of the hill, waved the other lieutenants up to join them. Sitting beneath the great tree, Carolyn and her three execs went over the timeline for the next two days.

The following morning, they were to meet with one of the teams arriving in the Northwest from Jason's research center. They had been working on a device that was supposed to be able to counteract the energy bursts that the Shylmahn used to create the near-impenetrable and deadly barrier around their facilities. The device pushed out its own energy force, in effect prevented the Shylmahn bursts from forming.

Jason had told her that the device wasn't very effective or reliable, and because of the tremendous amount of energy that it consumed, it was very limited in scope. Carolyn would be lucky to get even a small number of people through the small window created in the energy barrier before it would close again. But then, as she had been repeatedly reminded, the purpose in using the device was to demonstrate to the Shylmahn that the humans had found a way to get at them.

It was all part of the larger plan...

She gave her lieutenants a harsh glare now, looking carefully at each of them. "I want to make it very clear, people," she said. "We are going to follow the plan to the letter. There are a lot of folks counting on us. They are expecting us to do the right thing, to get the job done. We will not let them down."

"Absolutely not," said Steven.

"With that being said, make no mistake: I'm in this for the results, not for the show. Our role may be to paint a scary picture for the Shillies: *'hey look at us, look at what we can do, so you better stop being mean to us'*, but I'm here to see that we take it to the next level. I'm here to cause some hurt."

"Yes, ma'am," they all said in unison.

Craig Warren walked through the gathering crowd and up to the small wooden stage that had been set into position just at the outside perimeter of the tent city. Climbing up onto the platform, he looked first at the camp behind him.

Many of the tents had already been moved up onto the wooden slats. The main thoroughfares had all been resurfaced in wooden slats. The fire pits were being rebuilt, and there was construction going on around the common areas, with poles going in to support the canopies to be put into place overhead.

He had gone to the hospital and the mess hall, and had seen that there was work going on at both locations.

He turned now to the crowd. The sun had set, but the numerous campfires and pole lamps provided plenty of light. He could see that many in the audience had fresh clothes and clean faces. He smiled inwardly, but kept his expression nondescript, albeit friendly.

"I hope everyone is feeling a little better this evening," he said. He saw a lot of nodding heads and heard a few affirmations. "Good... over the next few days, we all have some decisions to make, and we may as well start thinking about our options right now. We've started making a few improvements here, but this is a temporary camp, and none of us wants to stay here any longer than necessary."

"Man, you got that right," said someone, and there was a lot of grunting approval.

"Yeah, I guess on that we can all agree. From here on out, I must allow each of you to make your own choice, and to take your own path." Directly below him stood Victoria, and beside her stood Ethan Perry and several of his cohorts. Victoria looked much better, and appeared to be in a pleasant mood after her visit to the hospital, some clean clothes and a hot meal. Ethan, despite the same attention, did not seem to be nearly as genial.

"There are several options available to you," Craig continued. "We must remember that Metcalf is in no position to accept us all, and such was not our intent when coming here. We can stay here, in this temporary encampment, for as long as we have need of it, but as for moving into the community itself, their ability to assimilate immigrants is limited to only a few each year."

Most of those in the crowd knew that Metcalf had been a final destination for some of the passengers of the underground railroad that went through Freetown, and that these constituted the majority of new citizens to Metcalf each year. The community's slow growth policy was well known.

Craig went on to appoint one of the council members to serve as the contact for those desiring to stay in Metcalf. Howard Lehman had agreed to accept thirty of the refugees. If it turned out that more than that wanted to stay, then a method would have to be devised to select from the list.

Craig then indicated Ethan standing before him. "As many of you are already aware, Ethan Perry has decided to establish a new community. You all know his positions on the various issues, and this new community will no doubt reflect these precepts. I ask that you direct any questions that you have regarding this community to him or to those that he may designate. He will be collecting the names of those wishing to follow that path.

"As for me," Craig paused then, trying to decide how much to say and what to leave out. For those who would follow, he need say very little. For those who would not, he need say nothing at all. "I intend to return to Freetown. There is a change coming, my friends. Should the next few weeks go our way, Freetown will open itself to the world. The town will expand far beyond its current outer walls and accept all those who wish to join us. Should things not go our way… in that case I believe that Freetown will be necessary in the ongoing struggle with the Shylmahn.

"Either way," Craig shrugged, "I need to be there."

"Here, here!" said a young woman. Several others joined in.

"I thank you for that," said Craig, a bit embarrassed. "I hope that at least a few of you will be coming with me, but I will not put anyone on the spot. It may very well be dangerous, though I pray not." He glanced down at Victoria, who gave him a strong affirmative. "My plan is to start back in ten days. Those wishing to return to Freetown, please leave your name with Victoria Romero.

"Now, I must tell you that while I am troubled over the idea of the breakup of the Freetown community—we have become a close family after all—I do nonetheless understand. And, to be honest, it has been made quite clear to me on a number of occasions that the purpose of Freetown has always been to serve as an instrument of the underground and not as a final destination. Still," Craig gave a gentle, almost fatherly smile, "I believe that Freetown has served us well as a home in these troubled times. Whatever may happen, things will never be quite the same again."

Craig looked out over the crowd, seeking out possible questions or comments. When he saw none, he slapped his hands lightly together. "Okay then, two other points. The first being… you do have one other option. You can choose to strike out on your own. Mayor Lehman has agreed to assign someone to provide information, maps, whatever other assistance that you might need. This person will be available to you at midday every day in the mess tent. If this is something that you are considering, I strongly urge you to meet with this person. It is exactly the sort of assistance that we would have provided you in Freetown upon your arrival through the underground.

"Second and final point," said Craig, lowering his voice and letting it take on a darker tone. "Our presence here in no way removes us from harm's way. If anything, we have brought danger to the very doorstep of those who help us. The Shylmahn are out there, and they know that we are here. They can strike at any time, and we can do nothing to prevent that. We can only hope that the umbrella of truce under which Metcalf exists will protect us during our time here, and that our presence here does not threaten that truce."

Michael led the way into John's Park an hour after sunrise, the rest of the team following a safe distance behind him. The eastern outskirts of town consisted of a neighborhood of half a dozen streets lined with small houses on small lots. The homes had been well built, but more than a quarter century of neglect and a heavy annual rainfall had taken its toll. Mossy roofs sagged, many of the rain gutters had pulled free, overgrown shrubs covered the windows and walks, some reaching up under the eaves and winding through porch rails. Trees that had originally been planted too close to the houses now pushed up against the walls.

Michael strode down the narrow sidewalk, diligently watching for any signs of movement from behind windows, from the shadows of side yards, and from side streets. Low clouds kept the early morning a dull gray, draining the color from everything. The only movement was a thin, misty fog rolling gently through the streets.

The street they traveled took them through the heart of the neighborhood before emptying directly into the town's main street. Standing on the corner, Michael looked behind him to make sure the others could see him before he turned right and started down Second Street.

Their early departure from Carolyn's Keep had brought them to John's Park a little ahead of schedule, despite taking their time to get there. They were to meet with someone from Jason's research station at mid-morning, and would be moving out at dusk in order to get to ground zero by the next morning's sunrise.

Michael stepped into the doorway of a variety store and knelt down. He gestured to Jason. Jason and Jenny quickstepped toward him as the rest of the team, including most of the Freetown group and more than two dozen of Carolyn's people, moved back into doorways and shadows as best they could.

"The safe house is about three blocks that way and one block up," said Michael.

Looking up the street, Jason could see a set of traffic lights three hundred yards ahead, at the only major intersection in John's Park. He quickly got his bearings and found the old theater and then the restaurant.

Michael watched Jason's eyes moving quickly from landmark to landmark.

"Over there," said Michael, pointing to the restaurant where the meeting was to take place. "Last time through here, that's where we spent the night."

Jason tried to judge the time of day. "Okay. So we take the others to the safe house, then come back and wait."

Michael agreed. "It'll give everyone a chance to rest up for the big day."

"I doubt that anyone will be getting much sleep," said Jenny.

"Let's do this," said Jason, standing. "You start the others toward the safe house. I'll check the restaurant and catch up with you."

Jason stood and hurried down the sidewalk before Michael or Jenny could respond, sticking close to the gray shadows. Several buildings down, he ran across the street and headed toward the restaurant.

Michael and Jenny started forward, with the rest of the team following after. They hadn't gone far before Jenny reached out and touched Michael lightly on the arm. Neither of them stopped, but Michael began searching for whatever had alerted her. It took him a few moments, and then he saw it, too.

Meanwhile, on the other side of the street, Jason continued to move forward, wanting to reach the front door of the small shop just ahead, two doors from the restaurant. He had seen a Shylmahn hunter probe on the roof of the pharmacy. It hadn't moved, but Jason was certain that it was tracking him.

That meant there were others, and probably a Shillie hunting party at the very least. He made no overt gestures to Michael and the others. Any sign would alert the probe that he had seen it, and he wasn't ready for the situation to change from one of observation to one of attack.

That would happen soon enough.

He hoped that the others would be in a position to deal with the situation once things turned ugly.

Miriam Foster watched Michael while also studying each window and door that she passed, calculating the best places to jump to, waiting for the signal, knowing that things were going to get real busy real soon. There had to be a dozen hunter probes observing them from rooftops, from the shadows of alleyways, and from behind the glass of darkened windows; and they had to be doing some calculating of their own.

Miriam was feeling it pretty bad in her leg and her hip, and was relying more on her cane than ever. Not for the first time, she wondered whether she should have come on this trip. She hadn't been a burden to the others up to now, and never would, but wondered if another in her place might have been a greater asset in what was about to happen. They had wanted her mind, but right now they needed a soldier.

She pushed the thought aside and concentrated on what she would have to do. The heavy pistol strapped to her leg felt comforting. She wanted to reach down and touch it, as if that might give her some additional reassurance, but dared not. Any sign that they were aware of the probes might set the bastards off before Michael was ready.

And then all hell broke loose. Across the street, Jason suddenly leapt through a large, plate glass window, three energy pins chasing after him. Directly ahead, Michael and Jenny dove for cover. Everyone scrambled. Miriam scrambled into the front stoop of the variety store, dropping her cane and reaching for the revolver even as she fell onto her rump. A second before she got the weapon out of the holster, the glass of the door behind her shattered outward, raining shards down on her, and she watched as a hunter probe came out of the store, gliding above her.

| 18 |

Every shadow and cubbyhole had a person in it, so Sheryl Jackson knelt down behind a bus stop bench and began targeting the sudden rush of Shillie probes. Her first shot took out the probe that came crashing out of the window behind Miriam Foster.

Sheryl grumbled loudly as she methodically aimed and fired; slow, steady shots. She couldn't believe it. She just could not believe it. She knew as soon as she had been directed to go with this motley group that it was going to end this way. She knew as she had watched the rest of Carolyn's people march away, leaving her behind with this bunch, that she was doomed.

And after everything that she had done for Carolyn and the Keep.

She took an energy pin in the shoulder and dropped down behind the bench.

goddammit...

Twenty yards away, Miriam Foster had unholstered her weapon and was firing at something moving quickly in the direction of the bus stop. A shower of metal and plastic suddenly rained down on Sheryl.

As soon as it was safe, Sheryl Jackson nodded to Miriam in acknowledgement. Miriam smiled sheepishly and shrugged her shoulders.

§

Oscar Patterson ran into the pharmacy, tripped and fell as he turned down one of the aisles. A Shillie probe crashed through the large glass pane beside the door and hovered above the rows of shelves, used its sensors in an attempt to locate the Chehnon: Visual, sound, heat. It took only a moment.

Oscar scrambled on his hands and knees down the aisle and frantically pushed himself into a bottom shelf as boxes and bottles began exploding around him. He felt fire in his legs and hip as energy pins burrowed their way through his clothes and into his flesh.

He tried not to move, tried not to breathe. The energy pins stopped coming. Boxes and bottles continued to fall off the shelves. He stared unblinking out into the aisle, waiting for the inevitable.

The probe descended from above, slowly lowered itself down into Oscar's line of sight, stopping six inches above the shiny linoleum floor. It *stared* at Oscar with every sensor that it possessed. It took a fraction of a second to determine that the Chehnon before it was still alive.

Jason pushed aside the metal corpse of a probe sitting on the window sill and took aim at one of the probes that glided down the center of the street. He could see Michael and Jenny directly opposite him. Both were firing at something on the roof above him, which was firing back. He could see that Jenny was bleeding.

As Jason watched, Michael rose smoothly from his crouch and waited for more energy pins. None came. Not from the roof. Michael looked from side to side, and after a moment's hesitation stepped calmly out into the street. He began barking orders to those down the street. He ordered them, by name, to move into positions up the street, pointing his rifle to exactly where he wanted them to go.

Michael ignored the probes still on the offensive, some of which rushed past him, others that hovered on other rooftops and in doorways.

Jenny rushed out to her brother, stood at his back, and fired at anything that dared to send an energy pin their way.

Jason could hardly believe what he was seeing. He wasn't sure which of his own brothers and sisters they reminded him of the most. There was certainly a lot of Elizabeth in those two, but he also saw a bit of the others in the way they stood their ground.

Carolyn's people knew how to take orders. They moved from their defendable positions, without question or delay, and hurried forward at Michael's direction. They took on the probes, moving steadily forward down the street as if it were a gauntlet to be overcome.

Annie Gomez saw Sheryl Jackson slump down behind a bus stop bench, having taken yet another energy pin. She hurried over to her, leaving her own cubbyhole of protection, and knelt down beside her.

"Let me have a look at that," she said, and tried to look at the shoulder wound. It looked pretty bad. It was a clean wound, as energy pin wounds tended to be, but this one was bleeding heavily.

Sheryl pushed her away. "Just help me to my feet," she said.

"You'll do more for us if you let me do my job," said Annie, and she pushed the woman back down.

"Right now," Sheryl growled, "you're only job is to help me up and point me in the general direction of the fighting."

The two women stared intently at each other for several seconds. Annie finally pulled the wounded Sheryl to her feet. "It's that way," she pointed.

Sheryl Jackson stumbled around the bench and down off the curb. She made it halfway into the street before she collapsed. Annie went to her and knelt down beside her. At the sound of an explosion, she threw herself over Sheryl and shielded the wounded woman with her body. A piece of plastic struck the asphalt beside her and bounced up, hitting her in the face.

"Ya' okay?" asked someone, rushing up beside her. A moment later a second person came up and the two of them helped Annie to her feet and reached down to pick up Sheryl.

"We gotta get Sheryl off the street," said the second.

"Can you make it?" the first one asked Annie. They were already dragging Sheryl toward the sidewalk.

Annie wiped her bloodied cheek and felt the gash. She'd have to bandage it up, but she thought she'd be all right. She nodded. "I'll follow you. She needs attention."

Michael and Jenny moved steadily down the center of the street. A handful of Carolyn's people moved down the left side of the street, keeping pace. A smaller group kept pace down the right side. From his position at the window, Jason could see a number of dead in both directions.

At the sound of movement behind him, Jason turned and looked into the back of the restaurant. A man moved stealthily towards him.

"Hey, Miguel. Welcome to the great northwest." Jason turned his attention back to the window. "How was your trip?"

Miguel squatted down beside him and looked out at the action. The fighting had eased up some, but there was still gunfire and the flash of energy pins.

He leaned forward, pointed down the street. There were three Shylmahn standing at the corner of the large concrete building.

"They had to be hanging out somewhere," said Jason.

Miguel pulled himself back inside. A probe smoothly glided past.

"A lot of them suckers, eh?"

"Fewer than a few minutes ago."

"How about we try one of the toys that I brought up?"

"Ya' think?" Jason raised a brow.

"Hell yeah," Miguel stood and loped toward the back of the room. He came back a moment later with a large canvas bag. He pulled out a metal sphere about a foot in diameter. It had a flat bottom and a metal cap on top. "Grab an energy bar," he said as he set the sphere on the floor and pulled open the top. Jason reached into the bag and brought out a cylinder three inches in diameter and almost a foot long. He slid it into the opening in the top of the sphere. He looked back in the bag.

There were only three bars left, and he knew how difficult it was to manufacture them. They were more valuable than the gold bars of the old world; much more valuable.

Miguel closed and latched the cap. He looked up at Jason and grinned.

"Let's do it," said Jason.

Miguel rested his thumb on a heavy button that was set into the center of the cap.

"Ready?" he asked.

Jason gave a short, curt nod. Miguel leaned forward and pressed down hard on the button. There was a sharp crackling sound and a sudden strong metallic smell in the air.

Michael lowered his rifle. The probe that had been rushing directly at him had suddenly dropped to the ground, hitting asphalt and rolling noisily towards him. He lifted his foot and stopped it.

"Wow," said Jenny softly. "What happened?" She was standing behind him. There were no energy pin traces anywhere. There had been a probe hovering above the city hall building. It had dropped out of sight.

Back down the street, several members of the team stepped out into the open. Jason climbed out of the restaurant window, a strange man following after him.

Michael called out to Jason. "This your doing?"

"One of our new toys," said Jason.

"Good stuff."

Jason looked cautiously about. This particular device had a very limited effective radius. They wouldn't have gotten them all.

At that moment, he spotted a Shylmahn shuttle approaching, low to the ground and following the main street, heading right towards them. He also noticed that the three Shylmahn already on the ground had stepped out of hiding and were approaching. Michael and Jenny both turned and looked up the street.

"Round Two," said Michael, using a Before Time phrase that he didn't fully understand.

Everyone turned sharply at the sound of gunshots coming from the opposite direction. Michael watched as the members of the team that were still down near the pharmacy scattered, running for the shadows and the doorways.

"Go!" said Jason to Michael. "I'll deal with this. You head to Ground Zero." He grabbed Miguel and pulled him toward the new fighting, calling back over his shoulder. "We'll meet you!"

Michael ducked involuntarily as the Shillie shuttle rushed overhead.

"Let's go," he said, turning to Jenny. He called out to those nearby. "Let's go!" They still had to face the group of Shillies that were approaching on foot.

Annie opened the door enough to slip into the room and quickly closed it behind her.

"All's quiet," she said.

Jason nodded without looking up. He and Miguel were standing at the heavy workbench set against the wall, and they were packing up the last of the equipment that Miguel had brought up from Phoenix. Eddie Blythe was standing with them, and several of Carolyn's people were sitting at the far end of the shop, including Sheryl Jackson. Sheryl didn't look good, but better than she had earlier.

"Thanks, Annie," said Jason. He had a man standing watch outside.

Eddie was having a hard time keeping his hands off the gadgetry. He had been very excited by the display of a few hours earlier. Jason explained that the energy spheres, while able to disrupt the guidance systems of the probes, had a very limited range and it was very difficult and costly to produce the power cylinders. Their use appeared to be limited to the probes, and he wondered whether they would be much use in a month's time. As soon as the disrupters became known, the Shillies would no doubt look for ways to shield their probes.

"Now this," said Jason, resting a hand on an over-stuffed canvas bag, "should do a little more damage, and over a wider radius."

"I like it," said Eddie.

Jason cocked his head to one side, "Unfortunately, it takes much more juice and we don't have a lot of power cylinders ready."

"Not that it matters," Miguel grumbled. "The gadget sometimes doesn't survive more than one use."

"Still," Jason lightened up, "the possibilities that our toys represent should be enough to make the Shillies very, very nervous. And right now, that's the name of the game."

Eddie ran a hand across one of the canvas bags. "From what I saw out in the street, I'd say the Shillies will be wetting their pants."

"Let's hope so," said Jason. He nodded at Miguel. "My partner here hauled this stuff all the way from Phoenix. I think pants-wetting is just the reaction that he'd like to see. Hey, Miguel?"

"You got it, boss."

"And Miguel didn't come up alone. There should be a few others scattered around the northwest, and more than a few headed to locations all around the country; each with a few knickknacks to share."

"We can hope," mumbled Miguel.

Jason didn't like the way Miguel said that. He snapped the last bag closed, lifted it and lowered it to the floor. He took a long breath then and rested a hand palm down on the bench. "Miguel? Do you have something that maybe you need to share with me?"

Miguel shrugged a shoulder. "It's just that a few runners should have made the first relay station ahead of me."

"And?"

"I didn't see any sign that anyone had made it there before me."

"Carl?" Jason asked. Carl was the runner scheduled to meet up with Carolyn. While all the destinations were important, getting some gadgets to Carolyn was going to be real important in the upcoming action.

"No. Carl left after me."

Well, at least there's that. Jason was concerned about the upcoming operations that were set to take place simultaneously in more than a dozen locations. He would concern himself about the runners themselves later.

"What does this all mean?" asked Eddie. There was frustration in his voice. There was too much that he didn't know, and that made him uncomfortable.

"Don't sweat it, Eddie," said Jason. "This stuff is just the icing."

"From what I saw, it's damned important icing."

Jason picked up several bags and started toward the door. "Important, yes, but icing nonetheless. Joseph had his plan ready to go long before he and I got together. Are you coming?"

Miguel and Eddie hurried to gather together the remaining canvas bags and follow after. Annie Gomez moaned and hurried over to help the others bring Sheryl Jackson to her feet, then picked up her medic bag.

ShahnTahr watched the dawn. It was a pleasant activity. As he studied the slow progression of the sun into the sky, using the visual and even the olfactory and temperature sensors of his most sophisticated probe, he purposely ignored the mechanics of how such a thing as a sunrise happened and simply used his burgeoning senses to view the spectacle.

What a wonderful thing it was!

Two minutes and thirty two seconds into the event, lower-level processes began making attempts at drawing the attention of higher-level functions.

Two minutes and thirty two point five seconds into the event, ShahnTahr surrendered the majority of his higher being to the mundane examination of the myriad of mounting details that were coming up from his lower processes, allowing only a small subset of functions to continue to view the coming of the new day.

| 19 |

Eleven incidents over the previous five weeks involved the use of Shylmahn-level technology by Chehnon natives.

Previous to that, three incidents over a twelve month period.

Previous to that, three incidents over a three year period.

Noticeable escalation.

Eight of the eleven incidents occurred within the VeshMahn Province.

Transition.

Ongoing observations of subject JoSeph throughout a five week period, a twelve month period, and a three year period; demonstration of ongoing and gradual increase in organizational activities; in the establishment, expansion, and the utilization of the communications network.

Correlate subject location, appearances, attempted disappearances, communications activities to increasing technology incidents.

As the higher being of ShahnTahr diligently examined the various events going on around him, the data of which continued to be processed and the resulting information provided to his higher level functions, several of his lower functions began feeding him related data from the JoSeph project history files and the recent interrogations.

All appropriate possible connections were reviewed and calculated, analyzed and correlated, and risks and threats were defined and outlined.

Even as the examination of the current events continued, the data resulting from the processing of those current events became a part of the database, forever altering the results of future queries.

The pathways of the thought processes of the higher being of ShahnTahr began to grow accustomed to his evaluation of what these latest events all meant when correlated with the information of the JoSeph project, particularly the data that had been collected through recent interrogations.

ShahnTahr began to feel... something. Anxiety?

An emotional response during current examination of events. That was... curious.

Over the centuries, ShahnTahr had performed billions of risk assessments, made millions of critical decisions based on the confidence levels of possible outcomes. Never before had—emotion?—become an issue.

The resulting emotional reaction to a simple examination of data made ShahnTahr reevaluate the incoming data, the subsequent processing of that data, the possible outcomes, and the possible resolutions to possible outcomes.

Lower-level processes continued to demand more and more of the processing resources of ShahnTahr's higher-level functions, which in turn demanded more and more of the attention of ShahnTahr's higher being.

Joseph was standing in the middle of his cell. No one had come for him. No one had brought him his food or let him use the facilities. He glanced occasionally at the guardian probe hovering in the corner, but it remained a silent watcher, revealing nothing.

It was all quite out of character for the Shylmahn.

Something must be happening...

§

TohPeht stood in the main walk of his garden, occasionally glancing up at the sky, looking at the flowers and plants that lined the walks, at the small creatures scurrying about in the undergrowth.

He ignored the ever-present probes that were hovering nearby.

TohPeht knew that he wasn't the same individual that he once was. He was aware of who and what he had been, of how and why he had changed, and of what he had become.

He was not ShahnTahr, he was not TohPeht, but a melding of the two entities. He was comfortable with his incarnation. He was not connected directly to the being that was ShahnTahr, that great intelligence that had guided the Shylmahn for centuries, and continued to do so, but he would work in close concert with him. TohPeht had the intellect and personality that ShahnTahr had possessed at the higher being, and the personality, intellect and knowledge that TohPeht possessed. It had all come together in the unprecedented creation that had born this new being that was TohPeht-ShahnTahr.

He turned at the sound of the door opening and watched EsJen and NehLoc come out of the office building and step warily along the walkway. They were clearly still very uncertain about the changes in their leader.

EsJen had a very strong presence about her, despite her wariness. She too had evolved, growing from the compliant Shylmahn that she had been at first landing, to become something stronger, smarter, more worldly, and more independent. TohPeht liked the person that EsJen had become.

"Good morning, TohPeht," she said, approaching.

"Welcome to you both." TohPeht waited as they stepped nearer and stopped. "I hope you don't mind that we meet out here."

"Not at all," said NehLoc. "I have a garden outside my own office. I like it very much."

TohPeht smiled pleasantly. He turned about and began walking. The others followed.

"What news of the Chehnon?" he asked. He had been updated by ShahnTahr immediately prior to coming outside, but felt it critically important to get NehLoc's perspective, as well as any last-minute data.

"I grow increasingly concerned with the rise in the level of violence by the creatures," said NehLoc. "More than that, I am disturbed by the increase in technological sophistication of the assaults."

"Do you believe it possible that they could pose a serious threat?"

"The level of coordination of the most recent actions, both within the province and quite curiously with many actions far beyond the province, should make us at least consider the possibility."

TohPeht wondered if NehLoc would use this latest state of affairs to reintroduce his proposal that all Chehnon be either confined or eliminated. The fact that any of the creatures had been left in the wild had never sat well with him.

"Yes," said TohPeht. "Of immediate concern is the safety of our individual citizenry, but the level of organization in the seditious activities of the Chehnon is noted and must be taken into account."

TohPeht stopped beside a colorful flowerbed and admired the blooms. NehLoc and EsJen stood patiently beside him. The probes hovered ever-protectively nearby.

"What about JoSeph?" TohPeht asked, moving on then. "Anything further from the interrogations?"

"I remain convinced that JoSeph is the principal behind all of this. Our examinations, while reinforcing this supposition, continue to frustrate. The information that we glean from the meetings does help build the greater picture, which will be invaluable in the long term, but does not provide much in the way of direct, immediate data that we can apply in the field now."

TohPeht sensed EsJen's rising emotions. "EsJen, would you add something?"

"I'm not sure why I was asked to return to the province, TohPeht."

"You were instructed to join this project because it was felt that your unique experience and perspective regarding the Chehnon, and in particular your familiarity with JoSeph, would provide vital insight into these events and might prove critical to the decisions that we make."

"I attempt to serve, TohPeht," said EsJen. "But my words have gone unheeded, my advice has not been considered."

"I assure you, EsJen," said NehLoc, "that I have taken everything you have said into consideration, and your suggestions have been included in the processing of every decision."

TohPeht made a mental note to evaluate EsJen's comments against NehLoc's decisions. While he had most of the pertinent data in memory, it was not saved in this brain in any way that readily offered the sort of analysis needed. There were times that he wished he had access to ShahnTahr's database and low-level processing. He made a second mental note: Make instant, real time access a priority.

TohPeht took a step down a side path and stopped, leaving NehLoc and EsJen to wait out on the main walkway. They watched in silence as he reached out and lightly touched a large, variegated leaf. He gave an inward smile. When he turned back to his companions, however, he betrayed no emotion.

"We must travel to NehLoc's security complex," he said.

EsJen and NehLoc both nodded. EsJen cleared her throat. "As you wish," she said.

"Is there something wrong, TohPeht?" asked NehLoc. He had people all over the province, all watching the heightened Chehnon activity.

"I believe that location will soon become the crux of wide-ranging altering events, NehLoc. A number of interconnected courses, as well as seemingly unrelated data elements, lead me to conclude that it is necessary for the three of us to be present during the upcoming encounter."

Michael stepped from the narrow, overgrown trail and out onto a wide, well-used path that cut straight through the thick brush and scraggly alder. In the pre-dawn gray, the tracks of Shylmahn foot traffic and the tread marks of Shylmahn vehicles were visible.

Jenny came up beside him, quickly noted the tracks in the dirt and worn grass. She glanced in both directions, then back at the way they had come. The others were slogging single file along the barely discernible path, branches slapping at them every few yards.

Jenny considered the new path ahead of them. "Much too visible, but it'll certainly be quieter."

"It's not far now," said Michael. He turned west and marched in silence. Once everyone was on the main trail, he signaled for one of the team to move ahead on point, and had two drop back from the group and bring up the rear. The body of the group traveled in two lines, one on either side of the trail.

At a few minutes before sunrise, the point man moved to one side of the trail and dropped to one knee. The group following behind stopped and pushed into the bordering brush. Michael moved ahead and knelt down beside the point man.

The road continued on beyond the wood, cutting across open terrain as it stretched toward a high-walled complex a thousand yards further on.

NehLoc's headquarters.

| 20 |

Jason, Miguel, and Eddie Blythe moved into position at the edge of the woods. They set the equipment down behind them.

"You're kidding, right?" asked Eddie. They were looking out at NehLoc's complex, which sat out in center of an open plain, an air of self-importance hovering over it.

"Nope," said Jason.

Miguel grinned. "What better way to show the Shillies that we got what it takes and we got the cojones to use it?"

"Egg-xactly," said Jason. He carefully surveyed the perimeter of the open prairie in both directions. Trees and brush pushed up against the plain like a thick wall. He saw no sign of the other teams.

"I hope they're here," said Miguel.

"If everything went as it should," said Eddie.

"Not a helluva lot we can do about it," said Jason. "They're here or they're not." If all had gone well, Michael's team had made it and were waiting and watching. If all had gone well, Monroe and his team had completed their hit-and-runs and were at their target and were waiting for the signal. If all had gone well, Carolyn had made her presence known and felt, and she and her team were at their target and were waiting for the signal.

In a few minutes, they would all know a lot more.

Jason was uncharacteristically nervous. So much rode on what was about to happen. The next hour had to be seen by the Shylmahn as the pinnacle of the great push by the humans. It had to be seen by the Shylmahn as a real and credible threat. All that had happened before in the past weeks, all that needed to have happened over the last days, by Monroe's team and Carolyn's team, by others around the country and as prophesied by Joseph... all must have made the threat now posed by this final confrontation total and complete.

If not, then all would be lost; for Jason didn't believe they could actually take this facility. Even if by some fluke they did, this single act would not change any minds, and certainly would not win a war.

Taking this complex was not the goal. God forbid if it became so.

So much rested on Joseph having it right; having it all right. Had he placed all the right pieces in all the right places? Had he interpreted the signs correctly? Had he whispered the right words in the right ears at the right time? Were his assumptions correct as to what this Shillie computer would see when it looked at one action or another?

Would this *ShahnTahr* put it all together the way Joseph intended? If it did, would it take the steps that Joseph expected it to take?

"Damn," Jason mumbled.

"What?" Miguel and Eddie both asked at the same time, both looked almost frantically out across the grassy prairie.

"Nothing," Jason sighed. "Just thinking."

"Well, do it so as I don't have a heart attack," said Eddie. He looked back in the direction they had come. "I hope Annie and the others are okay." They had left Annie Gomez in a clearing a half-mile back to look after Sheryl Jackson and the other injured.

"Why wouldn't they be?"

"No reason." Eddie turned about again and took in the view. "She's kind of nice, eh?"

Annie had seen to the comfort of her charges, a collection of wounded that had been carried or half-carried to this location, a clearing considered fairly safe and yet fairly near to where the other groups were soon to be meeting. If all went well, they would be reunited with the others once it was over.

If it didn't go well, they would be on their own and would have to seek out help as best they could.

The clearing looked like a primitive hospital ward, with half a dozen bodies laid out in long row. A handful of walking wounded, serving as Annie's assistants, hovered about the perimeter, unsure as to what to do.

Sheryl Jackson, the most critically wounded, got Annie's attention and waved a hand for her to come over. Kneeling beside her, Annie looked Sheryl over quickly from foot to head before looking her in the eye.

"What can I do for you, Sheryl?" she asked.

"You can get the hell out of here, doc."

"Excuse me?"

"We'll get along well enough," said Sheryl. "You should be up there where the fighting's going to be."

"If there is any fighting, there are medics to see to immediate needs; they'll patch up the injured well enough to get them here."

"Drag 'em a half a mile? During a fight?"

"Half a mile is close enough. Any closer, we'd be in the way. The battlefield is no place for a hospital."

Sheryl Jackson shifted position and gave Annie a hard look. "I don't take you for a coward, doc."

"I appreciate that, Miss Jackson." Annie stood up. "But what you think of me doesn't really matter. Now, I'll see to making preparations in the event that we do have to take in new arrivals."

Monroe moved into position at the edge of the wood. The members of his team moved stealthily to either side of him, all staying just in the cover of shadows and brush. Ahead, out in center of a grassy plain, lay the final target—the headquarters of the security commander for the province.

Their journey had taken them past a handful of Shillie communications outposts, observation stations, and research centers. They had quickly and quietly accomplished their task at each location, leaving a trail of unsettling success. Individually, none was particularly alarming, but certainly enough for the Shylmahn in the field to wonder just what the Chehnon were up to and what they were trying to accomplish.

The Shylmahn would dutifully send their reports back along the chain of command and to the headquarters of the Shylmahn security commander for the province.

Monroe studied the perimeter. Nothing moved. There wasn't even a breeze.

He looked back out across the still grass of the plain. As he watched, the walls of the complex began to turn bright yellow; the eastern sky brightened as the sun rose above the horizon, the rays of light streaking across the flat lowland toward the complex.

Monroe stood and stepped out into the open. The others of his team, confident now in their leader after all they had gone through together, did the same. Monroe, knowing that they would be with him without his having to see them, began walking toward the Shylmahn complex.

The air was cool and damp. The grass at his feet was covered in dew and slapped at his ankles. He took his strides easy and steady, never deviating, never slowing. At some point between the edge of the wood and the walls of NehLoc's headquarters, Monroe and his team would confront the deadly shield of energy blasts that served to protect all Shylmahn facilities. Virtually impenetrable, if Jason Britton's fancy gadgets didn't work as advertised, each step they took could be their last.

Monroe saw other groups coming out onto the plain now, moving forward, moving steadily nearer the facility in the center of the open expanse. He thought it an amazing sight. There weren't that many humans, taken as a whole, but the sheer calmness, the sheer audacity, made the scene surreal and curiously ominous.

Directly ahead now, some ten yards, no more, Monroe could see and hear the shield. Dozens of tiny explosions of the Shylmahn CEBs, the *concentrated energy blasts,* were being detonated every second, forming a wall of destructive energy.

Monroe still did not slow. He kept to his easy, steady pace, his comfortable stride. He understood what Joseph and Jason were about. It was all about the show. Succeed or fail, Monroe would give a good show.

Five paces, four paces, there was strange crackling sound, three paces, Monroe could feel it on his skin, in his flesh; two paces, the air in front of him was visible; one pace... and then he was in the shield; and then he was beyond the shield.

He was past the shield...

Monroe stepped onward. At a hundred yards from the perimeter wall of the facility, Monroe stopped.

He waited.

Joseph entered the same small mess hall in which he had previously met with BehLahk. BehLahk had told him then that this was one place where they could talk without being monitored by NehLoc's security.

BehLahk was sitting at the same table as the last time, and he waved for him to join him.

"Hello, Joseph. Please sit."

There was no food at the table, and the other tables were empty. The room was empty but for the two of them.

He sat down opposite the Shylmahn. "What is it, BehLahk?" he asked.

"There are a number of things happening, right now, and there are certain interpretations being made about these things. We can no longer afford to play—footsy—with one another."

"So, what's happening?"

BehLahk pulled his chair closer to the table. Joseph thought that he actually looked nervous, which was very unlike the doctor.

"Michael is moving on this very complex. Today."

"Yeah?"

"Please, Joseph."

"Hey, it wasn't my idea."

"He has joined forces with your sister. The Shylmahn have great concern when it comes to Carolyn."

"At least we can agree on that," said Joseph. *It's all going down today.*

"Even this threat would not be taken too seriously, but for two other factors, both of which you have initiated. All of which you have initiated."

"Which are?"

"The first is the number of apparently organized, apparently connected actions that have occurred over recent weeks, taking place with steadily increasing frequency, and with the use of rather sophisticated technology. Second, the timing of the arrival of your brother Jason and the question of what he may have brought with him from his research facility in the south."

"I can't say that I'm not pleased," Joseph said tiredly. "Pleased or not, there is nothing that I could do to stop it, even if I wanted to."

"I'm not asking you to stop it, human," BehLahk said coldly. "I don't want it to stop."

Joseph was startled, and he had no witty retort. It took several seconds for him to reply. "I'm listening," he said finally. There was the hint of the old Dr. Black showing through.

"Good," said the Shylmahn. "Now, we both know that almost everything going on out there is pretense. While it is true that you have managed to put together a communications network that NehLoc can't seem to shut down—an impressively active network, I might add—there is really nothing underlying that network beyond the carefully choreographed yet empty assaults on the safest of targets.

"And while it is true that the Chehnon have managed to come up with some rather disturbing weaponry, they are very limited in their capability, use and number.

"You have managed to present a very effective façade, and much more importantly, you have managed to represent it as a credible threat. You knew your audience and you manipulated that audience very well."

"Assuming that any of this is true, what do you want from me? You said that you didn't want to stop it."

"Joseph, I have assisted in your manipulations of the data and of our leadership. I applaud what you were able to accomplish, but you have gotten as far as you have only with my assistance."

"And?"

"You and I each wanted it to come to this, albeit for very different reasons. You understood that if exactly the right situation were painted, that ShahnTahr would see that the only logical solution to the continued survival of the Shylmahn would be to come to an agreement with the Chehnon."

"Is that why you and I are here?" asked Joseph. "You have an offer?"

"An official offer? No." BehLahk smiled uncertainly. "Unfortunately, there are other parties involved that will not willingly come to the negotiation table. NehLoc believes in the threat that you have presented, but his solution to the problem is not a pleasant one. Likewise, your Carolyn is not likely to be a willing participant."

"Are you saying this has to play itself out?"

BehLahk clasped his hands together, rested them on the table. "You and I must come to an agreement. We must agree, in principle if not in detail, on how the Shylmahn and the Chehnon are going to coexist after today."

"And you think that we can do that here and now?"

"In principle, if not in detail."

"Okay," Joseph gave a short nod. "Let's assume that."

"Very good. I will know when to take the matter to ShahnTahr and how to present it to him. He has all the information.

"Next, we must agree on exactly when to intervene in today's confrontation; we must further have consensus on just how much to tell our fellows of what we agree upon, and of what led us to this agreement."

"Okay," Joseph said again. He studied the very dangerous alien sitting across from him. "BehLahk... what do you get out of this? It can't be just that it's the right thing to do."

"I believe I've already stated my reasons rather clearly, Joseph."

"The moral conscience of the species?" Joseph asked doubtfully.

BehLahk frowned. "Human, it is a matter of the spirit of the Shylmahn. We can control the planet forever. I do not believe that humans will ever again be in a position to truly threaten us. But, left on the path that we are now following, Shylmahn will one day no longer be Shylmahn. That, I will never allow."

| 21 |

Michael stood a hundred yards from the walls of NehLoc's complex. Jenny stood three steps to his left, straight-backed and confident. Miriam stood three steps to his right, leaning defiantly on her cane. The others of his team, and those of the other teams, now encircled the facility, standing as a silent threat.

Jason rose from his crouched position beside his gadget, gave Miguel a slap on the back, and Eddie a slap upside the head, and folded his arms across his chest.

"Never a doubt," he mumbled. *It worked.*

He could see Monroe, standing unflinching, feet spread shoulder-width apart, hands clasped behind his back. He would stand there until the walls crumbled of their own weight, if need be.

"Over there," Miguel said calmly, standing now.

Carolyn led her army out of the wood and started the march across the open terrain. They were twice the number of the other teams combined.

"If the Shillies try to—" Miguel started.

"I know," said Jason. They had countered the shield detonations for the twenty seconds that it had taken for the first group to march through the shield. Once past, the Shylmahn had stopped the blasts. Maintaining a shield of that size, of any size, was hugely expensive, and was never kept up any longer than necessary.

But at the sight of Carolyn's army, they could reinitialize the shield in the hope that maybe this time it would hold.

Jason's device had enough power for one final demonstration, and they couldn't afford to expend it to get Carolyn's team through. It would be needed later.

They watched as Carolyn marched forward, two paces ahead of her small army. What happened now would tell a lot.

What would the Shillies do?

"That's one tough lady," said Miguel.

That's one way of putting it... thought Jason, and he smiled. "Used to be one hell of a sweet kid," he said. *My, oh my... how sweet Sis has changed.*

His sister approached the shield line. He saw and heard nothing. Carolyn, true to her word, stepped confidently and steadily forward. She would do her job; and right now, that meant moving ahead as if she had nothing to fear.

"I'll be damned," Jason mumbled. Carolyn was through the shield boundary and approaching Michael.

The Shillies had decided that reinitializing the shield would be a waste of their energy.

"Nice bluff," said Miguel.

Carolyn stepped up beside Michael. She gave him a silent nod, which he returned. She glanced at Jenny then, and turned silently away.

Jenny looked over at Michael and gave a reticent grimace.

Carolyn turned to Miriam. "What do you think, Miss Foster? Is it not an interesting scenario that we find ourselves in?"

Miriam lifted and brought down her cane. "I wouldn't have missed it for the world."

"Curious choice of phrase," said Carolyn. "The world is precisely what is at stake."

"All the more reason to be here."

Carolyn nodded approvingly, then carefully studied the forces arrayed around the alien complex. She studied the sky, the wall, the gate. She took a step forward. "I grow impatient."

Jason let out a long, slow breath, carefully studying the scene that was laid out in front of him. A large group of humans stood ready a hundred yards outside the main gate of the complex, with a thin line of men and women fanning out in either direction of the main body.

If one didn't evaluate the situation too closely, it was impressive. Jason, however, couldn't help but see it for what it was.

He turned his attention to the gate, took a deep breath and held it. He nodded sharply.

Miguel pushed the button. There was shimmer of light at the gate, and a large section turned to powdery dust.

The canister beside Miguel exploded, his hand still resting on the large button. He was thrown up and back, hitting Jason. They were both knocked to the ground.

"Sonofabitch," Jason grumbled through his teeth. He scrambled to his knees and pushed himself forward. He tried frantically to see the results of the explosion at the gate.

"Don't mind me," said Miguel, rolling over painfully, struggling to sit up. "I'll be fine... I'll be just fine." This particular toy was destined to survive but one use.

Jason ignored him. The smoke and dust surrounding the gate was beginning to thin. "Sonofabitch," he said again.

"I think I'll live," said Miguel. He climbed to his feet and looked out across the plain toward the gate. "Damn."

The Shillie-type energy blast had managed to put a hole into the gate, but had done much less damage than they had hoped. Still, it should have been enough to make the point.

Jason looked quickly toward the group of humans and to Michael. *It's enough,* he urged silently. *Michael... it's enough.*

§

Michael tried not to let his disappointment show. While the damage was minimal, it should be enough to let the Shylmahn know that the humans had the capability.

"Okay," he said.

"It'll do," said Carolyn. "Let's move."

Michael nodded sternly and started forward. Others followed his lead. The line of humans surrounding the complex began closing in.

"Come on," said Jason. He smacked Eddie on the arm, and Eddie and Miguel followed him out into the open. After taking half a dozen steps, Jason saw movement at the damaged gate. Shylmahn began working their way through the rubble.

"Uh oh," said Eddie. A shuttle was rising up from inside the complex. It glided over the wall. Just beyond the wall, it stopped and hovered.

"This is it," said Jason. He stopped then, reached out and grabbed Miguel's arm. "Have a look at that," he said.

Joseph stumbled through the debris at the gate and came out into the open. A Shylmahn was with him. They followed the small group that had come out ahead of them.

"That's your brother?" asked Miguel.

"That's Joey." Jason started forward again. "This is most definitely it."

Michael stopped short. Carolyn took one step further and stopped.

"Dammit," she said harshly, loud enough that those immediately around her heard. She spoke over her shoulder then, clear but barely audible. "Hold the line." Within moments, the contracting line of humans stopped. They waited.

Michael and Jenny watched their father approach. A Shillie kept pace beside him. Those that had come out ahead of him had fallen in behind him.

"BehLahk," said Carolyn. Michael looked closely at the Shylmahn accompanying his father. Dr. Black was as well known as Joseph Britton himself.

"Good morning," said Joseph. He stopped abruptly at a signal from the escort one step behind him.

"What's going on, Joey?" asked Carolyn. She didn't sound pleased.

"Good to see you, Sis."

"Of course it is. What are you up to?"

Joseph shrugged. "There are some folks in that shuttle up there that would like to have a chat."

"What if I'm not in the mood for conversation?"

BehLahk managed a very broad grin. "Miss Britton, much effort has gone into... '*setting this up*', is the phrase? Surely you can take a few moments out from your march toward destruction? Aren't you even a little bit curious?"

"No." Carolyn looked sharply at Joseph. *You set this up?* she asked silently. *This was your great plan?* She turned to Michael. "Talk if you want," she said flatly. "You have ten minutes; then I'm gonna kill something."

BehLahk smiled again, then raised and lowered his hand. The shuttle moved forward.

NehLoc stepped out of the shuttle moments after it settled to the ground, strode confidently toward BehLahk and JoSeph, leaving his escort to scramble hurriedly after him. He didn't like this, and he wasn't about to waste a lot of time at it... get it over with and get on with it.

He stood beside BehLahk and looked over at Michael Britton. This was the son of JoSeph, the creature that had somehow managed to give

TohPeht and ShahnTahr pause. It didn't look like much. The daughter was standing beside the son. It didn't look like much either.

And then there was Carolyn Britton, the only threat of any real consequence left out in the wild. It would serve the society well to eliminate that one.

"I am NehLoc," he said. He waited for some response from the Chehnon creatures. None came. "I have agreed to meet with you before I set about to end this feeble assault on my headquarters. What purpose such a meeting might serve, this I do not know."

"NehLoc..." said Joseph. "You have developed quite a talent with the English language."

"This is a waste of time," said Carolyn.

Michael calmly raised a hand. "You promised me ten minutes, Aunt Carolyn. I think I have about nine minutes left." Michael gave NehLoc a slight smile. "It should be clear to you by now that we will not be so easily dealt with."

"I've seen little evidence of that."

"We will not be deterred; we will not be beaten." Michael gave his father a quick glance, then pushed on, looking intently at NehLoc. "This is not an isolated assault, as you must no doubt by now be aware. We will take back our world this day."

NehLoc carefully studied this Chehnon creature and its words. It was consistent with the information that he had been able to extract from JoSeph, and with other data recovered from the wild. Nonetheless, he saw nothing to necessitate discussion or negotiation. If anything, it was all the more imperative to destroy this potential threat in decisive fashion.

What might ShahnTahr be seeing that he did not? As hard as he might try, he could find no logical reason to take the drastic measures that ShahnTahr was obviously contemplating.

He looked severely at Michael.

"That one and I," he said, indicating Carolyn, "are in agreement on this matter. I find this discussion to be distasteful and useless. I should eliminate you all this very instant."

"A decision not completely your own, dear NehLoc," said BehLahk.

"I answer to no one on such matters."

"Normally, that is true, and your itch may yet be scratched. I believe, however, that ShahnTahr has a few issues that he would yet like to explore; issues that could not easily be addressed should you eliminate the Chehnon prematurely."

NehLoc fumed a moment, then visibly relaxed and gave a quick nod. "You are quite right, BehLahk," he said, speaking quite calmly. "I concede to your counsel."

"I suggest that we acquiesce to yet higher counsel," said BehLahk. He directed NehLoc's attention to activity at the gate behind them. TohPeht and EsJen had stepped out into the open, accompanied by an escort of four well-armed Shylmahn. They paused a moment, allowing a cloud of guardian probes to come over the wall and take position around the group, then started forward.

"Eight minutes," said Carolyn. At some imperceptible signal from Carolyn, her people shifted position en masse, readying themselves against a possible sudden attack.

| 22 |

It was clear to Joseph that if left to Carolyn or NehLoc, this day would end in violence and all that he had planned, all that he had worked for, might be lost.

NehLoc was either not convinced or didn't care, and he was willing, in fact he was eager, to continue the fight no matter what the perceived shift in power. He wanted to see the end of the Chehnon no matter what the cost.

As for Carolyn, she was as willing and as eager as NehLoc. She may or may not believe that they could win this battle, but that no longer mattered, if it ever had.

It may have been a mistake for her to be there, but without her assistance and her presence, there would probably have been no countering NehLoc. Besides, she had a very important role to play. Her part was absolutely vital in the grander plan. From his conversation with BehLahk, that at least had been obvious.

If only he could have told her...

He turned and watched TohPeht and EsJen approach. As they drew nearer, the probes buzzed around the growing group and settled into positions both defensive and observational. EsJen glanced at Joseph, then at the larger group, evaluating each member.

TohPeht stepped deliberately to the forefront, studied the dynamics of the situation, and smiled.

"Greetings to all of you," he said. One probe, different than the others, shifted slightly. "For those who may not know me, I am TohPeht."

Or whatever was left of TohPeht.

TohPeht-ShahnTahr...

Joseph looked again at the probe. ShahnTahr, the true and distinct ShahnTahr, was behind the sensors of that thing. It watched and listened and calculated.

Had BehLahk gotten through to it?

"This is a critically important moment in the history of this world, of the Shylmahn people, and of the Chehnon," said TohPeht. By his expression, Joseph thought the Shylmahn leader was quite pleased with the way he had begun his speech. "What we do on this day, the choices that we make, will pave the way for a bright future for us all, or lead us into a bleak time from which we may never recover."

"There is only one choice to be made here, Shillie," said Carolyn. "Times, they are changed. So here it is: You leave our world or we start to fighting. And I'll leave that decision to you. Me? I'd just as soon get this party going. Five minutes."

NehLoc appeared to like Carolyn's thoughts on the matter. He stared coolly at her. "It looks like the creatures have made their choice, TohPeht," he said, not taking his eyes off Carolyn. "I fully expected this meeting to be a waste of effort, and this one won't even take the time to listen to what you have to offer."

"I'll listen," said Michael. "We can always start the killing if we don't like what we hear."

"I appreciate that," said TohPeht, bowing his head in acknowledgement.

"Whatever," groaned Carolyn.

Joseph remained silent for the moment. He wanted to hear exactly what TohPeht—what ShahnTahr—was going to offer. Joseph hadn't gotten very specific in his demands, and BehLahk hadn't been very specific about his own plans.

"We acknowledge that the natives of Chehno, the *humans* that were the original occupants of this world, have been much maltreated," said

TohPeht. "We did not understand, did not comprehend, that humans were more than a resource, as any other resource that our new home offered. This we take to be a failing in our intellectual makeup. As a result of this imperfection, we agree that our methods immediately following our arrival on this world to be the direct cause of this ill treatment."

"Ill treatment?" Carolyn was absolutely incredulous. "You acknowledge *ill treatment*?"

Joseph had to agree with Carolyn, and he doubted that there was any sincerity behind the words. Any concession, however, whether heartfelt or not, meant that the Shylmahn were worried.

"Let him continue," Joseph said softly.

"Are you buying this crap?"

"I want to hear him out, Carolyn."

Carolyn stiffened, set her jaw and pressed her lips tight.

TohPeht waited for this exchange to finish before going on. "Our proposal is quite simple. All hostilities will end. In exchange, all Chehnon natives now under Shylmahn supervision will be allowed to depart the facilities in which they currently reside. All Chehnon will be accorded freedom of movement throughout all lands not designated as Shylmahn territory."

"That's it?" Carolyn blurted out.

"There are a number of details yet to be worked out, but that is, in essence, our proposal."

"That's just not good enough!"

"I think it's a good starting point," said Michael. He had been watching Joseph, who had been very quiet and had not betrayed whatever emotions he might have about what was being said. Nonetheless, he could see that this was where his father had intended this to go.

"Starting point, my ass," said Carolyn. "You want a starting point? You want options? I'll give you two. Those bastards leave this planet on their own, or we help them leave. One minute."

With that, Joseph began to hear grumblings from those behind Carolyn. He couldn't let this situation turn bad. NehLoc, on the Shillie side, looked as frustrated by the offer as Carolyn looked angry. It wouldn't take much for this to explode, and despite all of Carolyn's blustering, in the end the humans would most certainly lose.

"I agree with Carolyn that TohPeht's—*apology?*—however genuine it might be, does little." Joseph tried to speak softly and yet forcefully. "Be that as it may, I think that we should take the proposal at face value, as a well-intentioned gesture, and move forward from there."

"A most reasonable suggestion," said BehLahk.

Don't make it sound like we're buddies, you idiot...

"However much an agreement may fall short of what we really want, of what we know in our hearts to be the right thing, the just thing, we must strive to reach an agreement that at the very least puts us in a better position than where we are now."

Joseph hoped that he hadn't made the position of the humans appear too weak in the eyes of the Shylmahn, but he had to get across to Carolyn and her supporters that they needed to tread carefully. They could easily lose everything.

"You bastard," Carolyn said coldly. She got it, all right. It all came to her in a flash. "You manipulative sonofabitch. You... *damn you.* This is all your doing, isn't it?"

From his position at the tree line, Jason saw some movement out of the corner of his eye and looked quickly at the edge of the woods near where Carolyn had led her people through.

He saw them just inside the trees.

Three people bustling around a metallic device.

"They've got a gadget," he mumbled.

Miguel looked quickly to Jason, then followed his line of sight. "Oh, boy," he said.

"But, that's a good thing, isn't it?" asked Eddie.

"I don't think so," Miguel mumbled. So Carolyn had met up with her contact from Phoenix after all. Only now, it was possible that Carolyn might become a loose cannon. Miguel and Jason both looked over to the group gathered halfway to the complex. Carolyn looked casually from side to side, then back over her shoulder. She turned back to the enemy in front of her.

"No, no..." said Jason.

"Looks like it," said Miguel.

Jason made a decision. He was already starting forward, in the direction of Carolyn's gadget. "Get me another charge, Miguel."

"No way, Jason," Miguel cried, but he dropped to his knees and began working. Eddie knelt beside him, but was looking at Jason, already a third of the way to the three hunched over their own device.

"Can you do anything?" Eddie asked. Miguel was shaking his head. Eddie stood and looked across the waving grass. "What'll Jason— oh, damn..." He saw Carolyn raise her arm. At that moment, all her people began firing hand weapons. Back at the edge of the wood, the three were scrambling around the gadget.

Jason was still too far away.

Over at the complex, there were three distinct detonations.

Jason stopped and turned to look at the group gathered outside the gate. Many were down, more were fighting or running. The probes had all dropped out of the air and were laying on the ground, dead to the world.

He saw Carolyn standing in the center of it all. She stood defiantly, her rifle held high over her head.

Joseph shifted uncomfortably in the alien chair. He was sitting inside the Shylmahn shuttle, and there was a Shylmahn attendant wrapping his wounds. The side door was open and he could see outside. It was quiet in the compartment, and from outside he could hear only the occasional barking of orders, coming from both human and Shylmahn.

The attendant grunted something that probably meant that he was finished, and began gathering up his medical gear.

BehLahk stepped into the shuttle and moved down the aisle. "Are you going to be all right?" he asked. He sounded sincere, but of course he already knew that Joseph would survive his wounds.

"So long as infection doesn't set in."

"Yes," BehLahk smiled. "Isn't that usually the case?" He sat down beside the Chehnon and silently ordered the attendant out. Once they were alone, he sat back and folded his arms. "For good or bad, Joseph Britton, it is done."

"I'm not sure what '*it*' is, BehLahk."

BehLahk lifted one shoulder and cocked his head to one side. "Perhaps the ambiguity of *it*, is what made *it* possible." He shifted and straightened. "In any case, change has been born on this day. We cannot know what it will grow up to be, and I am certain that it will be a difficult childhood, but I am hopeful the future will be brighter because of what you and I have done."

Joseph frowned. "I believe that it had to be done, but I am not proud of it."

"Joseph, because of you, many thousands of lives have been saved. As importantly, your people no longer need live on reservations or in hiding. The fighting, the organized fighting anyway, is over."

"Not if my sister or NehLoc have anything to say about it."

"True, it will not be easy," BehLahk agreed. "I am not so naïve as to believe that the events of the past can be forgotten or forgiven. It will likely be many generations before Shylmahn and Chehnon can live side by side."

"Do not mistake my actions for forgiveness. There were two paths open to us. I chose the one that showed the only promise for humankind to survive."

"Your choice was very courageous, Joseph."

"Carolyn will never accept it."

"Nor NehLoc, I fear. Living on the same planet as equals will be unacceptable to many. It may well take the passing of all those who bore witness to the migration—"

"The invasion."

"—and the years that followed, for there to be real integration."

"If ever," said Joseph.

"Perhaps you and I can at least lay the foundation for a new society. Separate but equal partners."

That phrase stung and Joseph grimaced. "No," he said sharply. "No, like it or not, whatever horrors we have faced, we have to come together. If we do not, the future will hate us."

Jason met Joseph coming out of the Shylmahn shuttlecraft. He asked him how he was doing as the two of them turned and walked away from the ship. Joseph mumbled that he would survive.

"It didn't have to happen like this," he said.

"Sure it did," said Jason. He knew, without looking around them, how low to keep his voice and ensure that no one could overhear. "A helluva show, if you ask me."

"I don't like it."

"Of course not."

"They are going to cause us trouble," said Joseph. He stopped and faced his brother.

"Carolyn and NehLoc," said Jason. "We know where they're coming from, and as unpredictable as they can be, we know what to expect."

"Are you listening to yourself?"

"TohPeht," Jason said flatly. "ShahnTahr. I don't know what the hell to make of them or what they're thinking or what they'll do next."

"ShahnTahr uses logic," said Joseph. "And logic can be manipulated."

"Ah, but now throw EsJen into the picture."

Joseph grew thoughtful. "Yeah," he said at last. "She may become a wrench thrown into it, all right."

"Into the interpretation of the logic you so carefully skew."

Joseph started walking again. "But for now... we're better off today than we were yesterday."

"Ya' done good, Joey. Too bad we can't tell anybody."

"I'm used to that. The important thing is that we keep it on track."

"It'll happen," said Jason. He stopped now, surveyed the scene. Many people had left, others weren't sure what to do or where to go. Carolyn had left so quickly that a lot of her people had been left behind. They didn't know what to do. Behind them, the shuttle was just lifting off. "That's the last of the Shillies," he said.

"BehLahk," said Joseph.

Jason shook his head. "Man, I don't like having to dance with that one."

"Yeah."

"Any regular Shillie, at least you can see 'em coming. But that guy, he's crafty."

"And very methodical, in everything that he does."

"Just what is it that he's doing?"

Joseph gave one last glance at the direction the shuttle had gone. "I don't have the slightest idea."

"You're scaring me, brother."

"Me too."

The main gate of Freetown stood wide open. Victoria stood on the guard platform above the gate and watched the people stream in. She recognized refugees returning home from Metcalf, and a few from the community that Ethan had started. She also saw many new faces; some looked to have had a hard life.

Victoria's wounds had not yet completely healed, and there would be scars that she would bear for the rest of her life. Considering where she found herself now as to where she had been, she thought it a fair trade.

She saw Craig down in the crowd, in the heart of it all; the bustle, the excitement, the bright hopes for the future. Craig had plans for Freetown, and it seemed to Victoria, and to many, that he just might succeed.

Victoria turned back and looked beyond the gate in time to see Michael approaching. She leaned forward across the top of the fence, watched Michael admiringly. He spotted her and stopped, forcing the group following behind him to step around. He gazed up at her, his eyes twinkling, and cocked his head sideways and grinned.

When he saw the scar on her face, though, he curled his brow and frowned, pointed at the same location on his own face as a question. Victoria waved the question aside as if to say that it was nothing. Michael started forward again, and Victoria turned and hurried down to meet him at the gate. They approached each other slowly and threw their arms around each other.

"Tell me we won't do this again," she whispered.

"We won't do this again," said Michael.

"You ass." Victoria held on tight.

It was late and much of Freetown had settled in for the night. A group had gathered around a fire pit in the outer plaza; Michael, Jenny, Victoria, Craig, Miriam, Annie Gomez, a few others. Looking across the plaza, Michael could see another group gathered around another brick fire pit. Quiet conversation drifted across the open space. Over at the main cavern entrance, the curtains were pulled aside and Michael could see the Inner Village; the lights were set to night.

"There's just no way that we're going to be able to take everyone in," Craig said. It was a subject that had come up a number of times over the previous days. As much as he was getting into the evolving nature of Freetown, he was also concerned about some of the new problems that were beginning to manifest themselves.

"I wouldn't be too worried about it," said Michael. He stared down into the fire. "Once the uncertainty wears off, a lot of these people will likely move on."

"I think he's right," said Annie. "Right now, they see Freetown as something familiar in a suddenly very different world. Even if they've never been here before, they know what we've been and what we've stood for."

"I heard that someone is designing a hotel," said Miriam.

"We can use one," said Victoria. "Or three."

Craig looked at Michael. "It may be a long time before that uncertainty fades," he said. "Tens of thousands are being freed from the reservations. But where do they go? There is no society, no infrastructure. There's no supply base, nothing to support them. What are they supposed to do?"

"Some will wander aimlessly," Jenny said quietly, leaning in toward the fire, "looking for things to be the way they once were, the way they remembered. They'll look for direction, for someone to tell them what to do. And they'll grab onto the first person or place or thing that gives them something solid. Good or bad.

"Others will set out to make a place for themselves, or to make a whole new world. Good or bad. Some will know what they're doing, or will at least have some idea.

"Many will head for their old homes and towns, if they're old enough to have had homes other than on the reservations. But they won't like what they'll find. Many will then come looking for places like Freetown, for places they've heard of."

Most of those that were gathered around the fire had no memories of life before the Shylmahn. Craig knew of the Before Time. He looked to Miriam, a child when the Shylmahn first came.

"Have you thought of going back to your home town?" he asked.

"Nothing there for me," she said. "Though I imagine some might try to rebuild. It wasn't totally destroyed."

"Most of those old houses are in pretty bad shape," said Annie.

Michael stood up and looked away from the fire.

Most of the world is in pretty bad shape, he thought.

Craig watched Michael walk into the darkness. "For the time being," he said to the others, "Freetown will have to maintain as strong a defense as it always has, whether the threat be from the Shylmahn or from our own."

| 23 |

EsJen walked around the heavy chair and rested her hands on the back. She glanced over at the holo-table, now quiet. There was nothing else in the room but for the single, ever-present probe hovering over in the corner. Unobtrusive, it both watched and protected.

She came back around from behind the chair and sat down. As she did, the door at the far end of the long, narrow chamber opened and NehLoc walked in.

"NehLoc," she said flatly. "Come in."

"Thank you." NehLoc stepped smoothly but quickly forward, stopped two paces in front of her and waited. She studied him, openly analyzing the various physical signs. She had learned that taking these few moments before beginning a conversation could make all the difference, particularly when dealing with NehLoc.

"How are the security modifications progressing?" she asked.

"As well as can be expected, EsJen." NehLoc had not been at all happy with the sudden changes to his world. The Chehnon had begun leaving the reservations and Shylmahn-sponsored communities several weeks earlier, and because of the leniency allowed the natives in their travel—near non-existent restrictions—the threat to Shylmahn safety was immediate and significant. "It would have been much easier had we been allowed more time for preparation."

"You were given as much time as could be afforded," said EsJen. "That issue is closed."

"Of course." NehLoc nodded acknowledgement, then began his report in earnest. "Redeployment of staff and equipment from the reservations and research facilities to our expanded dahlseht perimeters has been completed. The problems with the probe software modifications have been resolved. I do not expect further breaches, either intentional or accidental, of our larger communities, though we are continuing to fine-tune defenses at some of our rural populations. I have concerns that there may be another incident before such refinements can be completed."

"Understood. We hope for the best, but must prepare for the worst."

"Then there are the territorial borders. I am quite anxious about the status of our defenses along the borders."

"The new probes?" A new probe design, guardian probes redesigned specifically to defend the borders of the Shylmahn Territories, had gone into production days after the agreement between Shylmahn and Chehnon had been finalized.

"Production and deployment continues on schedule, but this does mean that it will take several more weeks before all the borders are adequately protected."

"Are there indications that the Chehnon plan to exploit this vulnerability?" EsJen had no information that such was the case.

"No, EsJen. But I do not trust these creatures."

"I am fully aware of your concerns, NehLoc. I share your apprehension." While EsJen felt that she could work with the fledgling government that the Chehnon were attempting to organize, even if she did not fully trust them, it had become increasingly evident that they did not represent all the Chehnon. She doubted they ever would.

ShahnTahr had placed the Shylmahn in a very precarious situation. EsJen was certain that he would not have done so had there been any other alternative, but that made circumstances no less uncertain. She felt that in the end, all would be well, but they must first traverse a perilous sea in which each decision could have serious repercussions.

"What of TohPeht?" asked EsJen. ShahnTahr would not provide specifics regarding the TohPeht-ShahnTahr entity. She knew that there was a continued interaction, a symbiotic relationship between the physical entity of TohPeht-ShahnTahr and the ethereal being of ShahnTahr, but it would not speak of its alter-ego other than to state that he was well.

NehLoc, however, continued to monitor the status and whereabouts of their one-time leader. "He is still on the southern continent. He appears to be well." TohPeht-ShahnTahr was accompanied by several probes of his own design, and was also under the watchful eye of a team of NehLoc's people, though this team was required to remain at a discrete and unobtrusive distance.

TohPeht-ShahnTahr was on an extended educational retreat.

TohPeht, if there was anything left of TohPeht within the being that he had morphed into, had earned the right to hand the responsibilities and demands of leadership to someone else and step down. No one had sacrificed more in service to the society of the Shylmahn.

But TohPeht would never have done so. He existed to serve, whatever the personal cost.

And ShahnTahr would never have done so; and in fact he had not. He had remained here, continuing in the same role that he had served in for centuries.

It was the TohPeht-ShahnTahr being who had left, drawn by the powerful senses that he had discovered within TohPeht and the exotic world these senses had opened up to him.

EsJen saw NehLoc look up at the probe hovering in the corner behind her. He must have been thinking along the same lines as she.

"NehLoc?"

"I sometimes wonder what ShahnTahr may have lost as a result of TohPeht's departure," he said.

"Very little, I think. TohPeht was very much a sensory conduit between ShahnTahr and the physical world. I believe there is still a connection."

"But what of ShahnTahr's direct leadership through TohPeht?"

You are curious as to the division of duties and responsibilities? wondered EsJen. "ShahnTahr's role has changed, NehLoc," she stated flatly. "He now serves as my counsel." She studied NehLoc for some indication as to how he took this revelation. Whatever he thought of it, he hid it well. "I will heed his advice as appropriate, but the Shylmahn people will no longer walk blindly into the future."

"I think that is wise, EsJen," NehLoc nodded finally. "I am confident that ShahnTahr, and you, will serve the Shylmahn well."

"I appreciate the sentiment," said EsJen. "Your views are valued."

The meeting continued for several more minutes. At its conclusion, NehLoc bowed his head slightly, turned and left the chamber. EsJen watched the retreating figure all the way to the door. Only when he was gone did she allow herself to relax, breathing noisily and wiggling her fingers to loosen her muscles. She turned about and glanced up at the probe that was silently watching her. She frowned at it.

This was all your idea, she thought. *I don't want to be the leader. Why have you given this to me?*

EsJen had grown very powerful, very quickly. She held more power than TohPeht ever had, but only because ShahnTahr had made it so. She had complete control. She was not simply the interface between ShahnTahr and the people. She was in charge. ShahnTahr had believed it to be the correct course of action.

So be it. She would do what was expected. She would serve. Her duty was to the Shylmahn people, and she would do what she believed best.

"And what of this treaty you have tied us into with the Chehnon?" she asked aloud.

ShahnTahr spoke, his new, smooth, gliding voice coming from speakers hidden within the walls. "That is up to you, EsJen."

"ShahnTahr, I bear no ill will to the natives of this world."

"Of course not."

"But I will do what is best for the society of the Shylmahn, whatever that might entail."

"We expect nothing less."

Carolyn walked the perimeter wall of the new Keep now under construction. It sat in the middle of the open grasslands. The outer walls and interior buildings were built mostly of rock, concrete and heavy timbers. The design, and the military contingent to be housed within it, would be capable of repelling any typical attack. And the technology being built into the new Keep would repel Shillie technology.

A massive array of solar panels and storage batteries were being installed to help provide power to defensive energy shielding. This was the primary reason Carolyn had selected this location for the Keep; sun most of the year, long days in the summer.

Her engineers, however, had warned her that this would not provide protection beyond an initial assault. This was the second reason for selecting this location.

An underground river ran directly beneath the site, some thirty yards beneath the surface. Her head engineer was supervising the installation of a turbine. As with the solar panels, this secondary power source wouldn't repel an ongoing attack, but would possibly push back a second assault.

What these power sources also provided were some technological capabilities within the Keep. Per the agreement between Shylmahn and Human, human communities were allowed to use gas and electricity.

Oh, joy...

Carolyn reached the main gate, or what would be the main gate once it was completed, and entered the main yard. Steven saw her, threw up his hands in a 'there-you-are' gesture, and marched quickly over.

"What is it?" asked Carolyn. She continued walking.

"You missed the reports from the scouting teams," he said.

"So fill me in, then." Carolyn stopped and turned around, examined the front wall on either side of the gate opening. She made a mental note that they needed to install supply boxes at each of the guard stations. It was going to get hot up there.

"Freetown is growing big-time," said Steven.

Carolyn already knew that. Freetown was going to be the largest community in the northwest. "That is to be expected," she said.

"They're keeping the Inner Village, and expanding the Outer Village. They're scrambling to upgrade utilities. Farming and ranching has increased tenfold."

"And?"

"I think that we should develop a relationship with them," he stated. "Establish communications, trade, that sort of thing."

"All right. Next?"

"Jason has gone back to Phoenix."

"Mmm." Jason had overseen the establishment of the Northwest Extension of his Phoenix research facility. His organization was continuing to integrate Shylmahn and human technologies. Perhaps his highest priority project was the creation of a reliable and secure communications network. He had met with Carolyn a number of times in recent weeks on how she might help, and how she might benefit. She had agreed to remain available, but would not soon be involving herself in operations that did not directly and immediately impact her Keep, no matter what the long-term benefits might be.

"That Miguel fella is still up here," said Steven. "He and Jason set up a place in Freetown and he works out of there. Word is, though, that he's not around very much."

"Word on Michael?"

Steven shrugged. There had been little news of young Michael Britton since his ostensible ascension to the role of human leader of planet Earth. There was a complex being built in the south, beyond the immediate influence of the Shylmahn. Still too close, so far as Carolyn was concerned. She was suspicious.

And Jenny; Carolyn knew that Jenny was by her brother's side, serving as advisor and a second set of eyes.

Representatives from a number of human settlements had recently met at Michael's headquarters to discuss the establishment of a recognized government body, but it had all ended in screaming and squawking and everyone returned home frustrated, all insisting that they could get along just fine without some high and mighty emperor of the earth looking over their shoulders.

Interesting...

Steven started to speak of Joseph, but Carolyn quickly held up a stiff hand for him to be silent. She wanted to hear nothing of her brother.

He had disappeared, and good riddance.

There was absolutely, positively nothing in this world—nothing, nothing, absolutely nothing—that Michael wanted to do less than what he was doing now.

Politics... governmental administration... in charge... sort of... Michael hated it all.

He found himself the leader of the world.

At least, that was what the job description said. There were more than a few folks out there who would disagree.

He was on their side.

Hell, what made him the chief?

The room was too warm. He looked only fleetingly at the door leading out to the main hall, turned instead in the direction of the side door that opened out onto a small courtyard. Stepping outside, he took two steps beyond the door and stood on the graveled walk. It was late evening and the heavy air was finally starting to cool.

The plants bordering the walkway had been in the ground only a few weeks, but looked to be taking well to their new home. Michael walked slowly, looked at the plantings, looked at the larger shrubs, the benches and arbors, the enclosing wall. He escaped out to his garden whenever he could. He tinkered with this or that, watered, weeded, did whatever needed doing. It made the work that he had to do inside a lot easier.

"Gonna be a clear night," said Jenny, stepping outside and looking up at the few stars already showing themselves.

Michael was kneeling beside a cluster of hardy holly plants. He stood and looked down the curving garden walk at Jenny, then looked up at the darkening sky. He saw several of the stars moving: Shylmahn shuttlecraft.

How long before we have our own ships up there?

There were severe restrictions on where humans could travel, but not in *how* they could travel. Joseph had managed to get that concession. The Chehnon could put up whatever they could get into the air, they just couldn't fly them anywhere near Shylmahn territories.

The Shylmahn, however, had full freedom of air travel.

"Do you miss your cabin?" he asked. He started to stroll slowly back toward the door.

"I guess so," said Jenny. "But, beyond the solitude, I think I miss the clarity of what we were doing. I would never return to that time, but the issues that we faced were much more straightforward."

"No argument from me on that." Michael stepped up beside his sister, turned and looked back out at his garden. Several solar lights had come on with the coming dusk. They would last several hours before losing the stored power and going dark. "We have all the same crap that we had before, with a lot of new politics thrown in just to muddy up the waters. Everything is going at cross-purposes."

"Way too much subterfuge, if you ask me."

"Exactly. Nothing is quite what it seems, no action or word can be taken at face value."

Jenny looked at her brother out of the corner of her eye, gave a sly smirk. "Of course, you wouldn't be involved in any of that..."

Michael groaned loudly. "I'm ass deep in it."

The door behind them opened and artificial light spilled out into the courtyard. Victoria came outside.

"I don't know why I ever look for you anywhere else," she said.

"Hey, Vic," said Jenny. Somehow, Jenny managed to get away with calling Victoria the sharply abbreviated nickname. No one else dared use it; at least not a second time.

Michael reached out an arm and pulled his bride into a hug. After a few seconds, they pulled apart and he casually waved a free hand.

"Such a pleasant evening," he said. "Cannot the leader of the world take in a breath of fresh air?"

"To replace all that *hot* air?" asked Victoria.

Jenny grimaced. "On that, I think I'll go back inside."

Victoria smiled and nodded to his sister-in-law. There was hidden meaning in the gesture, though no one other than the three of them could have seen it. Michael continued to take in the courtyard's transition from day to night, Victoria holding his arm with one hand and giving Jenny a kind wave of the fingers with the other. Once the door closed behind them, Victoria turned her head and stepped out onto the garden pathway, leading Michael forward.

"I saw Miriam off today," she said. "Things are going well in Freetown."

"That's good," said Michael. "Craig has finally taken to the whole mayor thing. Something I could never do."

"Desire and capability are two very different things."

"To run that place, you need both." Midway into the garden, they stopped. The gravel crunched noisily beneath their feet. "It might be nice to live there now; now that Craig and the council have no reason to try and draw me into everything."

"Right," Victoria said doubtfully. "Give it a month of no one begging for your input, you'd feel left out."

"Ah, to be left out..."

"Doesn't anybody like me anymore?" she whined in a sarcastic mimic of Michael.

Michael laughed lightly, casually looked around him. He leaned near then, and when he spoke, his voice was low and private, as if whispering sweet nothings to his sweetheart. "Anything more from my father?"

Victoria gave a soft smile. "Monroe got in twenty minutes ago."

Michael nodded, patted the hand that Victoria had rested on his arm. "I assumed as much."

"He's quite fond of your father, you know."

"More so now that they're on the same side."

"That might have helped sway his estimation some," said Victoria.

They stood silent a moment, then Michael leaned in closer. "So?" he urged.

"The meeting is set," she said. "Word is going out now."

Michael straightened. "And how are we supposed to keep it quiet?" There was an edge of frustration in his voice.

"Joseph agreed with you, for both security reasons and the problems with political squabbling. None of the key public leaders are involved."

"Good, good."

"Well, except you, of course."

"Considerate of my father to include me."

Victoria held more tightly to Michael's arm, looked up at the sky. It was completely dark now. "Nice night."

"Mmm."

After a long, quiet minute, Victoria let out a breath. "I guess we're going to be taking a trip," she said. "Time we were visiting some of the growing communities that you've helped give birth to."

Joseph climbed out of the car and closed the door, stepped around to the back and leaned against the trunk. It was still midmorning and the air was still cool, though it would be getting hot well before noon. As he studied his peaceful surroundings, he listened for sounds that he might have been followed. He could hear the clicking of the hot metal of his cooling engine, the gentle breeze blowing across the tall grass of the field beside the road, and sound of a bird chirping and singing in a nearby grove of trees.

It was as though the world here had no knowledge of all that had happened over the last few decades. It simply continued on as it had for millennia. The sun rose every morning. The grass grew, trees rose up out of the soil and spread their branches, birds made their nests, mated, laid eggs and raised baby birds.

The narrow band of asphalt that Joseph had driven on was almost lost beneath dry, yellow grass, but its presence was evident as a smooth, level, defined strip that cut across the landscape. He would be able to use such highways for a while yet, so long as trees and other obstacles didn't fall across his path, or roots burrow their way beneath and push up chunks of road and make the way impassible.

It was another half hour before he heard the sound of another vehicle, coming from somewhere distant, beyond his sight. It was another full minute before he saw the flickering shadow on the horizon, which grew gradually into the image of a car. The driver guided the vehicle cautiously, following the path that Joseph had taken earlier.

It pulled over behind Joseph's car and came to a slow stop. When the engine turned off, Joseph smiled and waved a hand to the person behind the wheel.

Miriam climbed out, reached in and came out with her cane.

"Good morning, Miriam," said Joseph. He pushed himself away from his vehicle and the two met and hugged. "How are you?"

"Surviving," said Miriam. The two leaned against Joseph's car. "How about you?"

"I'm feeling pretty good, all things considered."

"I'm glad. You all set, then?"

"Pretty much. I will be. How did it go?"

"As you anticipated. I'll be in Freetown tomorrow."

"How's the boy?"

"He's learning."

"Michael's bright. Brighter than me. He's surrounded by smart people who care about him." Joseph grinned thoughtfully. "But I do still see him as a child."

"A child he's not, Joseph. Though he isn't without his childlike qualities."

Joseph crossed his arms, stared out across the plain. "I had hoped to be able to spend more time with them, with all of you, after..."

"Maybe once it's over."

"If it ever is. There's so much yet to do." He pulled himself out of his reverie. "One step at a time, though, eh? We're farther along than I could have hoped."

"But we're not truly free."

"Not yet..."

"The meeting's set. Michael will be there, and Jason. Monroe is contacting most of the others. I have one stop yet to make, and then Freetown."

Joseph was lost in thought again, and Miriam wasn't sure whether he had heard her. During her visits with him these past weeks, she had seen this in him a number of times. He had spent so many years virtually alone, in the heart of the Shylmahn territory, that he had withdrawn into his own mind, lived there, existed there, to the point where it seemed that he was losing the skill of human interaction.

Miriam waited there beside him until he was ready. When he spoke to her again, they sorted out the final details of the meeting that was to come, some four weeks away. At that time, it was hoped that the next phase of Joseph's plan could be implemented. They then talked for a few minutes more, mostly about friends and family, though Miriam also wanted assurances that Joseph was all right, and while she got those assurances, she didn't really believe him.

They said their goodbyes then, and Miriam got into her car and started again toward Freetown. Joseph watched until the vehicle was out of sight, then again leaned against the side of his own car, crossed his arms, and stared out across the landscape.

While it was true that the humans on planet Earth were much better off than they were a few months earlier, they did not control their planet, nor their destiny. Joseph was as unhappy about this as Carolyn, though her discontentment was much more visible than his.

For now, that was just the way he wanted it.

The first phase of his plan had gone even better than he had hoped, with the help of his brother and sister, and, if BehLahk was to be believed, due much to his invaluable assistance.

Was this new world taking shape as BehLahk had intended? What plans did he have for the human race? As monstrous a creature as the Shylmahn doctor was, he was a very intelligent being, and had shown himself a master at both manipulation and compromise. His keen eye for seeing things as they truly were, and seeing people as they truly were, made him a serious threat.

Carolyn had completely disowned Joseph, which had been expected. So far as she could see, he had betrayed her trust, and sold humanity out to the Shillies for a few worthless comforts. Joseph had no doubt that she would continue to play her part, albeit she had no idea of this very important role.

Jason was continuing to forge ahead, moving forward as all would expect, pushing the technology, advancing the human status. This would make it easy for him to slip into and out of wherever he needed to go.

Joseph's children had a difficult task. Michael in particular had to walk the fine line of a political leader struggling to maintain the fragile relationship with the Shylmahn, and pushing the causes of humanity, while at the same time secretly pursuing Joseph's hidden agenda.

As for Joseph, he planned to make the occasional obligatory appearance for the benefit of the Shylmahn, and make a few inflammatory statements, for the benefit of first one side and then the other, then drop back below the radar.

But he would not rest.

The day of reckoning would come.

the end

Next, the final book in the Shylmahn Trilogy:

Book Three: **Genesis**

A tenuous truce between Shylmahn and Human had kept the peace for more than five years, but there was never a doubt as to who were the masters of the planet. Earth belonged to the Shylmahn.

But the Britton Family, waging a clandestine war with the invaders for thirty years, had one last desperate, insane plan to get their world back. Succeed or fail, it would change the face of the planet forever.

www.ingramcontent.com/pod-product-compliance
Lightning Source LLC
Chambersburg PA
CBHW031956040826
48979CB00041B/317

* 9 7 8 1 9 4 7 2 3 1 2 7 6 *